EVERY
HIDDEN
THING

Also by Kenneth Oppel

The Nest
The Boundless
Half Brother

The Airborn Trilogy

Airborn
Skybreaker
Starclimber

The Silverwing Series

Silverwing
Sunwing
Firewing
Darkwing

The Apprenticeship of Victor Frankenstein

This Dark Endeavor
Such Wicked Intent

KENNETH OPPEL

INTERNATIONALLY BESTSELLING AUTHOR

EVERY
HIDDEN
THING

SIMON & SCHUSTER BFYR

New York London Toronto Sydney New Delhi

An imprint of Simon & Schuster Children's Publishing Division
1230 Avenue of the Americas, New York, New York 10020
This book is a work of fiction. Any references to historical events,
real people, or real places are used fictitiously. Other names, characters, places,
and events are products of the author's imagination, and any resemblance to
actual events or places or persons, living or dead, is entirely coincidental.
Text copyright © 2016 by Firewing Productions, Inc.
Jacket illustrations copyright © 2016 by Dadu Shin
SIMON & SCHUSTER BFYR is a trademark of Simon & Schuster, Inc.
For information about special discounts for bulk purchases, please contact Simon &
Schuster Special Sales at 1-866-506-1949 or business@simonandschuster.com.
The Simon & Schuster Speakers Bureau can bring authors to your live event. For
more information or to book an event, contact the Simon & Schuster Speakers Bureau
at 1-866-248-3049 or visit our website at www.simonspeakers.com.
Jacket design by Lucy Ruth Cummins
Interior design by Greg Stadnyk
The text for this book was set in Adobe Garamond Pro.
Manufactured in the United States of America
First Edition
2 4 6 8 10 9 7 5 3 1
Library of Congress Cataloging-in-Publication Data
Names: Oppel, Kenneth, 1967– author.
Title: Every hidden thing / Kenneth Oppel.
Description: First edition. | New York : Simon & Schuster Books for Young Readers,
[2016] | Summary: In the late nineteenth century, a budding romance develops between
Rachel and Samuel, two teenagers from rival families of fossil hunters heading out to the
badlands in search of a rare dinosaur skeleton.
Identifiers: LCCN 2015045436| ISBN 9781481464161 (hardback) | ISBN
9781481464185 (eBook)
Subjects: | CYAC: Dinosaurs—Fiction. | Fossils—Fiction. | Paleontology—Fiction.
| Families—Fiction. | Love—Fiction. | BISAC: JUVENILE FICTION / Action
& Adventure / General. | JUVENILE FICTION / Social Issues / Dating & Sex. |
JUVENILE FICTION / Animals / Dinosaurs & Prehistoric Creatures. Classification:
LCC PZ7.O614 Ev 2016 | DDC [Fic]—dc23
LC record available at https://lccn.loc.gov/2015045436

For Philippa

PART I
THE TOOTH

HE WALKED THE BADLANDS FOR TWO DAYS WITHOUT
food or water. The boy was naked, painted in white clay, searching for the gift he had seen in his vision. With jagged stones he raked his chest, and still heaven and earth wouldn't open their secrets to him. He began to despair. He was lost and needed to be guided. He was a boy and needed to be a man. He staggered on into the night, hoping dawn would bring the fulfillment of his vision. But it came instead from the darkness.

Its eye was a gaping hole in a skull built from black bones. The boy struggled with the beast as it tried to drag him beneath the earth. Kicking, yelling, he pushed against the dark teeth to keep the jaws from closing on him. The teeth pierced his hands. He was pulled down to a place without moon or stars, but he fought on. Light disappeared, and time with it. Finally he was still and thought he'd died and would never see the dawn again.

When he woke, the sun was rising and he was walking, streaked with blood, a black tooth clutched in his fist.

1.
THE ELASMOSAURUS

I **WOULDN'T SAY MY FATHER WAS A VIOLENT** man, but he wasn't afraid to talk with his fists. And I was glad of it. Because if he hadn't belted Professor Cartland that night in the Academy of Natural Sciences, I wouldn't have had the chance to see Rachel's eyes up close.

When I first saw her in the lobby, I didn't even know her name. She was just an ordinary-looking girl, dowdily dressed with all the flair of a cabbage moth. Her nose and jaw were too big to make her face delicate. Fair hair, quite fine, reddish tinged, parted severely in the middle and pulled back from her face.

She stood out because there were only two girls in the entire lobby—and the other one was Anne Atkinson. I'd glimpsed Anne several times before. She was the oldest young person I'd ever seen. Bowed and strangled in bonnet and lace. Rickety as the aging uncle she steadied during monthly meetings.

And then there was Rachel. I wondered who she'd come with.

She left the crowded lobby, where people were talking before the lecture, and wandered into one of the galleries. Behind the giant Irish elk and prehistoric turtle was *Hadrosaurus foulkii*.

It was still an impressive brute, no matter how many times I'd seen it. Just sixteen years ago Joseph Leidy had dug it up. The first dinosaur skeleton unearthed from American soil. Mounted on its rear legs, it stood fourteen feet tall. Twenty-six feet long, head to tail. Forelimbs gripping a fake tree added for support. You could go and stand right underneath the rib cage.

She was staring at it intently, a vertical line between her eyebrows.

"Never seen it before?" I asked.

She only half turned, just enough to glimpse me, and then directed her gaze back to the hadrosaur.

"No."

Just no. "You're not from here?"

Since it went up several years back, the hadrosaur had become such a popular attraction that the academy had cut back its visiting hours and started charging admission. I figured everyone in Philadelphia had seen it by now.

"We're visiting from New Haven."

"Ah." She didn't seem at all interested in me. Most girls were. I wondered if I smelled like the pickle I'd eaten with dinner. More likely she was just shy. I wanted her to turn and look at me properly. "Those aren't the real bones," I said.

"I know. They're just plaster casts."

I studied her anew. "How'd you know that?"

"I read an article."

I looked around to make sure Professor Leidy wasn't nearby. Whispered anyway. "They never found the skull, so they had to invent one."

"They based it on an iguana."

She was getting more intriguing by the second. And then she looked at me straight on for the first time. Her gaze was frank. No flirtatious lift of an eyebrow, no smile. I got the feeling she'd be just as happy without me. Happier maybe. For a moment I couldn't think of anything to say. Unusual for me.

"That's a very pretty hairpin," I lied.

"No, it's not." She gave a little sigh, like she was disappointed in me.

I'd never met a girl reluctant to talk about her hair ornaments. I chuckled. For a second I thought she might too.

I added, "I just thought it was . . . unique in its . . ."

"It's just a regular hairpin," she said, touching it.

The tip of her left thumb and index finger were both stained with ink.

She saw my gaze and answered before I asked. "I draw my father's specimens for him."

Tonight, everyone crammed into this building was a naturalist of some sort. Probably her father was just another gentleman dabbler.

"He's a collector?"

"Yes. And he's quite exacting in his drawings."

"You must be very skilled."

There was no one who didn't like being complimented, but she showed no sign of pleasure, only tilted her head slightly and said, "It's very challenging. I hope to get better with more practice."

"My father's speaking tonight."

She looked genuinely surprised. "You're Michael Bolt's son?"

I nodded at the large display case against the wall. "That's his *Laelaps aquilunguis* in there."

My father might not have been the first to discover a dinosaur in America, but he was the second. What he found was only a partial skeleton, but I'd memorized every bone: mandible; clavicles; both humeri; femur; tibia; fibula; phalanges; lumbar, sacral, and caudal vertebrae. The pieces were enough to let him guess its size and weight and eating habits. And win him the right to name it. *Eagle-clawed terrible leaper.* A carnivore, with a curved claw to do its slashing and killing.

"There's talk of making a cast and mounting it one day," I said.

She walked over and looked solemnly at the bones. Completely absorbed. I worried she might've forgotten me altogether.

"You seem very interested in dinosaurs," I remarked.

Still not looking at me. "I am. I know more about snakes, though."

"Really?"

"I keep several," she told me.

I was delighted. "We have a tortoise at home. Horatio. He roams around. We also have a Gila monster."

She turned to face me. "Does he roam around too?"

"She. No, we keep her in a vivarium. She likes raw eggs and getting her head scratched. She's venomous, of course."

I usually got a dainty squeal when I said this, but she simply nodded, wanting more.

"We have a fernery in our back room with tree frogs and salamanders. Our housekeeper complains. She keeps finding them in the sink."

This time she actually smiled. "I adore salamanders."

"Did you know they can regrow lost limbs?"

"Yes," she said, which was a bit disappointing, since this was the one good thing I knew about salamanders.

"I know a fair bit about them," she said. "Of course, there are over four hundred species, so there's a great deal to know."

We talked about salamanders. She got fairly animated, and I think I did too, because I liked this kind of talk, and it was rare to have with anyone my age—and never with a young woman. I'd never been more aware of a girl's scent—not just the pleasant floral of soap, but the smell of her hair and heat of her skin. To my horror, I felt myself stiffening between my legs, and I silently counted backward from ten. Which usually worked, but didn't now, so I imagined Mrs. Shaw, my former history teacher, which *always* worked.

It did, but slowly. To distract myself—and her, in case she looked down—I asked how she'd gotten interested in the natural sciences.

"I spent a lot of time looking into puddles," she said.

That made me laugh. And then she told me how she got her first magnifying glass early on. I liked the way she talked, very direct and honest. For such a plain girl she was extraordinarily interesting. She asked me what sparked my scientific interests.

I shrugged. "I guess I had a knack with bones. No shortage in my house."

"Your building blocks and jigsaw puzzles," she said with another small smile.

"My father taught me their names. By six I could put a foot together. At eight I did a whole squirrel. Sometimes at parties he'd drag me out in front of everyone, give me a bunch of bones, and time me. Once I put together a raccoon in three minutes. I can put pretty much anything together."

She said nothing, then abruptly, "Well, I look forward to your father's lecture."

"Maybe we'll have a chance to talk afterward."

"Excuse me," she said, walking away, and I wondered if I smelled like pickle after all.

I went to the ladies' lavatory and splayed my fingers against the cool marble counter, waiting for the color to leave my cheeks. It was unusual for a young man to talk to me, especially such a handsome one, but I knew exactly why he had. I was the only young woman in the room, and no doubt he was bored and wanted to try his charms on someone. Certainly he was charming, and knew it. And all that talk about how fast he could sort bones: so boastful.

Still, he did not condescend when I revealed my interest in salamanders. I liked that very much. Our conversation felt like one between equals. Almost. That was rare.

He was tall, with a mop of wavy, coarse hair. He looked like one of those puppies that hadn't grown into its body yet but gave all the signs of its full size to come: the paws, the huge eyes. I'm not sure I'd ever seen a more perfect nose. It sloped at just the right angle, with a perfect set of nostrils at the end. How nostrils could be perfect, I didn't know, but his were.

Darwin talked about advantageous traits, how they're all divvied up and it's all random—and my portion did not favor physical beauty, and there was no point pretending it did. In the mirror I saw the perpetual disappointment that was my face. Every day, all around me, I saw beauty blooming in fields or flitting between trees or frozen in marble in an art gallery or simply walking down the street. But the closest I came to it was drawing it, line by line, in ink.

You fool. You felt bathed in the warmth of his eyes, but they've practiced that look on many girls, no doubt, that easy smile. He just wanted a bit of attention, and you would have to do.

There. My pulse was calm; the blotchy redness had left my cheeks. No more nonsense. Easy as slamming a gate.

When I returned to the lobby, I found Papa looking for me, could sense his impatience in the angle of his domed head. Everyone was going into the lecture hall.

"I saw you talking to a young man," he remarked.

"He's Michael Bolt's son."

"Ah. The spawn of our illustrious speaker."

And then we were inside and taking our seats. I casually looked around the hall but didn't find the boy, and then the chairman of the academy came out to give a tedious preamble and make the introductions.

"And now please join me in welcoming Professor Michael Bolt."

"Professor," my father whispered mockingly. "Difficult, without a university post."

Plenty of times I'd heard Papa complain that Bolt had no formal degree. That he was mostly self-taught, an amateur with no teaching position. In fact, I was quite certain my father had just rejected Bolt's application to teach at Yale, where my father chaired the paleontology department.

Professor Bolt bounded to the stage. He was very tall and had feet so large his shoes must have been specially made for him. He was in every way an overgrown version of his son. Or I supposed a *grown* version. He had an eager forward lurch, a sway of the shoulders that made him seem off balance. But he didn't stumble; he rocked and rolled. He had a well-tended beard and a slim jaunty mustache, which gave him the look of an eager fox, especially with his ample hair spiked out to either side like alert ears.

And when he spoke, Professor Bolt was a mesmerist.

He began by telling us how a series of crates had arrived from a certain Dr. Hawthorn from Kansas, a dentist by training, but an amateur naturalist. How he'd opened the crates like the Ark of the Covenant and drawn out, one by one, the bones hastily wrapped in newspaper. They were still burdened with the chalk they'd been dug from. Bone after bone, each of a size that promised a creature of huge proportions.

I was on the edge of my seat. This was exactly the kind of discovery I dreamed of making myself one day. But when I glanced at my father, he looked decidedly unimpressed.

And then Professor Bolt plunged the audience back in time, to the early history of the world, when Kansas was an inland sea, inhabited by creatures that no longer traversed our oceans. Much of this I knew already, but I'd never heard it described so vividly. In the skies wheeled creatures that we would think of as dragons now, pterodactyls like the ones they had recently found in Europe. And how, when all these creatures died, their bodies settled to the bottom of the sea and were covered by sediment that became stone that preserved their bones for millions of years until Mother Earth heaved up the continent and the ocean drained, and later glaciers scoured the softer rock away to reveal the bones of these vast serpents.

Then, with a dramatic flourish, Bolt had the curtains pulled back to reveal the elasmosaurus itself. Set out on a series of tables, the skeleton of this amazing sea serpent was thirty-five magnificent feet from head to tail: the ribs, its platelike fins, its surprisingly tiny head.

Applause reverberated through the hall, mine with it, but when I glanced over at Papa, his clapping was very tepid. A strange, smug smile was on his lips.

After he'd talked about the anatomy of the elasmosaurus, Professor Bolt invited comments and questions, and Papa wasted no time. I had the uneasy feeling he'd come fully prepared.

"If I may, sir?"

"By all means," Bolt said, with a tight smile.

"An impressively long chain of vertebrae, yes yes—prodigiously long."

Papa had a rather unfortunate verbal tic of saying "yes yes" in the midst of his sentences. And it rarely meant he agreed with you.

The two men chuckled together mirthlessly.

"The tail," Papa said, "seems twice the length of the neck."

"Naturally," Bolt said. "This creature, I believe, propelled itself primarily with its tail, with some assistance and stability from its flippered forelimbs."

"Remarkable," said my father.

"If I might just come forward, sir, it might be easier to illustrate my query."

This was not typical, and there were a few whispers in the audience. I felt my toes clenching inside my shoes. I wished Papa would sit down. But Bolt, with a rigor-mortis smile and a little wave of his hand, said, "By all means, by all means."

Helplessly I watched. Papa walked with his deliberate, almost prissy, little steps. When he reached the table, he clasped his hands behind his back and tilted slightly over the bones.

"It's completely understandable, Professor Bolt, that you would assume the creature's neck is shorter than the tail, as this is the case with *lizards*—which I believe is really your primary area of expertise."

I felt my face heat at my father's barely veiled insult.

"Well, Professor Cartland, it's true I've written many papers on herpetology, but they constitute only a small proportion of the one hundred and forty-six I've written in total."

This, I knew, was a very sore point with Papa, for he himself had published nowhere near this number.

"Might I finally suggest," Papa said forcefully, "that what you have assumed is the creature's *neck* is in fact its *tail*?"

Audible mirth bubbled up from the audience, and bolstered by this, Bolt chuckled.

"You might *suggest* it, Professor, but I'm afraid you would be disappointed. The creature would be out of all known proportion. As well, a neck of such length could not be practical or even functional."

"But let us not forget yes yes, that this creature is aquatic, and its long neck would not require the same muscular support as a terrestrial animal. Indeed, one might surmise that such a long neck might be advantageous for snapping up fish from below, unawares."

"These are interesting musings, I grant you," Bolt said, "but I think they might have been made just as well from your *seat*."

"I'm sorry," Papa said, "to try your patience, Professor Bolt, but we are all friends here. Truth is always our common goal. Please don't take my questions personally."

"I take them personally, sir, because you suggest my incompetence."

"Not at all, not at all."

The strain in the lecture hall was thick now. Someone called, "Please sit, Professor Cartland. So others can ask their questions."

"My apologies," said my father. "I am nearly done, but if I might just beg your indulgence one last time, Professor?"

Bolt nodded curtly. "Go on."

"I am just yes yes wondering," said my father, and the crowd gave a small gasp to match my own as he plucked up the elasmosaurus skull, "if the skull might just"—and he walked the thirty-five feet to the far end of the table—"fit more *naturally*"—and he picked up the final tail vertebra and slotted it inside the base of the skull—"right *here.*"

There was a loud click. Maybe just my imagination, but it was like two puzzle pieces snapping together perfectly.

Cartland held them high. "Which would indicate to me, Professor Bolt, that the *tail* is in fact the *neck*, and you have built your dinosaur *backward*, sir."

I felt like some important part of my chest had busted loose and plunged into my stomach. The stricken look on my father's face confirmed my worst fear: Cartland was right.

Father rose to his full height. "I will ask you to retract that comment, Professor Cartland."

The scoundrel rocked smugly on his heels. He was much shorter than my father, solid as a potbellied stove. Sparse hair began way back on his shiny head. His mustache took a sharp downward turn, obscuring the sides of his mouth, which I think was curved into a triumphant smile. I hated him. He'd come onto the stage to humiliate my father, to squash his reputation.

"Alas," Cartland said, "I cannot retract."

KENNETH OPPEL

Father's eyebrows were askew. His eyes, never pacific at the best of times, were fierce. His left eye had a slightly wayward angle to it and made you think that he wasn't quite looking at you—or that he was possibly deranged. Right now he absolutely looked deranged.

"Then, sir, I will ask you to put down my fossils and step outside with me."

Cartland laughed at this, but there was a pinch of alarm in his voice when he replied. "I will certainly *not* step outside with you."

"Put. Down. The fossils."

"There you go," said Cartland, placing them down. "Will you assault me here?"

Amused titters from the audience—but only from people who'd missed certain monthly meetings in the past.

I was already half out of my seat when Father punched Cartland. It was a good strong box to the eye—can't say I didn't enjoy it. I doubted Cartland was as practiced a scrapper as my father, but he was denser, and I almost shouted at Father to watch out, because he was too cocky. With a forward lunge Cartland buried his fist in my father's stomach, doubling him over.

I vaulted onto the stage. A chorus of disapproval rose from the audience.

"Gentlemen!"

"Shame! Shame!"

"Not *again*, Bolt!"

"Sir!" someone called out to my father. "Are you not a Quaker!"

"I am, sir!" my father panted. "But not a very good one today!"

And he took another punch at Cartland's face, which the other man dodged quite nimbly.

"Father!" I took him by the arm, but he shook me off.

"That skull," he panted to Cartland as the two faced off, "was found near the vertebrae I selected for the neck. My prospector was most clear in his notes!"

"That may be," Cartland said. "Nonetheless, they were *caudal* vertebrae, not *cervical*!"

He managed to seem calm and somehow dignified, standing still as my father fumed and circled. Like he knew he couldn't be struck down, because he was right.

"Father, stop!" I yelled again.

He lurched in close for another jab at Cartland, too close, and the cast-iron professor stamped hard on my father's oversized shoe. He'd paid a cobbler in Chicago a fortune for those shoes. Father jackknifed with a whoop, then butted against Cartland's belly with his full weight. They both toppled over, each trying to thrash and claw his way atop the other.

Suddenly the girl from the lobby was beside me, cheeks blazing. I'd never seen anyone look fiercer. She grabbed my father's ear and twisted like she was trying to yank a turnip from the earth.

"Hey!" I yelled. "Easy!"

"Get him off my father!"

Stupidly I looked from Cartland to the girl. "*That's* your father?"

"Yes!"

"Well, maybe you should remove *your* father from *my* father,"

I bellowed, and pointed down to the writhing mass: Cartland now had the upper hand and was strangling my father, who was drooling slightly.

We each took hold of our struggling parents and shouted and tugged. In all our grappling, her hands and mine got tangled briefly.

She looked at me, and I couldn't look away. Her eyes were extraordinary, not just for their piercing blue—it was the white and amber markings in her irises, like shooting stars and the aurora borealis radiating from the blackness of her pupils. I felt like I was witnessing the birth of the universe.

It took me completely by surprise: With absolute certainty, I knew I'd fall in love with her.

2.

THE CRATE

I FOUND THE CRATE THE NEXT MORNING.
It was unopened under Father's desk. The muddy boot prints on its lid told me he'd been using it as a footrest for a good while. Exactly the kind of thing my father would do absentmindedly. I dragged it out and cleared a space on one of the worktables.

A small crate, not much bigger than a shoe box, stenciled all over with the faded insignia of the Kickapoo Medicine Company. It was addressed to the "Most Esteemed Professor Michael Bolt" in a spidery hand. Clearly the sender was hoping flattery would get Father's attention. Which was normally an excellent plan. But in this case it still hadn't saved him from being used as a boot rest.

Tons of things got sent to my father by amateur naturalists. Ancient leaf impressions in sandstone, the giant toe bone of some extinct mammal, the skins of two warblers with unusual wing markings. And lizards. Plenty of lizards. Sometimes they were sent to him care of the academy; other times they came direct to our house. Our doorframe was splintered by the number of crates wrestled through. They stacked up in the hallway, in the long, narrow rooms of our ground floor.

The floors crunched with dried clay trimmed from fossils. You stepped around rickety towers of dusty books and papers, trays of things yet to be labeled—and tried not to tread on Horatio, our tortoise, who made his slow creaking perambulations around the house and somehow managed to turn up underfoot when you were lugging something tricky.

There was no parlor or living room or library. No comfortable room with great leather armchairs for guests to sit and stretch their legs. Our decorations were the skins of a vole, a snake slowly uncoiling in a jar of spirits, an antelope femur.

Mrs. Saunders, our cook and housekeeper, was forbidden from cleaning these front rooms—Father didn't trust her not to whisk up some treasured body part or scrap of paper with a brilliant note. Not that she'd ever set foot in here, even if ordered. She hated the chaos, our salamanders, and the sight and smell of our Gila monster, who had a habit of regurgitating her meals.

Often there were students over, or colleagues, helping father with something or other. Some days it was like being in a telegraph office. News and chatter flashing between tables. It was a museum upended, everything dragged out of its cases and cupboards. It was a zoo. It was a morgue. More dead things here than the local slaughterhouse. More pickling alcohol than the tavern down the street.

I loved it. But I was also glad that, upstairs, I had a bedroom with a door I could close. And there were times I needed to shut it tight and keep it shut. Against the dust and the roving salamanders. Against my father's cries of fury or joy.

Two weeks ago I'd been sent home from school. For the rest of the year. I'd been suspended, mainly because of the incident with Harold Thom. He'd asked me what my father had done during the war. It was a sneaky question, since most Quakers hadn't fought as a matter of conscience. But some had, including Thom's own father. When I told Thom my father had worked in field hospitals since he was a pacifist, Thom had snorted, said that was a joke since everyone knew my father was quick enough to use his fists when it suited him. And it was only for the war he decided to be a coward.

I kept hitting him until his nose and teeth bled. Which was not a good thing to do in a Quaker school. I got yanked off by several of his friends and marched to the headmaster's office. He lambasted me for my "deplorable violence." Also, I'd played billiards in the town, gambled, and scandalized several girls at the school with my "saucy poetry." "Moreover," the headmaster added, "your penmanship is atrocious." I think he found this the most despicable thing of all. I would not graduate this year, he said, and would need to reapply to return in the fall, if there was any hope of me being accepted into college. I didn't care about returning, and I didn't care about college. But I knew my father did. My first few days home had been explosive with his angry talk.

But that was past now. I think he was secretly glad to have me home. Since he wasn't an organized man, he quickly enlisted me to help sort and identify his specimens.

So all this morning I'd been dutifully opening boxes and letters and taking notes. Trying to stay focused.

But I kept seeing those eyes of hers. Rachel. I'd only learned her name from my father on our way home from the academy. She'd filled my head as I slept. In my dreams I was trying to schedule a train trip to see her. The Pennsylvanian from Philadelphia to New York, arriving at Penn Station, and then a quick change to the New England line that would bring me to New Haven in another two hours. She would see me, wouldn't she, if I showed up at her doorstep? But the train schedules didn't make any sense. Columns of jumbled numbers and letters, and anyway I was always running late and never getting to where I was supposed to be, and I woke up with my heart pounding.

I wanted to talk to her, tell her I wasn't a rash, cocky fool. Wanted to tell her I wasn't a mad brawler like my father. Quite a speech I had planned. I kept hearing her voice, catching her scent, seeing her looking up at me gravely. Just one meeting. No beauty, and an ass of a father. But she'd snagged at something in my heart.

I dropped a fossil shell to the floor and went scrabbling for it—and that's when I found the Kickapoo Medicine Company crate under my father's desk.

On the worktable I used a chisel to prize up the lid. Inside was a nest of prairie grass for padding and three separate burlap bundles. I'd only just started to unwrap the largest when I heard the front door burst open and slam shut. Father exploded into the room with a mighty sigh.

"It's too late, they say."

All through the night, holding a handkerchief bulging with ice chips against his bruised cheekbone, he'd furiously rewritten his elasmosaurus paper. It had already been slated for publication in the next issue of *Transactions of the American Philosophical Society*. He'd even paid (too much, I thought) for a set of lithographic plates illustrating the glory of his find.

"It's already gone to the printer's." He plummeted into his cane-backed swivel chair—the only chair without a stack of paper on it—and slouched, his long legs shooting out.

"You're sure Cartland was right?" I asked pointlessly.

"I knew the instant he said it. I blame that numbskull dentist Hawthorn for leading me astray. He assured me the skull rested near those vertebrae . . . but that was my mistake: relying on others. If I'd been there, if I'd dug it out myself, there'd be no confusion."

"What'll you do?"

"Buy up all the copies of the journal as quickly as possible."

He didn't need to say what a huge embarrassment this was. He had no degree. No professorship at an esteemed university. All he had was his work and what he published.

"Everyone makes mistakes," I said, hoping to cheer him. "Remember Agassiz, the Harvard man who fell for the Cardiff Giant?"

My father smiled only briefly. "Yes. It was Cartland who exposed that as well, of course."

"Well, you still brought the elasmosaurus to life, just a little . . ."

"Backward," my father said, and we laughed together.

Absently he touched his bruised face, winced. "That was a fair thrashing I gave him, eh?"

"You thrashed each other."

"I got in more blows, I think. The parasitic carbuncle. Did you know how he got his position at Yale?"

"Yes, you've—"

"He cajoled a wealthy relation into creating a department of paleontology, building it, endowing it. And now he is the chair of that very department!"

A series of rasping pants came from the Gila monster's vivarium.

"Have you fed her?" my father asked.

"Just an hour ago."

"That's her hungry sound."

"She's getting fat."

My father went to her, stooped, and scratched her head. "Old girl," he said fondly.

I felt sorry for her, pacing her small home with her splay-legged gait. Sometimes Father let her have the run of the workroom, but once she disappeared for several days, and Mrs. Saunders refused to come downstairs and cook until we'd found her and gotten her back into her vivarium. Father let her out less now, since neither of us enjoyed going hungry.

Father's distracted eyes turned to the crate I'd just opened. "Anything good?"

"Did you know you were using this as a footrest?"

He made no reaction. Not sure he even heard me. He already had one of the burlap bundles open in his hands and was staring. His face very still.

Slowly he laid it out on the table. It was a seven-inch span of bone, some stone still clinging stubbornly to it. Tapered at one end, much thicker at the other, like hardwood polished to a high sheen. I was trying to place it. Tibia? Part of an ulna? But the shape wasn't right. Both ends were jaggedly broken. I tore away the burlap from the second bundle as my father unwrapped the third. His piece was the thickest yet, with a broad oval base. He placed it near the thick end of the first piece. They clearly belonged to each other. And my piece . . .

My piece tapered to a very sharp point. The surface was smooth to the touch, but the pad of my thumb felt telltale serrations along the edges. I placed it in front of the other two pieces.

I felt a bit breathless. "This is the biggest tooth I have ever seen."

"Who sent this?" my father demanded.

I foraged inside the crate. "There's a letter!"

"Read it!"

So like him to command me to do something he could easily do on his own. So impatient he couldn't bear the idea of doing only one thing at a time. He handled the portions of the tooth and peered close as I ripped open the envelope. Yanked out the letter and started reading aloud.

KENNETH OPPEL

Dear Professor Bolt,

It is with great humility I write to you, as it's my truest wish to become a fossil collector like yourself. I am a section boss on the Union Pacific near Edford station, and—

"What's a section boss?" I asked.

"Takes care of a stretch of track. Go on!"

—I've been a dedicated collector for several years, and made a fair collection of leaves and flowers from the Cretaceous.

"Dear God," said my father, "hurry this along!"

"If you'll let me!"

While prospecting northeast of Fort Crowe, I came upon a portion of exposed femur and sacrum, which to my untrained eye, were so large that they could only belong to the Dinosauria. But what I think might be of greater interest to you, sir, is this tooth which I found. I have never seen a bigger one, and think this creature in the rock must be of enormous proportions. I did not have time to do much quarrying, but I think there is a great deal of bone here. I send you this tooth as a way of showing my

*interest and ability, in the hopes you might find a use
for me. I would like to continue work at the site, but
have no funds available to me. This work is God's
work for me, and my needs are few.*

Awaiting your advice, I remain yours truly.

Edward G. Plaskett

This tooth was a meat eater's. Those serrated edges helped sink the tooth deep into its prey and hold. Imagine it punching into you, gripping, bleeding you.

"What length would you say . . . ," my father was murmuring.

I already had the tape measure in my hands. "Eleven and a quarter inches."

With calipers my father measured its thickness and called out the girth at its widest and narrowest bits. I got out ink and a pen and noted the figures. He snatched the pen from my hand and began talking aloud to himself as he made his own calculations. "Our model will be *Laelaps* . . ."

Laelaps aquilunguis—practically a member of our family I'd seen it so many times. Sketched what it might look like with muscle and skin. But its longest teeth were not even a full inch.

Father inked more numbers. "Given the size of the tooth, we will assume the jaw . . ." He jotted again. . . . "Making the overall size of the skull five feet. Again, using *Laelaps* as our model . . ."

There was this French anatomist, Cuvier, who claimed you

could build an entire animal from just a single tooth. I knew this was what my father was trying to do. He was calculating the extent of the backbone, then the hips, then the humeri.

"And we have," he concluded, looking up at me triumphantly, "a bipedal creature of some fifty feet in length, whose height, measured from the ground, would be in the area of thirty feet."

Never had I imagined anything so big. There was the megalosaurus, which Buckland had discovered over in England decades earlier. It was big. But if megalosaurus could peep into my second-floor window, this new creature could crash right through the roof before swallowing me whole.

"It's like the king of dinosaurs," I said.

"A *rex*," Father said. "Ha! You've half named it already!"

For as long as I could remember, I'd been looking for things. As a boy it might be a warbler egg or the knuckle of an ox or the larva of a monarch butterfly. The thrill of the hunt, something lost now found. I'd kept shelves in my bedroom for my specimen boxes. They made me happy—but almost from the moment of the finding, that hunger rekindled and made me turn to something new, something more I needed to be discovering.

But anything, *everything*, I'd collected before now seemed like nothing.

Every other thought went out of my head. I knew instantly. I knew I wanted this creature, every bone of it. I wanted to chisel it out of the rock with my own hands and assemble it and see it mounted in the gallery of the academy.

"We will not speak of this to anyone," my father was saying

severely, like I might just telegraph his day's work across Philadelphia.

"The letter is dated April second," I told him.

"What of it—" he started to say, and then paused, his eyes wider. "What day is today?"

My father's head was so full of genius he sometimes had to jettison little things—like the seasons or day of the week.

"June fourth."

"Nine weeks ago!" He handled his beard a moment to soothe himself, then glared at me. "Why did it take you so long to open this?"

This was rich. "I told you! You were using it as a footrest."

"That's absurd!"

I lifted the crate lid, showed him his muddy boot prints. "Under your desk!"

He waved his hand dismissively. "Never mind that now. We've got to telegraph Mr. Plaskett immediately. Before he takes this to someone else."

By "someone else" I knew he meant Cartland. There weren't too many scientists who called themselves paleontologists. Even Leidy and Hayden thought of themselves more as geologists and biologists.

If—and it was a big if—we'd been the first people Plaskett told about this, we had to get in fast.

"Take this down," my father said, rocking on the balls of his feet.

I found a clean scrap and dipped the pen in ink. It was just as well I was doing this. I'd seen his excited handwriting—a hideous jumble, even worse than mine. Which was no small feat.

My father looked through me, addressing our invisible fossil hunter in Wyoming Territory. "Mr. Plaskett. I like your style. You're hired. Retainer to come. Share news with no one. Await further digging instructions by post." His eyes refocused on me. "That's all. I'll need to send him some money to bind his services. . . ."

"You're going to let *him* find it?" I blurted in dismay. "Just like that? *We* should be the ones! That way there won't be any mix-ups—like elasmosaurus!"

I knew I'd plucked the right chord. Could see his restless eyes trawling the room, trying to find anchorage. He brought his hand down hard on the table. "Damn it, but you're right. I want to go and dig it up myself! The teeth and everything attached to them!"

"Yes! Why don't we?"

His gaze meandered, losing intensity. "I'd like nothing more . . . but I can't afford to mount an expedition at the moment. Do you know how little I have in the bank?"

I nodded, because Father had also asked me to manage our bills. His genius did not extend to household finance. "Sixty-two dollars at present."

My father folded his lips over his teeth. "So very little?"

He hadn't had a paying job for years. For a while, when I was small and just after my mother had died, he'd taken a job at Daverford College, teaching zoology. But he'd lasted only five semesters before resigning in a fury, saying he couldn't work with such pedants. At the time I'd had no idea what a pedant was—thought it must have been something really unpleasant like a goblin. Since then, of course, my father had made me familiar with its meaning—and all its lively synonyms.

Grandpa had wanted my father to farm, like all the other siblings, had even given him a large portion of land. Father had rented it out, land and house, and for a while we got by on that. When that became too little, he'd sold the house, then the land, and we'd been living off the capital, shrinking year by year, boosted by articles my father wrote for encyclopedias and magazines.

"What about the academy?" I asked. "Can't they help?"

He scoffed. "The academy is a gentlemen's club for amateurs playing at science. What money they have is used to maintain their collections and publish their *Proceedings*. They don't pay for their fossils, and certainly not for expeditions."

He frowned and paced the room. "It's not like some," he said, warming up to a rant, "who work for well-endowed institutions like Yale, who can raise funds. Cartland, for instance, I know has been planning something—"

"What about the money Grandpa's set aside for me?" I interrupted. I knew this was a sticky matter, but it was all I could think of.

"That money is in trust," he said, "to be released only for your university studies." His gaze hardened. "Which you've imperiled by your recent delinquency."

"Why do I need to go to college?" I said. "Isn't this a much better education? Working the field alongside you? Laying claim to the undiscovered world of Dinosauria? That's better than studying in any classroom."

"Not anymore," said my father. "It's not enough to be self-taught. You need a degree from an accredited university."

"You have no degrees."

"That's right!" he said. "And the world is changing. It demands degrees if you're to be taken seriously!"

"You're taken seriously!" I said.

His nostrils narrowed. "Not by Cartland and his cohort. I'll never get a university appointment. No, that money is for college—which you will go to, after you finish school."

"But the expedition," I said, worried we'd veered too far from my goal. "If we could ask Grandfather to let us use the money *temporarily*—"

With force he said, "I will not ask my father and nor will you. And you *will* go to university—there is no question of that. Not this fall, clearly, but the next term."

"What if we had money for an expedition, though?" I asked him.

"There's no point entertaining such a question. Now take that note to the telegraph office. I'm off to the bank to get a check for Mr. Plaskett."

I took my coat from the hook. I'd send his telegraph.

But I was already planning a way to dig up the *rex* myself.

3.
THE EXPEDITION

I **AM COMING WITH YOU," I TOLD PAPA.**

I was in the library, inking in the vertebrae of one of his prehistoric horses, when he'd come to tell me the news. His summer expedition to the Western Territories had been fully approved. The army had offered an escort. Union Pacific had granted free rail passes. And he had twelve paying Yale students keen to delve into the earth alongside him. Normally Papa relied on amateur prospectors to send him fossils. But this was to be the first expedition he headed himself. I fully intended to be a part of it, and had been telling him for months, but he'd made no promises.

He patted my hand. "My dear, it's out of the question. The arrangements are made. Your aunt Berton has very kindly offered to host you here in New Haven, and she has planned your entire summer."

"Yes, and I can guess what her plans involve. Picnics and

church socials—and another debutante ball. I've done one, and I have no intention of doing another."

There is a realization you have as a young woman—and it comes very soon, maybe twelve for me—when you walk into the room and know you might as well be invisible. You are not the prettiest thing in the room; you are not even in the running. Men's gazes move over you as though you were a pattern on wallpaper or a pillar blocking their view of something more interesting. I knew what admiration looked like in a boy's eyes— but only directed at other girls, not me.

It was crushing at first and made me angry, thinking men so unobservant. How could you see anything with such a cursory glance? Church picnics found me alone. Skating parties and sleigh rides too. But by and by, I became resigned. Men did not care for me, so I would not care for them. I tried to think of it as liberating. I did not have to mind my appearance or my posture; I did not have to laugh at feeble jokes or feign interest in dull talk. Loneliness had its own rewards, for it left my mind and energy free for the things that were truly important to me.

"Your aunt has only your best interests at heart," said Papa.

"She hasn't a clue about my interests. The natural sciences. Fossil hunting. All she wants to do is trot me around town until she finds me a fiancé."

My father frowned at my bold talk, but with the vivid purpling bruise around his left eye, it only made him look like a sad clown.

"What on earth is wrong with being engaged?" Papa said.

"Nothing at all, except that I don't want to be engaged right now, and maybe not ever. I want something different, and marriage would only get in the way."

My father tilted back his head and rocked on his heels. "Ah, you're talking about university again."

"I can't see any man allowing me to attend classes and scrabble in the dirt looking for fossils."

Samuel Bolt, with his warm eyes and mop of hair, flitted across my mind, quick as a sparrow, and gone just as fast.

"Well, after marriage no woman should be scrabbling in the dirt," said my father.

"And that is one of the many reasons I may never get married."

Papa sighed wearily. "With attitudes like this, yes yes, I'm afraid you may end up a spinster."

The word had always been hideous to me. It was "spit" and "spider" and "spindly" all wrapped into one. It was an ancient cocoon, long evacuated, dried out, and barren. It seemed such a cruel name for someone who, in some way or another, was unlucky or unusual or just different.

"I'd be willing to have that word on my tombstone," I said, "so long as 'paleontologist' is above it, and in much bigger letters."

He gave a small grin. Encouraged, I picked up the magnifying glass I'd been using to examine the vertebra.

"*You* gave me this, Papa. When I was eight. You encouraged me to start my own collections, to make a museum of my bedroom. You never advised me on dresses or the latest hair fashions, but you taught me how to find a fossil and use a killing jar, how to skin a bird, and how to shoot. For three years I've been drawing your specimens and seeing them published alongside your articles—"

All this time my father was nodding and patting the air as if trying to shush a tiresome orchestra.

"You have been an excellent helpmate to me, my dear. And many women have made a contribution to science in an amateur capacity."

"I don't want to be an amateur. I've heard you heap scorn on enough amateurs. Including Professor Bolt. I want to go to university and get a degree. There are women doctors now. Berkeley has just admitted its first woman engineer. Miss Maria Mitchell—"

"Self-taught," my father interjected.

"—discovered a comet, and was the first woman admitted to the American Philosophical Society. That was some years ago! I would make a very good paleontologist, Papa. My school marks are excellent—"

"They are indeed—"

"So if you have any doubts about my abilities, let me come on this expedition and prove myself."

"Yes yes," he said, which, of course, did not mean yes. "And who would chaperone you?"

"I've never needed one before."

"When you were younger, it was acceptable to come on the odd trip with me around the county. Even then, people thought it inappropriate. Now it would be quite scandalous. You're not a child anymore—"

"Exactly—"

"You're a young woman. And think of the journey. Even getting there by train is many days, and my companions are all young men."

"I've met most of them already." His students sometimes dined with us, and my father would hold court at the head of our enormous mahogany table in our fine dining room in our mansion, as they took their nourishment in both body and mind. "They've never shown the slightest interest in me. So I think it's safe to say that I will not be wooed out west."

"Perhaps, but men are men, and I can't be at your side the whole time. We'll be sleeping on trains, and once we begin, we'll be camping with soldiers. Tents and crude latrines and army food. There's nowhere for a young lady in all that. The terrain is savage."

"I am quite capable of managing."

"There are the Indians as well. The Sioux are renowned for their savagery."

"But you're not going to Indian territory," I said.

"Ha! That doesn't mean we won't encounter them."

"We'll have the army with us. Anyway, I'm a better shot than you. I'll prospect and draw fossils for you, and I will help cook the meals. I will *shoot* the meals if necessary. You said I was an excellent helpmate, so *let* me help."

He was shaking his head. "It won't do. It's not safe, and it's not appropriate."

"Papa—" I began, but this time when his hand lifted it was like a shield.

"You will stay with your aunt and be a help to *her*, and spend your summer in New Haven. And that is an end to it."

I said nothing, but I thought, *Oh, no it isn't.*

I liked meetings. It was the one time in the week I could sometimes—not always, but *sometimes*—be guaranteed I wouldn't hear Father's voice for an entire hour.

Silent reflection. Quaker meetings could pass without a single word being spoken. You were supposed to listen and wait—and if you were moved by God's spirit to speak, you could speak.

I'd never spoken. Maybe because my mind was always roving about. In any case, I didn't think I had anything worth saying to the other Friends. Or God. But sometimes, in the middle of one of those big silences, I'd get a moment where I felt like there was a light spreading out from me. Across the room and beyond. It didn't have a name, this light, and it didn't have a shape or a meaning. But it was there, and I felt better for it.

Whenever Father cleared his throat, my gut clenched, because I knew what was coming. Most people, if they said anything, kept it quick. A prayer for a sick friend. A short Bible passage. Father made little speeches. Observations. Revelations. Dreams. Once he spoke about the beauty of God's creation and how each blade of grass and beetle wing was sacred, and his voice shook, and I stared at the floor until he stopped, my cheeks burning. There was quiet after that—there was always supposed to be quiet—but this was beyond quiet. This was the quiet you heard when people stopped breathing. Or maybe even died of embarrassment. No one else said anything that meeting. Father had used up all the words. Afterward some of the Friends looked at me sympathetically. Even pityingly. One fellow put his hand on my shoulder and gave it a squeeze, like I'd just suffered a death in the family.

This Sunday morning my mind was even more restless than usual. Not because I was worried my father would speak.

But because I knew *I* would.

And the words in no way came from God.

I'd planned them out the night before, scratching and scribbling over and over in my head.

In my seat, I started, then lost my nerve, making a little cough-grunt. My father looked over at me questioningly. I stared at the floor, then finally lifted my head, my eyes screwed shut. I had planned carefully, and everything, *everything*, rested on this. I couldn't back out now. My voice wavered.

"The Lord's creation is vast. And there is still a great deal of it unnamed. I feel called upon to name it."

I opened my eyes to the room's silence. It had a new attentiveness to it. No one was looking right at me, but I felt like they were all leaning slightly toward me, wondering and waiting. My pulse was fast.

"I feel called upon to go west and see all of his great works, buried and waiting in the earth."

I *had* them. I could feel it: the air before a lightning strike. They wanted to know more, to know what this normally silent boy had to say for himself. My voice wasn't shaking anymore.

"I want to find all his creations and name them. I will go west, and continue Adam's work!"

The big ocean silence lapped up my words, sucked them back into itself. I tilted my face to the floor. Now I did feel all the eyes of the congregation on me, including my father's. I tried to look pious.

As we left the meeting hall, several Friends nodded and smiled at me, and a few offered me their hands to shake.

Farther down the street, alone, my father said, "Adam's work. A stirring phrase. A fine speech."

"It just came on me, very strong and sudden."

Father was proud of his intellect. But I knew he was also a big believer in spiritual commandment. I wasn't a practiced liar, but I was hell-bent on giving it a fair shake. Despite the cool air, I felt sweat on the back of my neck. My father stroked the foxy tips of his mustache.

"I must say, I'm surprised at your sudden fervor."

"You speak out all the time!"

"When I'm truly moved—"

"And I can't be truly moved? I have a very spiritual nature!"

Which would have surprised my schoolmasters. And everyone, really.

When Father spoke again, his voice was severe.

"Samuel, the things spoken in the meetinghouse are meant to be inspired by God."

"We're meant to go west," I persisted. "What we're doing would be God's work—"

"Enough. Were you really hoping the Friends would contribute money?"

"No one values education like them," I said, "and they're always setting up schools and scholarships and—"

"You've embarrassed yourself, and me."

"At least I was trying something!" I said. "Not just giving—"

"Mind your tone with me."

"I thought it was our only chance. To dig it up ourselves."

"We'll just have to hope that our Mr. Plaskett has a good eye and a strong back."

Back home, Father and I ate in the kitchen without speaking. All afternoon I tried not to think of the *rex* lying dormant in Wyoming Territory. Tried not to think of Rachel Cartland. I kept talking to her in my head. Like I was writing her a letter.

Dear Miss Cartland. *Dear Rachel.* I liked talking to you very much, and wondered if we could correspond. . . . *Did you notice it, when we met, or am I alone in feeling . . .* I was particularly interested in your views on salamanders. *I don't really care about salamanders.* I'm sorry about what happened between our fathers, but don't see why that should stop us being friends, do you? *Ha ha ha!* It's rare to find someone who shares my interest in the natural sciences. *What did you see when you looked at me? Because when I looked into your eyes . . .* I hope your father wasn't too badly bruised. . . . *Actually, I hope his stupid head is swollen to the size of a pumpkin.* My father can be hotheaded. *I couldn't tell if you hated me or liked me by the end, as we hauled our fathers off the stage. Our hands touched. Did you notice?* Maybe we'll see

KENNETH OPPEL

each other again at a lecture or meeting. *I keep thinking of you.*

As we lit the lamps, I began to feel very hopeless. Father was right. My plan with the Friends was a failure—and a huge embarrassment. And I'd probably never see Rachel Cartland again.

When our bell rang, quite late, Mrs. Saunders went, and then summoned my father. I followed from a distance. My pulse gave a hopeful kick when I caught a glimpse of John Eddington, one of the Friends, in the doorway. I hung back in the front room so I could hear their conversation.

"We were all of us moved by your boy's words," he said to my father. "The contributions came unasked, and I've collected them, for you to use as you see best. Very stirring, this idea of Adam's work."

I sat down in my father's cane-backed office chair and stretched out my legs, resting my feet on an empty crate. After my father thanked Mr. Eddington profusely and wished him good night, he appeared around the corner. His face wore a look of utter bewilderment.

"How much is inside that envelope?" I asked.

He opened it and did a quick count. "Enough to mount an expedition."

I gave a whoop of joy, and Father looked at me sternly, but only for a moment.

"We can't disappoint the Friends, can we?" I said. "Not after all the faith they've shown in us."

"No, we can't," said my Father, his face becoming especially foxlike with his wide smile.

"It seems we're headed west," I said.

. . .

Papa delivered me to Aunt Berton's the day before he was to leave for the territories. We all had tea together in her parlor. I knew Father didn't like Aunt Berton any more than I, but he was painfully polite, almost groveling. He relied on her financial support and good regard. Uncle Berton had died several years ago, leaving his widow to watch over the family fortune like a gargoyle atop a jeweled spire.

After tea I said a curt good-bye to my father. A maid took my luggage up to my room. I did not unpack.

My aunt and I had a quiet and almost comically mirthless dinner. She would occasionally cast a disapproving eye at me, and I would smile back brightly, which seemed to irritate her all the more.

"You're disheveled," she finally said.

"Am I?"

"You are, child. You will not attract a husband at this rate."

"I suppose not."

"You mean to be a burden to your father his whole life?"

"I am not so expensive to keep," I said.

"Being motherless is a great misfortune," she said, as if I'd brought it on myself. "Your father has let you become odd. I plan to make you more presentable this summer. It's no easy thing to find a husband these days, after the war took so many of our young gentlemen. The men can have their pick. And who will they pick?"

"The prettiest and richest they can, I imagine," I said.

KENNETH OPPEL

She actually looked pleased. "Precisely. Now, the worst position to be in is to be both plain and poor. You at least are not poor. There is hope for you. You should take heart."

"Thank you, Aunt Berton, I feel very cheered up."

Aunt Berton went to bed early. Her room was just down the hall from mine.

None of the snakes I'd brought with me were poisonous, though one of them was very good at hissing and feinting like he meant to bite. I waited for an hour and then walked quietly down the hall, opened the door to Aunt Berton's room, and waited for my eyes to adjust to the darkness.

My aunt slept soundly, though noisily, her skull encased in a nightcap. I let the three snakes out beside her bed. Some enthusiasts have claimed snakes are affectionate, but I believe they are just fond of warm places. I wasn't sure how much heat Aunt Berton's wizened frame produced, but it was a safe bet my snakes would find it ample. They quite liked armpits. I returned to my room and read a book until the screaming began.

Early next morning, my father was summoned to take me away.

Aunt Berton did not come downstairs to see us off. She remained in bed, exhausted by all the screaming she'd done last night.

"You did this on purpose, of course," Papa said, as we drove off in the carriage.

I said nothing. I had learned his trick of just looking with an impassive expression. It was rare to see him flustered, but he was now, and angry.

"How could you do such a thing to your aunt?"

"I'll need to come west with you now."

"You think you should be *rewarded* for this escapade?"

"There's nowhere else to go. No one will take me in on such short notice. I don't imagine anyone would want to, anyway. Given the snakes."

The horse clopped along.

Helpfully I said, "I suppose I could get a job as a tutor, or a companion for an infirm—"

"Stop it," my father said. "Your aunt may change her mind."

"She said under no circumstances was I welcome to sleep under her roof in the foreseeable future."

He twitched the reins. "You have put me in a very awkward position."

"You can't just leave me unchaperoned. Think of the mischief I might get up to."

My father sighed.

"I am looking forward to being an excellent helpmate to you," I said, and took his arm.

4.
ABOARD THE UNION PACIFIC

THREE SLEEPLESS NIGHTS ON TRAINS, AND I was ragged when we arrived in Omaha on the overnight from Chicago. Father had bought coach seats to save money—*my money*, I liked to think of it—and they were about as comfortable as a pew. He'd promised we'd get proper berths in the Pullman car for the last leg on the Union Pacific.

The station was an enormous cowshed. A confusion of tracks. Clang of rolling stock being shunted in the rail yards. At least we were out of the sun. It was still early, but you could already feel the day's heat budding and blossoming. Hot wind carried the smell of creosote, and hops from a brewery somewhere.

At the ticket office, the clerk told us the Pullman Palace Car was already full.

"In its entirety?" Father asked.

I heard singing from somewhere.

"It's a large party, sir. They booked it two days ago. I can offer you comfortable seats and berths in the second carriage. You will, of course, have access to the parlor car and dining car."

The singing was getting louder. I slouched across the platform with our luggage, feeling like a yak.

"We should've booked in advance," I said reproachfully to my father.

Suddenly a dozen young men in college blazers burst onto the platform, belting out "Come in Old Adam, Come In." They looked so energetic and well rested that I hated them on sight. I wasn't sure if their arms were linked, but they gave the impression of moving toward us like a chorus line.

"Isn't that Professor Bolt?" one of them called out.

My father turned and squinted. He was nearsighted and too vain to wear glasses except when at work.

Abruptly the singing stopped. "Professor Bolt!" exclaimed another fellow respectfully. "What a pleasure to find you here, sir!"

My father smiled: Nothing made him happier than being recognized. Even though he really wasn't a professor, he was still quite famous. Or infamous, depending on who you talked to. I'd once heard some college students describe him as a "militant scientist."

"What brings you gentlemen to Nebraska?" my father asked.

"Well, sir, we just took a few days to get kitted out, and do some target practice, and now we're on our way west to search for fossils."

"Is that so?" my father said, and he looked at me with a sly grin. In that moment we were both thinking the same thing. A work crew, eager to toil for a well-known paleontologist.

"They're with me, actually," said Professor Cartland, emerging from behind the tallest of his students.

"Ah, I see," said my father, the goodwill instantly scoured from his face.

Cartland looked crisp and freshly shaven and as dapper as his sturdy frame allowed: vest, jacket—and one of those Western string ties like some of his students wore.

"Good morning, Bolt," he said.

"And a very good morning to you," my father replied, standing up straighter.

For just a second I wondered if they'd start brawling again, right here in Omaha Station. But they managed a few more pleasantries before I stopped hearing them. Because Rachel Cartland had just appeared beside her father.

Even after all the weeks of preparations, the busyness, my dreams of digging the *rex* from the rock—she'd still stitched her way through my thoughts. I'd conjured her many times, but the picture was always imperfect. Mostly it was just details. The gap between her teeth. Always the eyes, looking up at me so studiously. I couldn't piece her all together in my memory. After all, I'd seen her just the one night.

Now she was right in front of me. Taller somehow than I remembered—was that the boots? And she wore a hat. Her clothes were simpler now, a white skirt and a blouse in the hundred-degree prairie sun. Her face was flushed, and she looked healthier and prettier than she had at the academy.

I realized I was smiling. She stared back at me like a wary cat.

"Hello, Miss Cartland," I said.

"Hello," she replied.

I wrenched my eyes from her and took in the students with even more dislike. Here she was with these strutting fellows. They'd all be fawning over her.

Behind their party, several porters with dollies moved their luggage toward the train and began loading it into the baggage car.

"You're taking the Union Pacific westbound?" I heard Cartland ask my father.

"We are," he replied tightly.

"Ah," said Cartland. "Then we shall see you on board." To his students he said, "This way, gentlemen," and marched ahead to the Palace Car.

I stole one last look at Rachel and then helped Father heave our own modest bags onto the baggage car. We boarded and took our seats in the second carriage. I patted at the careworn upholstery.

"These seats aren't so bad," I noted cheerfully. My heart was still beating hard. I was absurdly happy. I was on my way out west, to lay claim to the biggest dinosaur on earth. And Rachel Cartland was on the same train. There'd be lots of chances to talk to her. I felt like I'd been given a Christmas present in the middle of summer.

My father stared out the window, his mouth moving like he was gnawing a bit of gristle. "We should get off this train."

"What?" I asked in alarm.

"We can take the next one."

"But why would we . . ." I leaned closer and lowered my voice. "You can't think he's following us."

"No?"

This was paranoid, even for my father.

"They booked their tickets before us," I reminded him. "The stationmaster said so."

Father seemed not to hear me. "He has a habit of moving into my territory."

When he saw my blank look, he hissed, "New Jersey!"

I remembered now. Father meant the marl pits where he'd found his *Laelaps* years ago. The pits were owned by a fertilizer company. And after Father's find, Cartland had quietly talked to the owner, slipped him some money so he'd alert Cartland if his digging crews uncovered anything juicy.

"But he can't know where we're going," I whispered, then frowned. "Have you told anyone?"

"Of course not. You?"

"No!"

"But where *is* he going?" He jabbed his finger at me. As if I knew the answer. "*That's* the question that should worry us."

His intensity was starting to alarm me. "Are you saying—"

But suddenly Father looked past me, lifted his hat. "Good day, ma'am."

I turned just as a woman passed us in a pleasant breeze of lavender.

"Good day," she said, and smiled. She was very attractive and seemed to be traveling alone. My eyes followed her to the end of the coach. With a slender, white-gloved hand she opened the door to the single private compartment and stepped inside. I turned back to Father. His gaze lingered outside her door, a private smile on his lips.

And just as quickly his attention was back on me. Warily he glanced all around. Like he was making sure none of Cartland's people were nearby. He leaned closer.

"I asked the conductor where they were going, but the fellow was tight-lipped."

"Let me get this straight," I said. "You're actually worried they're going to the *same* place as us?" It was a terrible thought—that they somehow knew the location of our colossal tooth. But impossible. The West was huge. States and territories stretching for hundreds of miles in all directions. "You said most of his finds came from Nebraska and Kansas. He's probably headed there."

"Maybe he's going farther afield this time. Maybe he's got a lead on a good bone bed." Father fingered the rim of his hat. "And he's certainly got enough free labor with those students."

"They'll probably smash more than they find," I said, hoping to console him.

Despite his boundless energy, Father often got despondent—and when he did, it fell to me to jolly him up. There were days he'd refuse to get out of bed entirely. But I'd grown used to these, and he always rebounded. Waking early, and waking *me*, to go for a walk and take the morning air, all energy and plans.

"There was another fellow with them," he said now. "Did you

notice? A little wisp of a man. Too old to be a student. He wasn't wearing a blazer anyway. Can't be a scientist; I'd have known him. And you saw he brought along that plain daughter of his."

I felt a sting of indignation. Obviously he hadn't noticed her eyes. "I think she's a keen collector herself."

"What was he thinking? Unchaperoned. Bringing her at all!" His eyes narrowed. "I want to know where they're going."

I sat back, straightened the crease in my trousers. "I could make conversation with her."

My father tilted up his chin, intrigued. "You talked to her at the academy."

"Just a little bit. Before your lecture. And, well, during the brawl."

He nodded. "She'd no doubt be grateful for your attention. She may let slip her father's plans."

"I'll do my best," I assured him.

The train gave an eager forward pull as it left the station, and I felt exultant. Everything I wanted was on this train. My geological hammer, the promise of discovery, and Rachel Cartland.

My father winked. "Hold your friends close, but your enemies closer, eh?"

"Much closer," I said, and chuckled.

"You are flushed," Papa said to me. "I worried the heat might be too much for you."

"I'm perfectly fine."

Seeing Samuel on the platform had given me quite a jolt; I'd honestly thought I'd never set eyes on him again, especially not after that disgraceful incident at the academy. Over the weeks, he'd barely entered my thoughts.

"I'll have some water brought," Papa said, stepping into the corridor to summon a porter.

I hadn't asked for a private compartment, just a regular berth like everyone else—but Papa had insisted. I should have objected more, because I didn't want anyone to think I required special treatment. It was quite luxurious. The upholstery was plush. There was deep red carpet and mahogany paneling and a gaslight. The shade had been pulled down to block the sun, but there was hardly any air coming through the open window. I was glad of the pitcher of water the porter brought. I took a long drink, trying to order my thoughts.

I heard my father's voice as he helped his students settle into their seats. It sounded like they were gearing up for another song. He returned after a few minutes and sat down in the other armchair.

"So it seems Professor Bolt and his son mean to do some prospecting of their own."

Samuel had just stood there on the platform, smiling at me, like we were old friends, like he wasn't the son of the man who'd assaulted my father. A family of brawlers.

"I had no idea old Bolt had the funds to cobble together an expedition," Papa said, fanning himself with his hat. "There must be something yes yes very promising out there, to get him traveling." He looked up at me. "Still it seems a meager enough effort, if all he's got is his boy."

I sniffed. "He told me he could put together any skeleton. Faster than anyone."

"Ah. Modest, like his father."

"Insufferable," I muttered.

"Now, listen," Papa said. "I've already warned my students, but if the Bolts try to speak to you, especially Samuel, tell him nothing of our plans."

"I don't intend to speak with him."

"Nonetheless," Papa said, holding my gaze with a rare grin, "Bolt is a talkative man, and his son's no doubt cut from the same cloth. Talkative people can be quite informative. And you've always been such a keen listener, my dear."

I stared at him in surprise. "You mean I should try to find out their plans?"

"Only if he should let something slip. Why not? I wouldn't be surprised if they were trying to follow us."

He must have seen me hesitate, because he added, "Only if you can bear it. I know you're naturally shy."

I wasn't afraid of being shy; I was afraid of being charmed. A foolish part of me still wanted to talk to him, to see his eyes and his smile. He was a distraction. I wanted—I *needed*—to impress my father on this trip, to prove myself.

"Of course," I said. "I'll see what I can learn."

All I had to do was close the gate on Samuel's charm. The problem with a gate, though, was this: Even though it slammed shut with a very impressive bang, you could still see through the bars.

EVERY HIDDEN THING

5.
KEEPING YOUR ENEMIES CLOSE

SHE WAS SITTING BY HERSELF AT THE FAR END of the parlor car, sewing something. She didn't look up as I entered with Father.

Outside the big windows, prairie rolled endlessly past. It felt spacious in here. Clusters of overstuffed armchairs, mostly filled with Yale students, humming tunes. Laughing. Comparing their bowie knives and pistols, so shiny they must've just bought them in Omaha.

Cartland was here too. Smoking a cigar and talking to a small wiry man. Must have been the wispy fellow my father mentioned. Balanced on his knee was a notebook, his right hand busy scribbling.

"Ah, Bolt," said Cartland, sighting my father and ushering us over. "Mr. Landry here is traveling with our expedition yes

yes, to write an article for *Harper's Magazine*."

"Is that so? Good afternoon, Mr. Landry."

"Professor Bolt, a pleasure to meet you, sir." The scribbler's enthusiasm seemed genuine as he shook my father's hand.

"Have you ever been out west before, Mr. Landry?"

Cartland chuckled. "There's no point trying to winkle our destination from Mr. Landry. He himself doesn't know where we're headed."

"It's true," Landry said.

His quick head movements and perpetually startled eyes reminded me of a meerkat I'd seen once in a zoo.

Cartland released a narrow plume of smoke. "He does have some questions about your extraordinary elasmosaurus, though."

Worriedly I glanced at my father, saw him raise his eyebrows. But he forced a grin. "Well, I'm sure your version of events is more amusing, Cartland."

"No need for *my* version when yours yes yes has been immortalized in print." And Cartland lifted from among some papers the latest edition of the *Transactions of the American Philosophical Society*. The locomotive gave a shrill whistle, and I started.

Father's grin hardened. "You were speedy in getting a copy."

"I had the editor send me one still damp from the press."

Cartland was the biggest fool to taunt my father like this. Dangling the journal like a red cape before a bull. My father's nostrils flared. I took a step closer so I could grab if he lunged. Though I wouldn't have minded seeing Father take another punch at him. I glanced over at Rachel, who'd looked up from her sewing. I hoped she was seeing this, how her father was hell-bent on provoking mine.

But Father just looked calmly at the journalist. "Well, Mr. Landry, I don't know what the good professor has told you about my elasmosaurus, but it's a difficult business, piecing together something that's been asunder for millions of years."

"I'm sure, I'm sure," murmured Landry, his pencil scratching paper.

"And Professor Cartland might not appreciate that, since he's only found . . . how many actual *dinosaurs* is it, Cartland? Ah yes: none. Not a one. Don't forget to put *that* in your story, Mr. Landry, and I'll be sure to read it."

The chatter of the Yale students dwindled. Their eyes focused on us.

Cartland waved his cigar in the air. "Let's be fair, Bolt yes yes. We've had our fossils found for us by quarrymen and amateur prospectors."

"No, sir," I said indignantly. "He was there when *Laelaps* was found. Dug him out himself."

"His birthday present," said my father with a grin.

"That's true," I said. "I'd just turned six."

"Oh, that makes a very nice bit," said Landry, jotting it down.

"It was there in the marl; I remember the day precisely," my father said. "It rained and rained, and they shouted down at me to come up; they were worried about a slide. I was soaked through, more mud than man. But I knew what I'd seen: a scapula, and attached to it, a humerus of a creature no human had ever set eyes on, and I was not climbing up from that pit until I had every bone the black earth was prepared to yield to me!"

He finished to an appreciative silence. The Yalies all watched, enthralled by this oration. Rachel was listening too, and our eyes met briefly before she looked away. The journalist himself had forgotten to scribble, was peering up at my father with his wide meerkat eyes.

"And where we're headed," my father went on, aware that the entire car was his audience now, "we're going to exhume even more amazing creatures, vast creatures that will be talked about and marveled over for centuries." He beamed at Cartland and Mr. Landry. "But Professor Cartland here, I know, won't be coming home empty-handed either. He's got quite a fine collection of horse fossils, you know. Some of them no bigger than a cat. Adorable little creatures."

Chuckling from all around the car.

"You're a fine storyteller, Bolt," said Cartland, "yes yes, but I think with all your showman's bluster you've missed the real story. And the real story yes yes is evolution. These horses of mine that you're so quick to mock span millions of years, and when I have completed my collection, they will provide the physical proof for our English friend Charles Darwin and his controversial theory of evolution. How life starts, how it adapts over millions of years. It's fun to *dig* things up and give them names, but evolution will explain the entire story and *nature* of life on our planet."

His sober speech didn't win him any chuckles, but it had a heft to it. What I knew about evolution and natural selection wasn't much, but I knew it was talked about more and more. Many of the students grunted and nodded seriously. Cartland had just called my father a digger, a foolish amateur.

"Well," Father said with a forced grin, "I will look forward to admiring your horses in the museum, if I can push past the crowds thronged around the behemoths I've got on display."

"Ha!" said the journalist Landry. "And where will you find these behemoths, Professor Bolt?"

My father was so lathered up now I worried he might give something away. So before he could speak, I said, "You'll know when we get off the train."

"Very nice!" said Landry, scribbling. "You're a secretive bunch! I love this rivalry angle that's emerging. Feuding paleontologists in the Wild West!"

My father stepped very slowly, but firmly, on my big toe, and when I looked at him in objection, he tilted his head in Rachel Cartland's direction.

I didn't need any encouragement.

Across the aisle, he sat down with a sigh of contentment, as if the chair had been designed for him.

"Miss Cartland," he said cordially.

"Mr. Bolt," I replied.

He lifted a newspaper from a side table and began to read. I attended to my sewing, but watched him sideways. When he'd walked over, he still carried himself like a boy, vigor and eagerness bundled into the swing of his shoulders and arms. He had a mild stoop, his head drooping slightly. I was glad of it, this hint of uncertainty. A little tarnish upon the prodigy.

Some of the Yale students were humming purposefully now, warming up to yet another song.

"Have they been singing the entire trip?" Samuel Bolt asked, looking over with a grin.

"Unfortunately yes." I glanced up from my sewing. His profile really was quite perfect. "I'm hoping they'll quiet down once we get into the field."

"A little heatstroke might do the trick."

"Or a snakebite."

He chuckled. Freckles were dusted across either side of his nose. I kept my eyes on my work. Would nothing extinguish that smile? It made it harder for me to think clearly. The singing started up, loudly enough so that I couldn't hear what he said next.

"Excuse me?" I said.

He started to speak again, then gave up, and simply crossed the aisle and took the chair opposite me. There was not a foot between our knees. "May I?" he asked.

"Of course."

His eyelashes were thick enough to make most girls jealous. His mouth was very well molded. And the outline of his jaw was strong, giving his narrow face a lupine look.

"Our fathers are quite a pair, aren't they?" he said. "The way they carry on. Philadelphia! Good thing we were there to save them."

He was being a bit too familiar for my liking, like it were all some big joke. I carefully jabbed my needle into the material.

"As I recall, it was your father who struck the first blow."

His grin dissolved. "Only after your father publicly humiliated mine and tried to destroy his reputation."

His temper was quick when it came to defending his father. I supposed I was no different.

"What my father did," I said more gently, "he should have done in private. I truly wish he had."

Samuel nodded, the storminess leaving his face at once. "Well, my father's a terrible hothead. And he took a pounding for it. Ice to his face for the next three days. He's quite vain. I heard him murmuring to the mirror about permanent disfigurement." He chuckled.

"He looks absolutely fine to me."

"I hope your father wasn't too badly off."

"There was a lot of bruising. But he's fine now. Thank you for asking."

I looked around the carriage, hoping some gallant student wasn't going to join us. I needn't have worried. It was a lucky fact of growing up half-orphaned that I was often unchaperoned. I had no older sister or mother to fussily shadow me. My father forgot, and I was allowed a lot more freedom than most girls my age. I was used to sitting alone, and I enjoyed it.

"What are you sewing?" he asked.

I was ready with the lie I'd prepared, but something made me tell him the truth. Maybe it was because I wanted him to

KENNETH OPPEL

trust *me*. I'd give him a small secret, and maybe he'd give me a bigger one in return. Something useful to my father. I glanced around, but no one else was listening. They couldn't have heard anything over the singing anyway.

"A split skirt," I whispered. "I found a pattern in a magazine, and it didn't look too difficult."

"Is it like trousers?" he asked, lowering his voice to match mine.

I put my sewing to one side. "A little bit." I watched him, wondering if he'd think me odd. It was odd. No one wore split skirts out east. Even in the West, I'd heard, it was still considered eccentric, even improper. "It just divides a skirt into two equal halves. So a woman can ride astride."

He leaned closer, a conspiratorial smile on his face. "You're going to ride like a man?"

"Yes."

"Does your father know?"

"Not yet."

His eyes widened. "What'll he say?"

I had several guesses, none of them happy, but I felt reckless right now. "I don't know, and I don't care. If I'm going fossil hunting, I need to be able to ride properly, not slide off like some silly lady in the public gardens."

There was a pause, and for a second I was very worried he'd disappoint me and say something stupid.

He said, "I always thought those sidesaddles looked really uncomfortable."

"They're treacherous!" I said, pleased. "They don't hold you well, and sitting twisted in the saddle is terrible for your back. Not to mention the horse. I've seen them cinch those saddles so tightly the horse can hardly breathe."

"A split skirt makes total sense to me," he said. "Why not?"

I looked at him anew. I couldn't imagine too many men, if any, liking the idea of a woman riding astride. Was he just humoring me? No. For all his confidence and charm there was a guilelessness to his face. I didn't think he'd make a good liar.

He looked out the window at the endless grassland, hammered flat by the sky, and for a moment I was at a loss for what to say.

I nodded at a basket on the side table beside me. "There are some games here," I said, sorting through them. "Do you know this one?"

It was a word game, which was my forte. Samuel didn't know it, so I quickly explained the rules. There were sixteen cubes, with a different letter on each face. You shook them up in a little cloth sack and dumped them into a four-by-four tray, and then tried to write down as many words as possible using the adjacent letters.

"Like prospecting for words," I said.

"I should be good at this, then," he said.

"We'll see." Still cocky. I handed him a piece of paper and a pencil and turned the small hourglass upside down. "We have three minutes. Go."

When I played this game with Papa, we did it in complete

KENNETH OPPEL

silence, so intense was our concentration. So I was surprised when Samuel said, "Your father has a lot of hands working for him on this trip."

"Twelve students," I said, jotting down another word. This was no secret—anyone could count them right now in the parlor car.

"Don't forget you," he said.

I felt pleased. "I've done more prospecting than most of them. Some of them hardly know how to hold a geological hammer."

I heard him sniff sympathetically. "I hope they don't smash anything good."

"The soldiers will be even worse; I'm hoping Papa doesn't let them help."

Too late I realized I'd just let something slip.

"How many soldiers will you have?" he asked conversationally. It was a natural enough question, but I knew he was prospecting for information—just like me.

"No idea really. They're giving us an escort because of the Indians."

"Good idea," he replied. "That didn't ever occur to my father."

"Well, we'll certainly attract a lot more attention."

"With the singing and all."

I laughed. "Yes. It's just you and your father?"

"Pretty much."

We were quiet for a little bit, jotting down our words.

"Will you spend the whole summer out west?" he asked.

I didn't look up; I'd found a good clump of letters. "Yes."

EVERY HIDDEN THING

"Your mother won't miss you too much?"

"I have none."

When I glanced up, I saw the frank surprise in his face.

"Me either. She died of influenza."

"Mine in childbirth."

Eyes back on the game, he said, "So we both grew up mother-less."

I glanced at the dwindling sand in the timer, then back at the letters. "With only the influence of our fathers."

"For better or worse."

He laughed, and I laughed with him.

"I suppose that's why you're such a tomboy."

"The last person to call me that was punched in the nose."

"And who was that?"

"Matthew Kyles, in the schoolyard when I was nine. The timer's out."

He put down his pencil. "Interesting. So my father's not the only one who has a quick fist."

I was aware of the heat in my cheeks and hoped I wasn't blushing. I got splotchy when I blushed. "*I* was a child."

"So why did he call you a tomboy?"

"I took an atypical interest in a worm that had been cut in half."

Samuel nodded eagerly. "I ate one once."

This was good. "What did it taste like?"

"Dirt mostly. Dirt and . . ." His brown eyes looked up and to the right. "Cucumber. Did you get in trouble for punching Matthew?"

"He cried, and I had to stay in at recess and lunch all the next week. Which suited me fine. I got to read undisturbed."

"Well, I hope you won't punch me," he said.

"I might, if you call me a tomboy again. Maybe you'd cry too. I'm going to read out my words. The ones we have in common we cross out, and then I'll show you how we score the rest."

I could already see my list was much longer than his. He hadn't done very well. It was very satisfying trouncing him.

"How are you so good at this?" he demanded.

"A youth misspent on word puzzles and reading."

"I imagine you were quite abnormal as a child."

"Very."

"Did your friends enjoy losing over and over?"

"I didn't have friends."

"Not even at school?"

"I spent recess reading under a tree."

"The teacher's pet, I bet."

I shook my head. "That would've involved being helpful and chatty."

"I'd have sat with you under the tree," he said, and I raised my eyebrows doubtfully until he added, "if you ate a worm."

"Another game?" I asked, shaking the letters up again, because I could feel my cheeks redden, and I knew I was doing a very poor job closing the gate on his charm. What I really needed was more a windowless dungeon door, very thick.

"Yes," he said. "I'm determined to beat you at this."

I set the timer going again. He glared at the letters—as though he could order them into shape with the same uncanny ability he said he had with bones. He was very clever, and he knew it, but this was something I was undeniably better at. I got to work.

"Well," I heard him say, "I'm glad you won't be riding side-saddle. I've heard the terrain can be pretty punishing. Especially around the South Platte."

"Is that right?"

"So's your father hoping to complete his horse collection out there? He's had good luck in Nebraska."

"That would please him no end."

I kept my answers vague. Was he fishing again? Was that the real reason he'd come to talk to me? The only reason? I was surprised by the prick of hurt I felt, even though I'd been asked to do exactly the same thing.

"Time," I said, more sharply than I'd intended, and started reading out my words. He'd done better this time, but halfway through he said, "*Salvage?* You got *salvage?* Where?"

I tapped out the letters with the tip of my pencil. "That's worth seven points, by the way."

He shook his head in bewilderment. "I can't believe I missed it."

"Maybe you're not as sharp a prospector as you thought."

He frowned at his word list, and I felt a bit sorry for him.

I said, "I'm sure your expert eye will help your father find his king of all dinosaurs."

He glanced up at me so sharply I sensed I must've touched on something.

"All his talk of behemoths." I nodded over at his father. "He seems to have his sights set on something big."

He shrugged, but he still looked guarded. He was poor at hiding his thoughts. "Bigger is best with my father," he said.

I wondered if I'd made a discovery. Did they truly know about something vast waiting for them out there?

"Another lead from your dentist in Kansas?" I made a joke of it.

He grimaced. "I don't think Father would trust him to dig up a potato for him now. Anyway, Kansas is mostly aquatic reptiles—we're looking for true Dinosauria."

So he wasn't looking for any more reptiles. Nor was he going to Kansas. . . .

"If you could find anything out there, what would it be?" I asked.

"Oh, I don't know. Not another hadrosaur, not something that's already been discovered. Something amazing!"

His enthusiasm was so genuine I smiled, because it reminded me of the feeling I had when I thought of prospecting.

"Will you be able to put it together again in three minutes? Like the raccoon?" I made my eyes wide, wanting to flatter him, to make him talk even more. It surprised me when his face reddened.

"Well, the story didn't go quite like that. I left a bit out. My father had a stopwatch and gave me three minutes. I had it nearly put together, all except a pair of bones, and I didn't know where to place them." Even as he retold it, there was a faint echo of frustration and even panic in his voice. "It made me question all the work I'd already done. Was it even a raccoon? I started undoing everything and my father called time and I was still holding these two mystery bones, and I said, 'What are these?' And he laughed and said, 'I just added those to throw you off.' And everyone laughed with him, and I was furious."

"How old were you?"

"Eight."

"That's a cruel joke to play on a boy."

"It was a good lesson, I suppose. Taught me to trust my instincts and not get flustered."

The fact that he'd told me the real story—and not the bragging feat he'd related when we'd first met—made me like him much better, this new, more vulnerable boy.

"Was your father a good teacher?" he asked me.

"He was. I don't think he knew any other way to talk to me."

"Gave you your first magnifying glass."

He'd remembered. "Yes. And showed me my first dinosaur fossil. He woke me up early and took me to a field where a farmer had plowed up some sandstone slabs." I could still feel the chill in the morning air, see the long light through the trees. "There was a line of huge bird tracks in them. The farmer said it must've been Noah's raven; he'd never seen a bird so big. My father told him it was no bird. They were dinosaur footprints. It had been walking on two legs, dragging its tail behind it through the wet mud. You could see the tail marks. Millions of years ago. It was one of the most incredible moments of my life."

He nodded, saying nothing, eyes on mine. He knew how it felt. I had the sense I could say anything without baffling him, so unlike the people at my father's dinner table, with their thin-lipped smiles of disapproval or even pity. So I said, "I started looking at everything more carefully after that, for longer, too. The magnifying glass helped. A snail. A moth. A beetle. Even things that seemed ordinary or ugly at first could be beautiful."

6.
LET ME KISS YOU SWEET GOOD-BYE

WE TALKED AND TALKED, NEBRASKA swelling gently past the windows. We played one more round of the word game—and I played my other game, trying to learn as much as I could about Rachel's expedition. It would've been nice to win at least once. But I would've played any game that kept her near me.

The only thing reminding me of time was the train, stopping every so often to let people on or off. But Cartland's party showed no signs of leaving.

It was Father who eventually halted our conversation, by coming and introducing himself.

"I believe the last time we met," he said, smiling his most charming smile, "you had a very good grip on my ear."

I was glad to see she didn't fall victim to his grin and crinkled eyes. Solemnly she let her hand be taken and pressed.

"I have an appetite for lunch," Father said to me.

Reluctantly I said good-bye. We walked back to the dining car. My mind was singing with my long conversation, and I listened to little bits of it again and watched her laugh and frown and look at me gravely. Each thought and image of her was like one of those river rocks you held before putting it back so it stayed wet and beautiful.

The dining car was filling up when we arrived. We were directed to a free table and warned by the headwaiter that others might be seated with us if the need arose. My stomach rumbled happily. The food we'd been eating at station stops since Philadelphia was disgusting. Gray meat cunningly hidden beneath puddled gravy. It looked like something already chewed and rejected. I'd heard the Union Pacific's food was supposed to be good.

Father leaned in. "You two had a good long chat. What did you learn?"

I told him how I'd asked her leading questions about Nebraska and horses. But she'd been evasive.

"But," I said, "did you know they have an army escort?"

"Do they?" he murmured. "Trust Cartland to strum all the moneyed strings. But this is a very interesting bit of information. Because the soldiers have to come from somewhere. . . ."

"So we know he's getting off near a fort." I was quite pleased with myself.

"Precisely." He pulled the Union and Central Pacific map

from his jacket. He consulted his pocket watch.

"We've cleared Silver Creek," he muttered. "We've got North Platte coming up. That's near Fort McPherson. That situates them perfectly for excursions into both Kansas and Nebraska. He's found a lot of his horse fossils in that region. Even up into southern Dakota. After that there's Cheyenne—there's a fort near there as well. And next would be . . . well, that would put them at our station stop." He looked crushed.

"It's most likely North Platte," I said to cheer him up, though I hated the idea of Rachel getting off the train.

"That means they'll be getting off at two a.m.," he said, looking at the timetable. "Let's hope."

Just then the lavender-scented lady from our car was escorted to our table by the headwaiter. Both Father and I rose and said, "Good afternoon, ma'am."

"I hope you don't mind my joining you?"

"Not at all, please," said my father, pulling out the chair next to his.

We sat and introduced ourselves. Her name was Mrs. Cummins, and she was traveling from St. Paul to live with her sister's family in San Francisco. She'd lost her husband during the war. She must've married very young, because she couldn't have been thirty, and was uncommonly pretty.

She talked mostly to my father, who'd angled his chair toward her. He was trying to subtly stroke his mustache into some order. To straighten the lines of his train-rumpled jacket. No one could be as attentive to women as him. It was positively cosmic. He turned on his full solar attention, and they actually seemed to lean closer, like they were gravitationally pulled.

Despite Mrs. Cummins's lush mouth, and the pleasing swell of her blouse, I was thinking only of Rachel. Watching for her to come and have her lunch. I only half listened to my father's conversation with Mrs. Cummins. Mostly to make sure he didn't reveal too much about our expedition. He told just enough to impress the widow with his fame. Our food arrived, and the two of them seemed scarcely interested in it. She liked to touch his arm when she made a point or was surprised by something he said. She was surprised a lot. I saw Father sit up taller, his smile spread roguishly across his face. He was never at a loss for words, asking her question after question, which she eagerly answered.

Cartland and Rachel arrived and had their lunch with Landry and one of the students. She did not look over. Which was maddening.

When we were finished, Mrs. Cummins shook our hands and excused herself and went back to the second carriage.

"Well," my father said, inhaling as if enjoying a fresh breeze, "she was a very pleasant lady. We should return to the carriage as well."

"But shouldn't we try to learn more?" I asked. "About the Cartlands."

"Never overplay your hand," he said wisely. "Our best chance will be after dinner, when the bar opens in the parlor car. Until then, we have our own plans to discuss."

A big wintry gust of disappointment moved through me, but

I followed Father back to the carriage. When dinnertime finally came round, we returned to the dining car. Much to my father's disappointment, we weren't seated with Mrs. Cummins. She was already with three Yale students, who mostly stared at her in stunned silence while she made sunny chitchat. I noticed she liked touching the arm of one of the handsomer students.

We ourselves had the bad luck of being seated with two waxy-looking stationers. The more talkative one, very slowly and in excruciating detail, told us about the challenges of the job. I was shoveling food into my mouth so I could get away fast, but my father seemed to enjoy interrupting the fellow to pepper him with questions. I kept looking over at Cartland's table, hoping Rachel would look over and see me. She did, just once, and held my gaze for an electrifying moment before turning her attention back to her father.

By the end of the meal our stationers thought Father was a capital fellow and gave him their cards. They parted with hearty handshakes and invitations to visit next time we were in Sacramento.

"Ah, that was an ordeal," he said. "I believe the parlor car will be serving restorative beverages by now."

As we entered, the attendant was just unlocking the liquor cabinet. Its mirrored shelves were filled with festive-looking bottles. As diners finished their meals, the car filled till there were no more seats. People stood about, holding their cigars and drinks.

My father ordered whiskey. Many Quakers disapproved of

liquor, but my father wasn't one of them. He pressed a drink into my hand; I was still unaccustomed but took it back in two slugs. It seared sweetly all the way down. A hot bloom started through me. I felt the train's restless pulse through my feet. *Rex-ex-ex, rex-ex-ex, rex-ex-ex* . . . My father soon had a group of Yale students around him, asking about his finds. Tumblers hit the bar and were refilled. Mine included. Cigar and pipe and cigarette smoke thickened. A group of students began to sing, and I smiled this time.

Let me introduce a fellah, Lardy dah! Lardy dah!
A fellah who's a swell, ah, Lardy dah!

From the corner of my eye I saw Rachel, sitting in a corner by the window. She was not drinking, nor was her father. I wanted to go talk to her more than anything.

Suddenly the singing seemed louder, a familiar voice yodeling above the rest. Sure enough, when I looked, my father had joined arms with four other Yalies as they swayed back and forth, belting out:

As he saunters through the street,
He is just too awful sweet;
To observe him is a treat, Lardy dah! Lardy dah!

He had a terrible voice, my father, but it never stopped him from singing with huge enthusiasm.

In his hand a penny stick,
In his mouth a quill tooth-pick,
Not a penny in his pocket, Lardy-dah!

Which might be our situation, if Father kept buying everyone drinks. He was slapping another bill down on the bar for the attendant. Much cheering and backslapping and raising of glasses. Someone pushed a glass into my hand. I had to admit, Father knew how to commandeer a room.

"How much have you spent?" I shouted into his ear, pulling him aside.

"A pittance," he said, grinning. "And a small price to pay for what I just learned." He winked. "North Platte."

Just like he'd hoped: Cartland's group would be getting off the train at two in the morning. And I was headed on into Wyoming. Leaving Rachel far behind.

Father was elated. "And when we find our *rex*," he said, leaning close to me, face flushed, "I'm naming it after you."

A jolt went up my spine. "Really?"

"Of course! You practically funded this expedition! And you'll be at my side with your keen eye!"

I wasn't sure I believed him, especially in his current state, but it didn't stop the ballooning of happiness in my chest. My name. The perfect piece in my collection. Before I could even thank him, he was swallowed back up by Cartland's adoring students, who were embarking on the well-known temperance song "Dinna Forget yer Promise, Jamie."

Dinna forget yer promise, Jamie,
Dinna forget to think o' me.
Let me kiss ye sweet gude bye,
Let me kiss ye sweet gude bye.

The Yale students were making a big show of grasping their pals and planting big smacks on their cheeks. Someone kissed my cheek too, and my heart kicked. *Rachel.* But when I looked over I saw that it was Mrs. Cummins. She laughed at my surprised face, and then my father took her hand and led her in a dance. They seemed very cozy with each other.

I looked back at Rachel, alone now at the table, and was seized by the panic I wouldn't see her again. I'd never felt anything quite like it. I downed my drink, started toward her, not having a clue what I'd say.

I sat down next to her. Bold, since she hadn't invited me, but this was the Wild West and there was singing and I'd had whiskey.

"I wanted to say good-bye."

"Are you getting off soon?" she asked. She looked genuinely surprised, which made me surprised for a second until I realized she was playacting. I chuckled.

"No," I said, feeling very suave. "We're not getting off till *after* you." Her eyes widened. "How do you know that?"

"One of your students just told my father where you're going."

"Oh dear."

"It's funny," I said. "My father wanted me to talk to you and try to weasel out where you were going."

She hesitated a moment. "Mine too."

I sat back. "Really? So we were both spying on each other."

She smiled. "Is that the only reason you talked to me?"

For a moment I wondered if I'd hurt her feelings. I shook my head.

She looked unconvinced. I knew her father might return at any moment, so I hurried. "Would you write to me?"

"Yes," she said right away. "Where do I send the letter?"

"Just the post office in . . ." I caught myself. Too much whiskey. "Ha! You're very good. I almost told you where we're going."

"So why don't you?

What was it about her gaze that made me want to tell her the truth? Tell her everything in me. Maybe she'd make sense of it all, keep it safe. Maybe I thought the more I told her, the more she'd like me. At school girls had seemed to like my talk, but usually I was just flattering. I saw what they liked, and the look in their faces made me want to please them better than they'd ever been pleased.

Right now I wanted Rachel Cartland to stay and like me. I wanted her to *trust* me. I leaned closer, though there was no risk of anyone overhearing, it was so noisy. "We're getting off at Crowe, working the badlands to the north."

She nodded calmly, but I was pretty sure she was surprised.

"Can I tell you a secret?" I said.

She smiled. "You are a terrible spy."

"I shouldn't tell you."

"You don't need to tell me. I'll say good night." She made to get up.

"Wait," I said. "Wait, wait." I told her about the tooth, all about it. She listened with rapt attention. Our faces were close, and when I finished talking we watched each other expectantly. Her mouth was not lush, but her upper lip had a very precise and pretty notch at its center, and I knew I was about to kiss it. I didn't care who'd see or what would happen afterward, and I had the feeling she didn't either. But from the corner of my eye, I saw her stolid father approaching. The sour sight of him made me lose my nerve. I knew I only had a few more seconds alone with her.

"Don't forget to write," I said. "I like talking to you more than anything." My heart was beating fast, and I couldn't stop myself adding, "You really do have the most extraordinary eyes."

My appearance has gone uncomplimented, almost entirely.

Certainly my father praised me for good schoolwork and my scientific drawings and observations—and I valued these a great deal. But without a mother I was never told I had lovely hair or a pleasing figure or striking eyebrows—or any of those things one is supposed to hear as a girl, even if they're untrue. My aunt Berton's few remarks usually involved a criticism of some kind, like my hair looked as though it needed washing.

The first and only time I remember being complimented for my appearance was in school when I was nine. I was asked to read a passage of Tennyson's poem "Ulysses," and I was shy to do it. I did not like people's eyes on me, and I read it as quickly as possible. Mrs. Hansard, who was always kind to me, nodded and said, "Rachel Cartland, that was quite clear and correct, but

I find it hard to believe that you can't read such stirring words with more passion, when you have such bewitching intensity in your face."

Bewitching intensity. I had clutched that phrase to me the rest of the day, and then wrote it down in my best writing and laid it in the bottom of a drawer, which I'd vainly reopen just to look at.

But it didn't burn as brightly as Samuel Bolt's compliment, or the secret he'd just given me.

"Our stop," Father said. He stood beside my berth, shaking my elbow.

His hair was all askew, eyes bleary. Breath a pungent fog of spirits and tobacco. I didn't imagine I looked or smelled much better.

The whiskey had given me a fitful sleep. I'd been aware of each jerking station stop, knowing Rachel was getting off at one of them and feeling a spasm of loss. Also anxiety. I'd said too much last night. I'd told her all about the *rex* tooth. And where we were going. Stupid.

Head pounding, I dressed hurriedly, looking out the window at the great grass sea, still pale in the early morning light. The Cartlands were already far away; it didn't matter if I'd confided in her. She said she'd write. That was something. That showed she cared about me. I felt a bit cheered up.

As the train slowed, a few other people in our carriage headed for the door. I saw my father cast a quick backward glance toward the private compartment of Mrs. Cummins.

Many of the stations we'd passed in Nebraska were just a platform and water tower and shed built on the shore of the prairie. But Crowe was a proper town. As we pulled into the station, wood smoke rose from the low houses near the tracks.

Father hopped onto the platform before the train had even come to a complete standstill. Impatiently he stalked back toward the baggage car. But my gaze was pulled in the opposite direction, where four blue-uniformed army officers stood stiffly at attention. One of them had a captain's insignia and looked curiously in my father's direction.

"Professor?" he called out.

Abruptly my father turned and squinted in confusion, looking more like a crazed desperado than an esteemed scientist.

"Are you addressing me, sir?" my father asked.

"I'm Captain Longman of Fort Crowe. You are Professor Cartland, are you not?"

My father patted at his hair and stood to his full height. "No, sir, I am not Professor Cartland. I am Professor B——"

From the Palace Car, a blazered Yale student hopped down, followed by another and another and another. They looked like a scurry of bright-eyed chipmunks, darting eager glances at the town, the sky, the officers, their waiting horses and wagons, like they might burst into song.

Stunned, I watched as Rachel Cartland was helped down by the porter. Next came the journalist Landry. Professor Cartland brought up the rear.

"Ah, Captain Longman," he called out to the officer. "Delighted to make your acquaintance, sir. And thank you very much for the welcome."

As the captain strode eagerly toward Cartland with his hand outstretched, Cartland looked down the platform at my father and tipped his hat.

7.
CROWE

ONLY A MARCHING BAND COULD HAVE made Cartland's reception any grander. The little receiving line of stiff blue-coated officers shook hands with the professor and his beaming students, then Landry and Rachel. I wouldn't have been surprised if the soldiers had fired off a salute and the professor been presented with a medal. Mr. Landry scampered here and there with his notebook, scribbling.

Rachel waited patiently on the platform as her father talked to various officers and nodded officiously. I tried to meet her eye, but either she didn't notice me, or was ignoring me, which was much worse. I felt betrayed.

"This can't be a coincidence," Father muttered darkly.

His worst fear come true. I tried to douse a hot flare of guilt, telling myself I had nothing to do with this. Yes, I'd told Rachel where we were going, but just hours ago! What was happening now had been planned in advance. Before Cartland even set eyes on us in Omaha, he'd *known* where he was going. Or else how could the army be here to meet them?

I told all this to my father, but I wasn't sure he was listening. He kept glaring at Cartland's entourage. I felt like I was managing a trained lion who still sometimes mauled people.

"There's our things," I said, hoping to distract him. I nodded at the battered bags deposited on the platform. My father seized two and jerked his head at the others. I grabbed them and followed him inside the small station building.

"That student lied to me last night," he muttered. "On Cartland's orders, of course. Like a fool I fell for it."

Rachel hadn't lied to me exactly, but she'd let me keep thinking she was getting off earlier than us. I felt another pang of hurt and humiliation.

"Should *we* have an army escort?" I asked, staring back at all the soldiers.

"Not at all," he said. "It's the army the Sioux hate most of all. Having them along would just antagonize them. I worry about Cartland's safety, not ours."

I wasn't sure if he was lying but didn't feel like questioning him.

Inside the raw-timbered waiting room we looked around for our man Plaskett. No one stepped forward to greet us.

"You sent the right time in the telegram?" my father asked sharply.

"Yes."

There was a clock in the station agent's booth, and we watched miserably as a few more minutes ticked by. It would be hard to miss the arrival of the train, since the tracks ran right through the town.

"Let's go find lodgings," my father said. "Then we'll make inquiries for our Mr. Plaskett."

"You don't think . . ." I began before I could check myself.

"What?" So sharply I knew he'd worried the same thing. "That he just took the money and disappeared?" He yanked out a nostril hair and winced. "I'm a good judge of character. I trust the fellow. He's genuine. Like the fossil he sent us."

"Maybe he's waiting for us on the street."

We hefted our bags out the door. I was blinded by the light off the sun-bleached facades. A far cry from the cobbled, leafy streets of Philadelphia. The dusty thoroughfare was treeless. The town looked like it was making things up as it went along. Buildings of wood, buildings of canvas, empty lots marked out with stakes. Horse manure mingled with the sweet scent of fresh-milled wood. Every other establishment was a saloon. Right now at nine in the morning things looked fairly sleepy, but I bet it would be wild at night.

Two boys loitered with a hopeful look, so Father paid them to carry our bags to the hotel down the street—one of the few two-story buildings in town.

Inside my father asked the reception clerk where we could find Edward Plaskett.

"I see him in town from time to time. He doesn't live here. Can't remember the last time I saw him. Maybe a couple weeks . . ." He finished writing in his ledger. "Now, sir, if you could pay for your room in advance."

My father balked. "Do we look like paupers?"

"No, sir."

"Is this customary?"

"In Crowe it's customary."

"Very well." He pulled out his billfold and stared inside for a moment too long. "Excuse me a moment," he said, and then ushered me a few steps away.

He whispered, "Did I give you some of our money?"

"No. I asked you to, in Chicago, but you forgot."

"Ah."

A hot tingle of alarm moved across my shoulders. "What's wrong?"

"Nothing." He returned to the clerk. "Your simplest room is fine. My son and I can share a bed if necessary."

He paid out some coins very slowly. Like it meant he was paying less.

"Room's not ready yet," the clerk told us. "You're welcome to wait in the parlor, or they're serving breakfast in the dining room."

We retreated to the empty parlor. A plank floor, a few chairs, and one sofa with a distressingly large stain on it.

"What's the matter?" I demanded.

My father stared intently out the window, like a man having a vision. "I appear to have been robbed."

"What? On the train? How much is gone?"

"Not so bad, really. . . ."

I took the billfold from his inert hands and riffled through the notes.

"This is less than half!" I hissed.

Piously he said, "I have been the victim of a criminal plot."

"Who?"

"She was good enough to leave me some at least."

"She? Who do you—" My voice so low it was little more than a vibration: "Mrs. Cummins?"

Last night, after Rachel and Cartland had left, I'd headed off to bed. Leaving my father still carousing with a few students, and Mrs. Cummins. My last sight of them was cuddled up together on a love seat.

He lifted a hand. "We'll talk about this later. Possibly never."

"She *robbed* you?"

"I had some doubts she was a war widow, but I didn't think her capable of such deceit."

"We have to do something . . . the sheriff. Is there a sheriff in town?"

"No point. She's long gone by now," he said. "What we have will be enough."

"How?"

"We will be frugal. . . ."

"*Frugal?* Like buying drinks for everyone on the train!"

"I can have money wired from . . ."

"Who? Your father won't send you a cent."

He stared out the window again. "What we have, we will make last."

"We don't even have our guide," I grumbled. I was on my feet, suddenly furious. I'd fought for this trip. *I'd* gotten the funds—yes, other people's money, but by my own plan! And my father had just lost most of it to a thief. With my anger came a stormy surge of panic. The *rex* was out there in the badlands, waiting to be claimed, and we were stuck here.

"What's our plan now?" I said, more to myself than my father. I didn't trust him to salvage the situation.

"Yes," my father said absently, pulling at the bit of beard under his mouth.

Mr. Plaskett was supposed to take care of our arrangements. But where was Mr. Plaskett? Did he even exist? And if he didn't exist, was there even a fossil waiting for us out there? No. The tooth at least was real.

I said, "We need horses, a wagon, a guide, a teamster, provisions—"

My father stirred and sucked air through his nostrils. "Good." From one of his pockets he took a pencil and a scrap of paper and handed them to me.

"Provisions for . . . thirty days. Write this down."

I wanted to throw his pencil back in his face, tell him to be his own secretary, but I didn't. I just took dictation.

"Bacon, beans, rice, apples, onions, canned tomatoes, flour, hard bread, salt, pepper, and vinegar. And let's add to that: canned peaches, ham, and oysters."

I rolled my eyes and left that last one off. Next he'd be wanting caviar.

"Get that filled." He pointed out the window to a weathered sign that said GENERAL OUTFITTERS.

"What'll you do?" I asked.

"Make further inquiries about our Mr. Plaskett and hope I don't find him in a saloon. I'll also see about a wagon and team."

Outside, I squinted into the heat and glare. I found the least muddy place to cross the street. When I walked into General Outfitters, it took a moment for my vision to adjust.

No shelves, no barrels of goods, no promising smell of cinnamon. Just a deep and arousing musk of perfume. At one end was a caged bar and a tired-looking man within it. Behind him a long hall lead back into gloom and the muffled squeal of women. I was curious about the sounds, wanted to listen more. But the man behind the counter was watching.

"What's your pleasure?" he said.

"You don't sell provisions?"

"You'll want Smitherman's."

I left the bordello and walked the sidewalk. In my city trousers and shoes and jacket I stood out. Not nearly dusty enough. Some of the planks underfoot were wobbly, some dark with stains. Maybe urine and vomit, given their ghostly smells. Outside a saloon there was one reddish-brown patch that still looked sticky. I stepped carefully over it. I crossed the street toward a store that proclaimed:

T. SMITHERMAN

FIREARMS & AMMUNITION

HARDWARE TINWARE LUMBER

And then, like an afterthought, on a painted cloth banner below:

GROCERIES PROVISIONS

It was a welcome sight to walk in and see the place so well stocked. I handed my list to the proprietor, and he tilted his chin up to peer beneath his spectacles.

"Quite a list."

He looked up questioningly, which confused me. Didn't this happen every day? I wondered. People striking out for the wilderness from here? Homesteaders and gold diggers and soldiers? What else was there to do in Crowe—except leave?

"Let's see now. Bacon, no. Coffee, no. Beans, some, but not as many as you want. Apples, sold out, rice, no . . ."

In confusion I looked around the bursting shop. "But that's rice there," I said, pointing at a mighty pile of sacks. "And onions!"

"Spoken for."

"Well, that flour, then!"

"Spoken for in advance."

Maybe he was punishing me for being from out east. "What about salt? Can you spare a few grains?"

He grinned. "Salt we got."

At that moment the door opened and Rachel Cartland entered.

"Good afternoon," she said to the proprietor before seeing me. "I'm here for the Cartland order."

"It's all ready for you, miss," said the shopkeeper, stepping into the back. "I'll go get the boys to bring it out."

KENNETH OPPEL

"So," a voice said, off to my right. "You've bought the entire store."

Turning, I saw him and felt terribly awkward. I'd avoided meeting his eye on the platform, because he'd looked so astonished—and hurt.

"We telegraphed ahead," I explained. "You can't buy anything?"

Gone was his usual smile. He seemed angry with the whole world. "We both ended up in the same town. What a strange surprise."

"It shouldn't be! Last night you said you knew where we were headed."

"And you let me go on thinking it."

"You didn't give me any time," I retorted—and felt dishonest because this was only partially true. I'd been overwhelmed by his confidences, and his compliment, and hoping it was true, despite the whiskey on his breath.

"You could've told me," he said.

"What does it matter? What would anyone have done differently? We'd still be here at the same station. Our fathers would still be going about their business."

"And what's your father's business in Crowe, exactly?"

"He's been planning this expedition for months," I said, offended by his accusing tone. "The reason we have food, and you don't, is because we planned ahead. We are *not* following you."

He was being pigheaded. He must have known all this. There was no other explanation for it—and certainly no sinister one.

"But your father, he must've picked *this* area for a reason."

I hadn't thought anyone could be so annoying. "Yes, he'd heard there were excellent Cretaceous hunting grounds around here."

"Who told him that?" So insistent!

"I don't know. He corresponds with lots of people. Just like your father."

"You told him about the tooth, didn't you."

It was not phrased as a question. I didn't like him very much at all right now, and I wanted to say, *Yes, of course I told my father. We were spying on each other, weren't we? And you're not good at games.*

It hadn't been an easy decision. It was something I could give my father, something to prove my value on this expedition. I would be his helpful spy. But Samuel had told me in confidence, and it seemed a shameful thing to betray someone's secret. And the *way* he'd told me, so reckless and excited, so eager to share it. What good would it do my father anyway? He had his own goals for this expedition. He didn't need to poach someone else's.

"No," I told him. "I said nothing about your tooth."

His shoulders dropped as he exhaled. He looked embarrassed. "Thank you. I'm sorry I was rude. This day has—"

Mr. Smitherman returned with two boys carrying crates. I did feel sorry for Samuel, even his reckless father.

"Perhaps we could decrease our order a bit," I told the shopkeeper.

He pulled in a breath. "I'd need to get the okay from

Professor Cartland or Captain Longman to do that, miss."

Hurriedly Samuel said, "It's all right—please don't."

"Are you sure?"

"Yes, it's fine." I could tell he was proud and didn't want to be beholden to us—to my father anyway. "I'm sure there's somewhere else—"

"There's Mr. Powers just down the street," Smitherman said.

Samuel nodded. "There. He'll take care of me, I'm sure."

I bit my upper lip. "We've placed a fairly large order with him as well."

He sagged a bit. "We'll be fine."

To the shopkeeper and his boys I said, "The team's just outside. The driver and his man can help you load."

"You're striking out today?" Samuel asked.

"To Fort Crowe first; it's several miles to the south. They've invited us to spend a day or two there."

"Seems you'll have quite an escort. Where are you headed after that?"

The question was direct, his gaze intent.

"Why should I tell you that?"

"Like you said, what'll it change, since everyone has their plans made already?"

I glared at him; he glared back defiantly, like he'd won a victory.

"Fine," I said. "North. Father says there's a big river valley and badlands where bone's been spotted. And you?"

Samuel didn't say a word. His face gave his reply.

8.
NED PLASKETT

I **WALKED INTO THE GLARE OF THE STREET,** furious at my scatterbrained father. Why hadn't he telegraphed ahead for his order? Furious at myself, too. Why hadn't *I* thought ahead for him? But how could we've known our guide would betray us or that Cartland would land in Crowe at the same time? It was too cruel a coincidence. And our *rex* just sitting there, waiting to be discovered. Not picky about by whom.

Halfway down the street I met my father.

"No one's seen Plaskett today," he reported. "And every horse in town is spoken for."

"That'd be Cartland and his crew," I said. "They bought up most of Smitherman's."

We looked back as crate after sack was loaded onto the wagon.

"We should've ordered ahead," I said accusingly.

"Plaskett was supposed to take care of all that," my father replied tightly.

"Do you think we've been had?" I demanded.

"I'm not ready to entertain that possibility," said Father.

"Listen," I said. "I just talked to Rachel Cartland. They're headed to the exact same place we are."

He stared at me, one hand gripping his beard.

"Badlands to the north. River valley. Cretaceous bones." I nodded. "Plaskett's crossed us. Cartland's bought him off, or something, and he's working for *them* now."

I couldn't stand still. Father followed as I headed toward Powers' Grocery. Panic pounded at my temples. We'd spent four days getting here. We'd been robbed. We had no guide. Still, we had to move, to try to find the *rex* before Plaskett lead them straight to it. I felt like something precious was being wrenched away from me.

Inside Powers' Grocery, the proprietor shook his head sadly. "I'd love to help you, gentlemen, but—"

"It can't all be spoken for," my father protested, looking at the well-stocked shelves.

"The army was short supplied this month. They had to lean heavy on me and Mr. Smitherman. Good business for us, but not good for my other customers."

Father straightened his stooped shoulders and said, "I am Professor Michael Bolt from Philadelphia, and I am on a scientific expedition of great importance."

At this news the man looked almost suspicious. "Well, now, if I'd known you were coming, sir, I could've set something aside." He began to whistle softly and look around his shop, like he was wishing we'd evaporate. "Maybe in a week or so, when I get my new stock in . . ."

Outside the shop I said, "There must be other places in town."

But Father wasn't listening. He was squinting at a man limping down the middle of the main street.

"Who's this, then?" he muttered.

My eyesight was better than my father's. Whoever this fellow was, his trousers were caked so thickly with mud they were rigid as stovepipes. A buckskin vest hung crookedly on his shoulders; one sleeve had a big tear down it. A trampled wide-brimmed hat. A full white beard. He looked ancient. Leaning heavily on a stick, he was like a character plucked from the Bible. A half-mad prophet returning from the desert.

As he limped closer, I saw the stick was actually a long-handled pick. He was looking straight at us. I had the uneasy feeling he was coming our way. Likely he'd rant and rave and want to baptize us. Wearily he thrust a hand high, a gesture that looked as much like surrender as greeting.

"That's Ned Plaskett," said Mr. Powers, who'd come out of his shop to stand beside us.

"Ah! Is it now?" said my father angrily.

I couldn't believe this derelict was the man who'd written us.

"Looks like he's had himself an adventure," said the shopkeeper before going back inside.

"I didn't think he'd be so . . . old," I murmured.

He walked right up. I could see why people on the street had been giving him a wide berth. The mud—or worse—caked to his clothing gave off a high stink.

"Professor Bolt?" the man said, looking genuinely pained.

Up close, he was not so old. Maybe early thirties. His face was tanned, but fairly unlined. His hair and beard were actually black, just coated in dust. He took his hat from his head and, after shaking hands with my father, clutched that hat to his chest and worried the frayed edges with his fingers.

"Professor Bolt, I can't tell you how sorry I am, sir, to be late for you. I was headed into town yesterday, and my horse took a wrong step into a badger hole. She went right over and me with her. I got straight up, but she'd broke her neck, poor girl."

He wrestled a pack off his shoulder and set it down with a heavy thunk on the planks.

"So I took what I could and set off by foot."

I had no idea what to make of him. Was he telling the truth? Or was he just spinning a lie?

"You must be Samuel." He grabbed my hand and shook it heartily. "A pleasure to meet the both of you. I'm awfully glad you haven't given up on me!"

"Seems it's you who's given up on us," I said. I couldn't help it. My head and thoughts were so overheated.

Astonished, he gazed from me to my father. "I'm not sure I—"

"It's come to our attention," Father said, "that my colleague Professor Cartland is in town and seems to have his sights set on the same hunting grounds you described to us."

Ned Plaskett licked his lips like a parched nomad. His head lolled forward. I'd never seen a guiltier-looking fellow in my life.

"Professor Bolt, I should've told you earlier. But I didn't think anything would come of it—really I didn't. I can see how wrong I was now."

He started pacing back and forth, limping slightly. He ran a hand through his sweat-matted hair.

I waited for him to continue and confirm the worst. I felt sick.

"When I didn't hear anything back from you in so long, I thought you weren't interested—and to be honest, I was worried I'd lost my fossil in the bargain."

"Yes, well, my boy misplaced the crate," Father said.

I was too crestfallen to even object to this lie.

"Well," said Plaskett, "someone said I should write to Professor Cartland at Yale, so I did that."

My pulse pounded in my throat. "And what did you tell him?"

"Only that I'd found some interesting Cretaceous fossils in the area of Fort Crowe and asked if he'd be interested in me digging them up. He wrote offering me employment, but that very same day I got your telegraph. So right away I wrote back to Professor Cartland saying I was sorry, but I was honor bound by my original offer to you."

"And that's all you told him?" Father asked.

"That's everything."

My heart lifted hopefully. "Nothing about the tooth?"

Plaskett shook his head. "I had no idea he'd come out this

way. Truly, I never thought he'd end up in Crowe the same time as you."

"We're not so badly off," I said. "We've still got our guide."

Father stroked his mustache. "Cartland's got a small army." He looked severely at Plaskett. "And your leg's injured, by the looks of it."

Mr. Plaskett peered down at his legs, and then said, "Oh, my limp. No, I've had that since I was six. It didn't heal right after a fall. All the walking's bothered it some, I guess."

Mr. Plaskett swatted a fly on his face, leaving a bloody smear. He left it. His pant legs bristled with burrs. His matted hair rose in a series of damp spikes. I was getting worried his fingers would claw right through his hat.

"Ah," said my father. His eyes were darting here and there, and I could tell he was having a panic. I knew what he was thinking, because I was thinking it myself—unkind as it was. What kind of guide and helper would this beaten-down fellow be?

Father said, "Mr. Plaskett, forgive me, but I'm more than a little concerned about your general state of health."

"Because of my *leg*?" At this he actually laughed. A very generous laugh that opened his face right up and made him seem much younger suddenly. "It's never slowed me down any."

"Can you actually mount a horse, sir?"

A brown horse with a white diamond on its nose was tied up at a post. Plaskett put his hand reassuringly on the horse's muzzle, murmured something, and then with a quick flick of his hand, had the lead free of the hitching post. In a single fluid motion his good foot was in the stirrup and his body swinging into the saddle. Before his backside hit the leather, he wheeled the horse round and went charging down the street full tilt, scattering a couple soldiers and veering around a wagon. He made that horse pirouette and come galloping straight back to us. Before the horse was even fully stopped, he was off its back and hitching it to the post.

"That was fantastic!" I said.

With a wink he said to me, "Your pa's turn now."

"Very impressive, Mr. Plaskett," my father said. "Our big problem now is supplies, which I'd assumed you would take care of. But every horse and bean in town is spoken for."

"Tom Powers'll take care of us," said Ned simply.

"He says he's cleaned out," I said.

"Some things you can't see coming," said Plaskett. "Like that badger hole that killed my Clairie. But I always plan ahead. Come on."

He lead us back inside the shop, where Mr. Powers was wiping down his counter. "Tom, you got it all set out for us?"

Without a word Mr. Powers led us back through the store and out into a yard with a big shed. He unlocked the latch and left the door open so we could see. A wagon, already loaded up with what looked to me like enough provisions to last the summer.

"That's all ours?" my father asked.

"And the wagon."

All I could do was smile in sheer relief, but Father asked, "Why didn't you tell us you had our provisions? After we said who we were!"

"Ned here told me to be cautious and not sell to any out-of-towners until he could vouch for them."

I laughed, and my father nodded solemnly. "Very wise, Mr. Plaskett. I approve of your prudence."

"It was a good thing he did, or the army would've cleaned me out entirely," said Powers. "And I've got a good driver for you. My son Hitch."

"He's excellent," said Ned Plaskett.

"Well, let's meet this son of yours," my father said.

Mr. Powers shouted out, and from the back of the house emerged a short, stocky lad. As he came closer with his choppy walk, I saw he wasn't a lad at all. His large eyes had a childlike innocence, quite out of tune with his silvering hair and lined skin. I'd seen a few people in Philadelphia with the same unusual eyes.

"Hitch," his father said, "you remember Ned. And this is Professor Bolt."

"Hello. How are you?" he said with practiced formality, shaking my father's hand.

"I'm well, Mr. Powers," Father replied.

"I'm Hitch," he said, as we shook hands.

"Samuel," I said, wondering what his real age was.

"Yep," he said, and then smiled and went back inside the house.

"Is he simple?" my father asked the storekeeper quietly.

"Yes," said Mr. Powers. "But he's good with horses. Good hunter and cook, too. He's strong. He'll take care of you."

My father looked at Ned for corroboration.

"It's true," said Plaskett. "And he's got the best heart in this town. Not too many people here I'd feel safe sharing camp with."

"He doesn't talk much either," added Mr. Powers. "He's soothing company. And he'll only cost you a dollar a day."

"Done. Now what about horses?"

Ned Plaskett scratched some caked mud from his beard. "That's a bit trickier."

"But you've got a team?"

"Isaiah Collins has the only team left, but he won't rent it out. He'll only sell."

"How much?" I asked.

"Five hundred."

"*Five* hundred," Mr. Powers snorted. "Double its value!"

"Yep. Might be able to beat him down fifty, but no more than that."

"And we can sell it at the end of the season," I said.

"For a fraction!" my father muttered.

"We need horses," I reminded him.

"Is it a good team?" he asked Plaskett, as if my father knew anything about horses.

"Not bad. The wheelers are mustangs, a bit worn out. The leaders are solid enough; there's a colt who's a bit rambunctious. Isaiah's also got three saddle ponies he'll loan us in the bargain. It's not so bad. All things considered."

Father asked how much we owed for the provisions and wagon.

Ned Plaskett told him the price he'd arranged with Mr. Powers. My heart gave a thump.

"We're a hundred short," I said.

"We have a temporary shortfall," my father said. "I was robbed on the train."

"Pickpockets?" said Ned Plaskett, all sympathy.

"Indeed," my father said. "I'd like to meet with Mr. Collins and see if we can come to some arrangement."

"No point. He's awful stubborn," said Ned. "He's only holding them for me till tomorrow."

"Do they play billiards here?" I asked Ned.

"They do, especially at the Pioneer."

"I can win us a hundred."

Astonished, Plaskett asked my father, "What are your feelings on gambling, Professor?"

"Everything in moderation, and in desperate circumstances, in excess. The boy's excellent. He got suspended from school for it."

We took our lunch at the hotel and by then our room was ready and we all tidied ourselves up. Father adjusted my tie.

"We are witless city folk looking to be fleeced. We proceed with caution."

I'd never been in a place as wild as the Pioneer. It wasn't just a gambling hall. There were upstairs girls, too, bright as cockatoos. And even at three in the afternoon it seemed to be doing a good business. A couple of billiards tables to one end and a small crowd around each. There were card tables and faro tables too. The place smelled a bit high, all the bodies in it, and some of them not too well washed. My stomach clenched and unclenched nervously.

I watched Father play a couple of games. He won one, lost one. I knew he wasn't doing his best, was just trying to show me the competition. I didn't really know how to talk to these people, or how things were done, so I just watched and listened. When Father moved on to the next table, I let them know I was looking to play.

The first fellow I played looked like a farmhand with a day off in town, and he was good-natured enough. I let him win a dollar off me and then went double or nothing and got it back with interest. I was much better than him but made sure to win by just enough.

After that, a fellow with a big blunt red face, a beard squaring off his skull. I took five dollars off him and was a bit nervous about him getting angry. But I was more worried about some of the fellows watching. One had a burlap bandage over one eye. It blended so well with his pocked skin he looked like a Cyclops. Scariest of all was the shortest fellow. He reminded me of those small dogs who snap without warning. Wiry, all sinew and bloodshot eyes.

After an hour or so of playing, I was up thirty-five dollars, and I figured I'd better take a break and maybe try someplace else in town. Ned Plaskett was sitting at a table, drinking coffee, keeping an eye on us. I found his presence comforting. I looked across to my father at the other table, wondering how much he'd taken, or lost—but he was still in the middle of a game, and I didn't want to disturb him.

I went to the back to find a privy and came face-to-face with Mrs. Cummins in the hallway. She was dressed in the colors of an exotic bird. Her waist seemed impossibly thin. Her face was painted, and she was so beautiful I almost forgot that she'd thieved from us.

Her eyes met mine, then slid away. She tried to walk right past me. I surprised myself by taking hold of her arm.

"Remove your hand. Or I'll have my boys at you."

"I want our money." It came out as a strangled whisper.

"I don't know what you're talking about."

I cleared my throat. "You stole from my father."

"I don't believe I know you, but you're a bold young man."

"I'll get the sheriff." I had no idea if there was a sheriff in this town, so just to be sure, I added, "And Captain Longman, too."

"The captain is a regular," she said with a smile. "And are you sure you want to call the sheriff? Have it known your father consorted with a woman of ill repute?"

I let my hand drop from her arm. It would be ruinous. For a Quaker, for a man of science, for anyone who wanted to be called a gentleman.

She went on. "And can you prove I took the money? Is there a witness? The trains are filled with cutpurses from what I hear."

I must have looked forlorn, because her face suddenly softened.

"Come in here," she said. She rapped on a door, and when there was no reply, she ushered me inside. There was only a bed and washstand. I knew what happened in this room and felt pretty agitated.

"Has your father seen me?" she demanded.

"No."

"I liked him."

I snorted. "So you took away the money we needed for our expedition."

"He gave the impression you were very wealthy."

"No."

She looked me up and down. "How much do you need?"

I frowned. "All of it!"

She shook her head. "If I give you two hundred back, will you promise to leave here and not mention this to your father? Forget you ever saw me here?"

There was a trace of sadness in her voice. It wasn't a fair deal, not one bit, but I knew there was no way of forcing her to return all the money. Or proving she even took it in the first place. With what I'd already won at billiards, two hundred dollars would get us our team, with enough left over to see us through another month.

"Okay," I said.

From some hidden seam in her dress near her breasts she drew out an assortment of bills and counted two hundred to me—then added a dollar.

"What's that for?" I asked.

"For one of the girls here, if you'd like."

"No. No thank you," I said, blushing.

"Shame. I doubt they often see such a handsome young man."

Hurriedly I shoved the bills into my pocket. "Thank you," I said, and it felt strange to thank your thief, but I *was* thankful.

I walked back to the big room, eager to tell my father we were done, we could go, but he was in the process of being head-butted.

He sprawled backward against the wall. Facing off with him was the small, wiry, dog man I'd been sweating over earlier.

Ned Plaskett was on his feet and hurrying over. I ran too.

My father dragged in a breath, and there was a crazed look in his eyes, which I knew was elation.

"Come on, then!" he shouted. "If you're such a sore loser, sir, I'll blacken *both* your eyes!"

"And I'll gouge yours right from their sockets!" bellowed the little terrier, and the way he flexed his thumbs made he realize he was completely sincere.

What happened in the next seconds was impossible to describe in any orderly way. I knew I was throwing myself at the little man from behind, as was Ned. We were dragging him away from my father, and then all I knew was a flurry of fists against me, and boots, and I was lashing out at I don't know who, just trying to keep myself from getting dragged to the floor. A great crack silenced everyone.

Swiping blood from my nose, I saw a man standing on the bar with a smoking shotgun.

"That's enough!" he bellowed. "Now, you, sir." He pointed at the dog man, whose eyes bulged from his skull. "You pay what you owe! And both of you"—the gun swung to include my father—"get out of my place!"

The vicious little terrier spat and then took some money from his pocket and threw it on the floor at my father's feet. With as much dignity as he could muster, my father picked up the bills and counted them.

"This is not enough," he said.

I pressed up close to him and whispered, "We have enough. Let's go."

For a scary moment I thought he was going to keep brawling, but he looked at his torn lapel and ripped sleeve and let Ned and me escort him to the entrance of the saloon. We made our way toward the hotel. I turned back to see the little man standing outside, smoking with two of his friends, watching us.

"You did well?" Father asked me.

I nodded. "Between us we've got enough for the team, plus a little extra." I decided I wouldn't tell him how much I had exactly. I'd keep the rest to myself, in case of emergency.

"Now, before we head out," said Plaskett, "we need to get you and your boy a rifle, maybe a pistol, too."

I was nodding, because I wanted a pistol of my own. I knew it was in vain. My father inhaled regally. "That won't be necessary, Mr. Plaskett. I hate the things. I'm a pacifist."

I said nothing, just pinched my nose to stop the blood. Father did hate guns, though. It wasn't just Quaker belief that made him feel this way. During the war he'd worked in field hospitals and treated his share of men left limbless.

"You've got an excellent left hook for a pacifist," said Plaskett. "Anyway, the Sioux can be savage."

"Seems it's the white man we've got to worry about," Father replied.

"There's them, as well. You're sure?"

Father nodded.

"Well, if you don't mind, sir," Plaskett said, "I'll be holding on to my rifle."

"By all means, Mr. Plaskett."

"Let's go settle things with Mr. Collins, and then I'd stick to your hotel tonight. Just to avoid any unpleasantness. We'll head out first thing tomorrow."

PART II

THE

BADLANDS

HE RETURNED TO HIS PEOPLE A MAN. THEY MADE A sweat lodge with buffalo robes draped over willow branches. In the middle of the sage-covered floor, rocks hot from the fire were set down. Water was poured over them. Afterward his body was anointed with sacred sage and his hair braided. He performed a dance, because he could not understand or use the power of his vision until he had acted it out.

In his dance he told the story of how he had fought with a horned serpent that had escaped the lightning of the Thunder Birds. The serpent tried to drag him down into the earth, but he defeated it and took one of its teeth as his trophy. It was the length of a man's foot, sharp at the tip. He called it, and the creature it came from, the Black Beauty.

He made a special pouch so he could carry it with him on the hunt. With each buffalo that crumpled before him the tooth would get heavier, until his horse tired from the weight. He had once been weak, but now he was strong, and a great hunter.

When he rode into battle naked, he slung the tooth across his chest and was never wounded. Some said the tooth could be shot magically like an arrow. At least two men swore they'd seen him pulling it from the chests of those he had killed.

He was beloved but also feared. Only he could use the tooth, because he had found it in his vision.

9.
BURIAL OBJECTS

EVEN FROM A DISTANCE I COULD SEE THEM
rising above the plain: wooden platforms supported by
slender posts with a few cross braces. They appeared
weathered and rickety, and I was amazed they hadn't
collapsed or been toppled by some animal. The sun
had bleached them so that they seemed almost like natural formations, emanating a forlorn power. Our two Pawnee Indian
scouts circled around them and started riding back toward us
to report.

I was riding astride. Some of the Yale students and cavalry
had looked mildly horrified this morning at Fort Crowe when
I'd mounted a pony in my split skirt. But Father had been distracted with something or other and had just said "yes yes" a
few times—maybe to comfort himself—and left it at that. Landry
the journalist had made a note. I liked the idea of being written
up, my boldness proclaimed in a magazine.

I was quickly growing accustomed to this new way of riding. My thighs ached a bit, and the small of my back, too, but there was a great pleasure in being aligned with the horse, balanced, my gaze dead ahead, with both legs able to grip the horse's flanks. This was the way women were meant to ride.

I rode at the forefront of the column with Papa and Lieutenant Frye. Behind us were Mr. Landry and the students, and then the cavalry. And behind them came six wagons. Bringing up the rear were more soldiers. In all there were fifty-four of us, and I worried we looked more like a military force than a scientific expedition.

All day we'd made steady progress across the rolling prairie toward the badlands. We'd reach it tomorrow, the lieutenant said. Every so often I thought I saw a horse and rider on the wavering horizon, and sometimes my imagination shaped it into Samuel Bolt.

I kept remembering his discouraged face at the grocer's; it was such a different expression from the one he'd had in the parlor car when he'd leaned in close and told me about my eyes. Had he found the provisions he needed in the end? I felt sorry for him, but it wasn't my fault. And I needed to remind myself I had more important things to think about. I was here to dig fossils and dig my heels into the future I wanted—a very different one from the one Papa saw for me. So, this summer I was going to prospect and find fossils and make him realize I was better than any of his students. Still, I hoped Samuel had been able to get kitted out, and go find the owner of his tooth.

The Pawnee scouts had returned now and were talking with Lieutenant Frye. When I'd first seen the Indians at the fort, they were wearing US Army uniforms, but a few hours out, they'd replaced them with their traditional breechclouts and leggings. None of the officers seemed to mind. I'd seen illustrations of Indians in books and magazines, but these were the first I'd seen with my own eyes. I was very struck by their appearance, their fine dark hair parted in the middle and gathered into two braids, their skin like burnished wood.

"Sioux burial platforms," Lieutenant Frye told us. "That's what they do with their dead out here."

Closer now, I made out a body-size bundle of hide atop the closest platform. Ten yards distant were two more burial platforms.

"They're Lakota," said one of the Pawnee scouts, whose name was Duellist. The lieutenant had told me his Pawnee name earlier but too quickly for me to remember it. Duellist, apparently, was a reference to his skill as a warrior. He had a high forehead, a proud straight nose, and a wide mouth that always had an amused tilt to it. He was almost a head taller than his fellow scout, a burly fellow named Best-One-of-All, after his abilities as a hunter. The pictures I'd grown up with had always made the Indians look very fierce, and in the stories they spoke very little and in broken English. I was surprised and impressed at how well both our guides spoke. And they talked as much as anyone, though mostly to each other in their own complicated-sounding language. I'd heard plenty of laughter.

But I still felt shy when I asked, "Why is one platform apart from the others?"

Duellist looked at me. "Maybe sickness. Or he was a bad man maybe, and they feared him."

"Let's have a look, gentlemen!" said my father enthusiastically.

"You won't want to see this," Daniel Simpson said to me with a sympathetic wince. He was a doughy Yale student with punishingly bad breath.

"Do you think I've never seen a dead body before?" I asked.

"But a dead human?" asked Hugh Friar. He was the handsomest of the students and knew it. His shoulders had a pleasing breadth, and he had a fine brow and the profile of a Roman emperor on a coin. He pointed at a lone tree. "There's some shade over there, Miss Cartland. While you're waiting."

I urged my pony to the nearest platform, the solitary one, and stood up in the stirrups. The platform was at chin level, but I wanted an even closer view. There were many benefits of being raised by a distracted father, and one of them was tree climbing. My pony was a steady little fellow, and I kicked out of my stirrup and swung my leg over the saddle. Grabbing hold of the platform, I pulled myself up.

It swayed alarmingly, and for a moment I worried I'd bring it all crashing down. The students below may have gotten a flash of my calves, but I didn't care. I was up and crouched beside the shrouded body.

With satisfaction I saw Hugh and Daniel looking up at me askance.

"You'll injure yourself, miss!" called Lieutenant Frye.

"Well, she's up there now, and faster than any of you lot," my father said to his students.

I smiled to myself, glad my father had noticed. But I was a bit wary now. I'd never actually seen a human corpse—unless you counted Aunt Berton. There was no smell except the leathery odor of its shroud.

"Unwrap it!" called out my father, who was bringing his own pony alongside one of the other platforms.

I took hold of the shroud, and then hesitated, not so much because I was afraid, but because I caught sight of Duellist watching me from a distance. His mouth no longer had an amused tilt. I felt suddenly ill at ease. I'd just clambered on top of a funeral platform to prove I wasn't some squeamish girl, to please my father, to satisfy my own curiosity—and for the first time I wondered if I'd done something disrespectful.

"Is it all right?" I asked.

"Go ahead, yes yes," I heard my father cry out.

But I wasn't looking at him; I was still watching Duellist, and it was impossible to read his expression. Part of me wanted to come down, but I was worried if I did, my father and the others would think I'd lost my nerve, that I wasn't cut out for life in the field.

"You needn't worry about offending our scouts, Miss Cartland," said Lieutenant Frye pleasantly. "The Pawnee and Sioux are longtime enemies. Isn't that right, Duellist?"

At this, Duellist nodded and turned his horse away. That

nod was something at least. Hesitantly I parted the shroud. The body was mummified, the flesh and tissue tautened to a thin gray film over the skull. It looked as if his skin had been painted red. A burial ritual? The head was twisted at an odd angle on its corded neck.

I glanced over at Papa and some of his students clambering atop the other platforms.

"I'd say this body is about two years old," Papa bellowed. "Buried with his shotgun, and a deck of cards." He lifted these things high with a chuckle. "No doubt customary for them yes yes to be buried with their prized possessions."

I parted my covering some more and found a small bundle against the chest. I was curious to see what was inside, but again I felt a prick of shame at the idea of handling someone's treasured things.

Standing tall in his stirrups, Lieutenant Frye did it for me. "A harmonica," he said as he pulled items from the bundle. "And some kind of ceremonial dagger. Looks like stone. Quite handsome!"

"Well, boys," Papa called out, "these bodies aren't exactly the prehistoric specimens we've come for, but we'll never be able to determine the origins of the Indian race without their heads. Pass me up a hacksaw, will you, Hendrickson?"

I looked over at Papa in shock. "Don't you think we should leave them in peace now?!"

Some of his students looked uneasy, but none said a word.

Irritably Papa shaded his eyes and squinted over at me.

"They're already at peace, my dear. We're simply studying their earthly remnants for the benefit of science."

"You'd never dig up bodies from the New Haven cemetery and decapitate them."

My father laughed heartily, as did some of the soldiers and students. I felt my cheeks heat up. They thought me a silly little thing now.

"I would if there was any scientific need, my dear. Right here we have a completely different race that needs studying."

"What about common decency?" It cost me to say this, since I could tell his patience with me was already worn thin. He simply ignored me.

"I'll tell you a tale, if I may, Miss Cartland," said the lieutenant softly, still astride his pony beside the platform. "The Sioux are fierce warriors. Several months ago, during a night skirmish, we were outnumbered and had to retreat. We had two dead and didn't want to leave them in the open for the Sioux to massacre, so we dug graves and wrapped them in blankets and buried them. We scattered branches and grass on top to conceal the fresh earth. But when we came back for them next morning, we found the bodies dug up and stripped of their blankets and possessions. One man was scalped; another had his finger cut off for the wedding ring. Now, that is not what I call common decency. The fact is, they play by different rules than us."

"Maybe so," I said. "But it seems we don't really know very much about their rules at all."

He smiled and said nothing, and I did not find him quite

as handsome as I had last night at dinner in the commander's house.

"Where's that saw, boys?" my father hollered. "Never mind, my bowie knife should do the trick. There's not much sinew left."

"Please, don't!" I cried out.

Our Pawnee scouts looked on impassively as my father hacked away, and I wondered what they must be thinking. Even if the Pawnee and Sioux did despise each other, they were both inhabitants of the Great Plains. Surely they had more in common with each other than with us. Here we were, taking heads like something we meant to mount on a wall. Did Duellist and Best-One-of-All wonder if we might just as easily do the same to their people?

My father snapped the skull from the neck and passed it down to Roger Kinney, who was ready with a burlap sack. I felt disgusted by all of this, by myself, up here scrambling around on someone's grave. I wanted to get down now.

From the corner of my eye, I thought I saw the silhouette of a horse and rider atop a distant ridge. But when I turned, there was nothing there but an oily smear of heat.

"Did you see that?" I asked the lieutenant. "On the rise?"

He looked back at me with a shake of his head.

"A horse and rider, I thought."

"Could be." He stepped his pony over to Duellist and Best-One-of-All and had a word with them.

"Leave their trinkets alone," my father told his students. "We're not grave robbers."

Under my breath I said, "No, just headhunters."

I started to close the bundle on the body's chest and took a last look at the stone knife—and then looked harder. It was nearly eight inches long, silvery black, remarkably smooth. The hilt appeared to have been snapped off, leaving a jagged base, and then I realized it was not stone at all. The sun was hot on me, and the crescendo of the cicadas made me feel even hotter and suddenly sick. I hoped no one was watching. I knew I shouldn't, but I couldn't stop myself. I became a grave robber and took it.

On my hands. On my neck. On my face. *Smack*. Down my collar, up my sleeves, under the damp brim of my hat. *Slap*. The mosquitoes came at me like a biblical plague. In the hammering heat, as we crossed the prairie, I breathed them in and spat them out. They were the biggest I'd ever seen. Surprisingly muscular as they hunched against my skin. No matter how I swatted and cursed, they came. As maddening as my buzzing thoughts.

I wanted to get to the badlands fast. But there was only so fast you could trot or walk a pony all day, especially with a heavy wagon at the rear. I kept looking back over my shoulder. Worried Cartland and his students and his army would come storming past, whooping and singing and leaving us in their dust. No. They were going to the fort first. We'd have a day or two on them. But they were coming. *Whack*. Not Rachel's fault. But I couldn't help feeling outsmarted. Made no sense. I eased my chafed bottom off the saddle for a second. Wasn't used to riding for so long. I didn't want Cartland here, but I couldn't help feeling glad Rachel was.

"Those bugs seem to have a taste for you," Father said, riding serenely alongside me.

I looked at him, bewildered. "Why aren't they all over you?"

He shrugged. "There's no explaining some things. Amazing creatures, mosquitoes. There was an incident I once read about, of a cow that died of exsanguination."

I slapped again at my blotched and blood-streaked face. "Which means?"

"Total loss of blood. It was found completely withered."

"Why are you telling me this now?!"

"It's a curious fact. I thought you might enjoy it."

"If a cow can be bled to death, I don't like my chances!"

On my other side Mr. Plaskett looked over and winked. "There's things you can do. Bacon grease, applied nice and thick."

I nodded eagerly. If it worked, I'd gladly smell like a rancid frying pan.

"Not much longer now," he said.

We'd set out from Crowe at first light, and the grassland seemed endless. But after another few minutes, a crack appeared in the prairie. As we trotted closer, with every second the crack widened and deepened into a vast canyon that spread to the horizon.

A sunken world within our own. Water and glaciers and time had scooped it out, leaving behind a windy river and tall weathered buttes and mazes of ravines. The steep slopes showed all their ancient layers—tawny, black, gray, red—like the diagrams in Father's geology books. It was a landscape I'd never seen, but the rock formations had a weirdly familiar architecture. Some of the stepped buttes looked like Mayan temples. There were gaunt castles. Archways and spires of a great Gothic cathedral. A domed mosque with teetery minarets. It was like the whole history of mankind and all its creations were already here, seventy million years ago, and now ruined.

"There's an easier way for the wagon," said Ned Plaskett, leading us along the rim of the prairie. "We'll likely still have to help ease it down."

I could barely tear my gaze away. Neither could Father. It was a fossil hunter's paradise. All that stone with its deep secrets. You could look and dig for years and discover only a fraction. I wanted to get down there and start right away.

But there was the wagon to get down first, and we spent an agonizing hour easing it with ropes. As promised, Hitch was strong and very good with the horses.

The prairie above us quickly disappeared from sight, and it really did feel like we were entering another world. At first it was rocky, just scraggy brush and small cacti. Lower down it got greener. There'd been plenty of rain this spring, Ned said, much more than usual.

It was surprisingly lush along the brown, slow-curving river lined with cottonwoods and tall grass and flowers. In the sun's low evening light, the stone was rich yellow and peach and purple. The wind made a pleasant dry rustle in the cottonwoods. The grasshoppers were so loud they could've been snakes. Birds trilled and chuckled.

KENNETH OPPEL

"There's a good spot up ahead to make camp," said Plaskett, and he led us to a grassy patch near the river. Two antelope looked up, unconcerned. "We won't go hungry, either," he added.

"Can we see where you found the tooth?" I asked.

Plaskett looked at the sun. "Only got an hour or so of light left."

"Is it far?" Father asked. He was as eager as me, I could tell.

"Fifteen minutes."

"Just a quick look," I said. "If Cartland's coming, we'd better lay claim as fast as we can."

Hitch was already tending to the team. It was a wonder to watch how quickly he could remove the tack from the horses, his hands quick and confident with the straps and buckles. It was obvious he loved the animals, stroking and talking to them as he worked.

The three of us set off on our saddle ponies, Plaskett leading us along twisting ravines. My heart beat fast. We were about to see the owner of that colossal tooth that had bewitched me the moment I'd held it.

The ground was scattered with rocks of all shapes and sizes, gray basalt and pink granite and yellowy limestone and great speckled silver hunks and creamy pebbles, all broken and crushed by glaciers and rounded and smoothed by rivers over thousands of years. There were green sage and spiky cactus and clumps of perfectly spherical deer droppings.

"Almost there," said Plaskett.

I looked over at my father and could see the same impatient

excitement in his face. After a day's riding from Crowe, my shirt was plastered to my back, the headband of my hat sodden. Nearby a grasshopper rattled and made me feel thirstier. Almost there. It would be the biggest dinosaur ever to be discovered, and, if Father kept his promise, it would bear my name.

Finally Plaskett stopped and dismounted. Father and I swung ourselves off our ponies, then clambered up a butte to a ledge. Scaly rock was piled up on either side of a shallow excavation into the slope.

My heart gave a big happy contraction. A long stretch of purplish-brown femur, fractured in only a couple places, had been partially exposed. Its big knobbed head rested close to a massive piece of pelvic girdle. At the opposite end of the femur were the twin swells of the lateral and medial epicondyle, made to grip the tibia. It wasn't just the length of the bone, but the sheer girth. Stand it up and it would be half of me.

"It's a mighty big thighbone," Plaskett said proudly.

"It is indeed," said my father, but right away I knew something was bothering him. His eyes darted back and forth across the span of the bone.

"How long would you say it is?" he asked.

"Three and a half?" Plaskett guessed, and I knew he was off.

From a pocket my father took his cloth measuring tape and held it end to end. "Not even. Three feet, one and a half inches."

I let out a big breath. "You think it's too small."

"It should be at least four and a half by my reckoning. And much, much thicker."

I remembered all his detailed calculations when we first got the tooth.

"Still," I said, "that method only gives an esti—"

"I'm sure," he snapped. "Anyone could see that. The proportions are all wrong."

I hated it when he told me off, but right now I was far more crushed that the *rex* might not be where it was supposed to be.

Looking baffled, Plaskett said, "I don't understand. What are you saying, Professor?

"That these *bones* do not belong to the *tooth* you sent us."

"But I found it right here!" he protested.

"No doubt," Father said, scratching at his beard. "But that doesn't mean they belong together."

"Where did you find the tooth exactly?" I asked Plaskett.

He pointed to one of the spots where the femur was fractured. I leaned in close in the fading light. Near the broken edge of the femur was a sizeable, smooth-edged puncture mark. I waved my father over.

"Tooth mark?" I said.

He nodded. "Good."

"There was a battle here," I told Plaskett. "The owner of the tooth must've fought this creature. Bit him in the leg, here. See? Might've snapped the bone clean through, but he lost a tooth in the bargain. That's probably why it was in three pieces when you found it."

"I'd never considered that," said Plaskett. "But maybe he got wounded himself. Fatally. We might still find him here. Mixed in together."

I hoped so too, but my father grimaced.

"Doubtful," my father said. "It's unusual in the animal kingdom for the predator to be killed by its prey. Our *rex* would have eaten what he wanted, left the carcass scattered, and moved on. But if these were his hunting grounds, there's a fair chance he died in the area."

Ned looked utterly crestfallen. "I'm sorry I misled you, Professor. I feel I've been nothing but a disappointment to you so far."

"Nonsense, Ned," Father said graciously. "A common mistake. And this is a good find. An excellent find. We'll quarry it out. Whatever this creature is, it'll bear your name."

I glanced at Father. Was he going to hand out dinosaurs to everyone?

"Thank you, Professor, but that's not necessary."

"Nonsense. Fair's fair. Now, let's get a good night's sleep. At first light we'll start quarrying and find out what this is."

I lifted my eyes to the hills and buttes that rose all around us, creating labyrinth after labyrinth of rock. So many surfaces. And behind one of them, maybe just an inch out of sight, were the bones of my *rex*, curled up like a colossal baby nestled in a stone womb.

10.
BONE

T'S A TOOTH," I SAID TO PAPA.

Firelight ran like liquid over its smooth surface. We'd pitched our camp for the night and were sitting by a fire after dinner. I'd been waiting to present it to him in a quiet moment when he could appreciate it fully—and also appreciate that it was my find. He took the massive tooth in his hands and looked at me wonderingly.

"It was wrapped up with the body," I said. "I thought it was a knife at first. It's been snapped off—look—or it would be even longer. You can feel the serrations here." I moved the pads of my fingers along the sides to the tip. Little notches for gripping prey.

I felt out of breath as I watched Papa's face for his reaction. Our expedition had barely begun, and I'd made an incredible discovery. I felt queasy about how I'd gotten it, but it was too amazing a fossil to pass up.

"My dear," he said, "this is quite, quite extraordinary."

"A saber-toothed tiger, Professor?" one of his students asked, coming closer.

"No," I said. "The canines of the saber-toothed have a much sharper curve at the tip. And aren't nearly as thick."

The student looked at me doubtfully, until my father said, "She's right. This is the tooth of a carnivorous dinosaur."

"Imagine its jaws!" I said. "It must have been a brute."

There was a small group around us now and a moment of silence as we all conjured the creature in our heads.

"Why is it black?" asked our journalist, Mr. Landry.

My father said, "Manganese oxide perhaps, leached into the bone over millions of years. What a find it would be. It would dwarf anything seen so far."

I thought again of Samuel and the tooth he'd told me about on the train. I didn't know if this tooth, *my* tooth, could be from the same species, but I was startled by how badly I wanted to tell him about it. He'd admire it, compliment me, understand my excitement. I felt like my discovery could be fully complete only once I shared it with him.

"Why was it with the Indian's body, do you think?" I asked.

"An excellent question. Where's Duellist? Could one of you find him and ask him to come?"

Our expedition was so large that our campsite had almost a fairground atmosphere, with several large bonfires and little groups of soldiers and students smoking and singing bits of Western songs and telling lies about the things they'd done and seen. Earlier some of the students had even cajoled Best-One-of-All to show us a Pawnee dance, which was very impressive.

"Duellist, yes yes, very good," said my father when he arrived. "Look here. Have you ever seen a tooth this big?"

Duellist crouched down to take a good look, but I noticed he didn't touch it. He shook his head. "Where did you find this?"

"It was buried with one of the Sioux."

Duellist took a step back. He glanced up at my father, and then over at me, and I felt another stab of guilt.

"We see these bones in the earth sometimes," he said, "but most people will not touch them."

"Why not?" Landry asked, pencil poised.

"They are from the giant men that Tirawa first put on earth."

"Giant men, not animals?" my father asked.

"Men and women. And when they displeased Tirawa, he sent a flood and fire from the sky to destroy them."

At the fringes of the campfire I could see some of the students and soldiers smirk at one another, but to me, this Pawnee story didn't sound very different from Noah's flood or the Greek Titans getting replaced by the Olympian gods.

"Ah," said my father. "So your people will not touch the bones because they're afraid of being punished like the old giants?"

"Unless they have a vision," said Best-One-of-All, who'd come closer to the fire, but still kept his distance from the tooth. "Like Strong Calf."

"Will you tell us about him? Please?" I asked. I'd noticed

some of the students had lost interest and wandered off now, but I wanted more.

Best-One-of All's face was lively as he spoke, his eyes wide, his hands helping him tell the story. Strong Calf was a Pawnee man, not so long ago, who dreamed one of the old giants told him to dig up his bones. In the dream Strong Calf was given directions to a hill. And when he dug into the hill, he found a mound of bones so big they could only belong to a giant. After that, apparently, Strong Calf became a great medicine man, and the bone was kept at the back of the lodge in a sacred bundle beside the buffalo skull. He would scrape dust from the bone and make tea that cured the sick. Some said his medicine even cured small pox.

"Do the Sioux use the bones in the same way?" I asked. To steal a knife from a grave was one thing, but something believed by its owner to have mystical powers—that was much worse.

Duellist shrugged. "I don't know."

"Where might that Sioux have found this tooth?" my father asked, hefting it in his hand.

"Where you're going, the earth is full of bones."

"So I hope. Don't worry yes yes, we won't make you touch any giant bones!" he added, chuckling. "Thank you for your help."

My father might not have noticed, but I saw Duellist's mouth harden as he stood and walked away with Best-One-of-All.

"The bones of giants!" said my father. "Fascinating, these savage superstitions."

I did not believe in magical bones either, but Papa's insulting dismissal irked me—maybe because I knew often enough how it felt to be dismissed.

"Are they any more savage and superstitious than that circuit preacher we met at the fort yesterday?" I reminded him. "He didn't even believe in dinosaurs. He thought they were just the bones of animals heaved off Noah's ark during the Flood."

"Ha! Not the most enlightened man, perhaps," Papa said.

"He called them devil's chopsticks," said Mr. Landry, "put here only to lead us astray. I wrote that down."

He looked at me and gave me a sympathetic smile, and with surprise I wondered if I had an unexpected ally in the journalist.

Father cleared his throat and turned to the lieutenant. "What are the chances of talking to some local Sioux?"

"Not good. They're the worst of the Indians. Where we're headed is awfully close to unceded Indian territory."

"Still, they might be able to tell us where the tooth was found, if we offered them some gifts."

"Anyone in uniform's likely to get a very unfriendly reception," the lieutenant warned.

"Especially if you tell them we cut off the heads of their dead," I said to Papa.

"And robbed one of their graves," he replied pointedly.

He didn't need to remind me. What I'd done stained my thoughts; it was just as bad as what my father had done, maybe even worse.

"I see no reason why we'd need mention either," he said.

"But if that tooth was special to them somehow," I said, "they'll figure it out, won't they?"

My father ran his hand possessively over the tooth's enameled surface, like he'd already forgotten it was mine. "Well," he said, "we'll just have to find the jaw it came from, then."

"Bone!" I called out. "It's bone here!"

My heart hammered. I stepped back as Father hurried over.

He knelt and said, "Good. Let's have a look. . . ."

With his awl and hammer he carefully chipped away. I looked over at Ned, who watched expectantly, holding the butcher knife he favored for the fine work of sifting through sandstone. Heat battered the back of my neck. By tonight it would be scalded red. I didn't care. Restlessly I watched as my father exposed more of the bone. It was tapering to a point.

"A tooth!" I cried.

Father had been wrong. This *was* the *rex*. Ned had found it! The tooth we were uncovering right now was, if anything, bigger than the first one.

We'd spent all yesterday with pickaxes and shovels, cutting into the slope where Ned had exposed the first femur. All the overburden sitting atop the fossil needed to be removed. We'd started high, so we wouldn't accidentally break bones, creating a deep ledge. And then we'd started digging down, inch by inch. This morning we'd traded our shovels and picks for awls and geological hammers and chipped down more carefully. And then I'd spotted the bruise-colored bone.

I watched now as my father chipped and chipped, and the base of the tooth grew larger still.

"Not a tooth," he said, looking back at us.

"You're sure?" I said, which was always a foolish thing to ask my father. He hated being doubted. A heavy disappointment sank through my body. I'd wanted another colossal tooth. I'd wanted the *rex*. Stupid maybe, when I had another dinosaur right here in front of me and was surrounded by a buried treasure trove of new fossils. But it still didn't stop me wanting the *rex* more than all the rest.

"I believe," Father was saying, "this is horn."

"Horn?"

"See the base here? That's not the jaw it's connecting to, it's the top of the skull. I can see the arch of the antorbital fenestra. There."

"Do dinosaurs have horns, Professor?" Ned asked, wiping the back of his hand across his brow.

"None that have been discovered," he said, a smile sweeping his face.

My excitement came flooding back, and I gave a hoot that echoed off the ravine. "The first horned dinosaur!"

"We're the first," Father agreed. "Now back to work."

He had me work on the skull with him, while Ned kept on around what we'd guessed was the hip. Each time I uncovered bone, I felt another jolt. *There it is.*

We forgot our lunch. We kept working. The mosquitoes were in ecstasy because of all the rain. Even with bacon grease slathered over my face, hands, and wrists, and with my socks pulled over the bottoms of my pant legs, they came relentlessly. They loved it when you stayed in the same place; it gave them plenty of time to settle down to a nice leisurely suck, twenty or thirty of them draining your blood like that cow my father told me about. Couldn't stop thinking of that blasted cow (even if it was made-up) and how its sides would start to pucker and flap as its blood drained away until it just folded up like a tent, bony legs all askew.

The outlines of the skull began to emerge. Behind the eye sockets with their spiky crests, the skull didn't start curving down as I'd expected: It swooped up.

"What's this?" I asked Father.

"Some kind of bony frill," he said. "Incredible."

I'd once seen drawings of Michelangelo's unfinished sculptures. Like something struggling to be born from the stone. I couldn't help thinking of them now as I stared at our bones waiting to be free of the rock so they could thrust themselves into the world.

By the end of the afternoon we had quite a spread. I stood, my back and knees burning after being crimped and crunched so long.

Still half-submerged in stone, the creature's skull was large. A fox could curl up inside it. It had a compact beaked jaw, like a parrot, and teeth starting well back along the jawbone. The broken horn jutted up from above its nostrils. Might have been a massive rhinoceros, except for the bony frill at the back of it skull, which seemed to have two hornlets curving from it. Ned had uncovered a broken chain of cervical vertebrae, a few ribs, big as barrel hoops, and part of the pelvic girdle—next to the original thighbone he'd first discovered.

"It must have put up a good fight against the *rex*, with that horn," I said.

"It's in remarkably good shape for something that was eaten," my father commented. What kind of creature do you make of it, Samuel?"

I stood at the edge of the quarry and surveyed the jumble. It was not like looking at a labeled picture in an anatomy book or a mounted museum skeleton. Millions of years of rock had collapsed the creature so that spine and ribs and pelvis and limbs were splayed and scattered in unusual patterns. My eyes darted from one bone to the next, just like my hands had done as a child, handling my father's jigsaw specimens.

"He's big bellied," I said, "a quadruped, maybe twenty feet in length. Not built to be a hunter. He's slow. A crest to protect his neck, a horn for defense. Jaws and teeth for mashing plant matter. An herbivore. But I bet that beak could give a nasty bite! He would have stood . . . four feet off the ground."

Father was nodding. "Yes. Very good. I think this one will be . . . *Monoclonius crassus*. Single-horned fat one. And of course, in honor of its finder, we will append Plaskett."

Ned beamed. Like a child unwrapping a Christmas gift. I couldn't remember the last time I'd seen a happier face. I tried to hide my envy—and disappointment that it wasn't the *rex* we were naming right now.

"Professor, I don't know what to say."

"Say you'll find more for me, Ned!"

"I certainly will!"

"Let's cover it with the tarp and return in the morning."

The sun hovered above the hills, sending long shadows across the badlands. We'd made an incredible find, but my *rex* was out there somewhere, and Cartland would soon have a small army of prospectors at work.

As we rode our ponies back toward camp, I was glad Ned was in the lead, because I still hadn't mastered the maze of ravines. I was startled when he raised a hand and came to stop.

"Voices," he said.

What I thought was breeze became garbled human speech. Then came the soft whinny of a horse. I thought: Indians.

I didn't know much about Indians. The only one I'd ever seen, at a circus back home, turned out to be a man in face paint who was actually speaking Latvian. But I'd read plenty of magazine stories about Red Cloud's War. The Fetterman Fight. The Hayfield Fight. The attack on the new railway lines. At school we talked about the ambushes. And the scalping. The Indians were savage. They were fearless.

Then, unmistakably, I heard singing. Down here in the coulees and defiles it was hard to tell where sound came from. It bounced around the slopes, drifted overhead like mist, and then eddied back from another direction entirely.

With Father and Ned, I scrabbled up a sandstone rill. Crawled across the flat summit on our bellies. Down the other side we could see the meandering river. Along its bank were dozens of uniformed men arranging wagons, building a corral for horses, pitching tents. Enough blue uniforms and flashing gold buttons to make you

KENNETH OPPEL

think they were establishing a fort. A couple fellows were setting up a big cookstove. Then my eyes caught Rachel, helping pitch a tent with her father, driving in a peg with quick steady blows.

I shouldn't have been, but I was: I was happy to see her. Very happy. I looked at Father's grim face.

"Well, we knew this was coming," he said, "but I didn't think he'd have the temerity to set up camp a few miles from ours." He stood tall. "I'm going down to confront the scoundrel!"

"Is that a good idea?" I asked in alarm.

"I won't have him here on my doorstep. This is the New Jersey marl pits all over again!"

"Yes, but what will you—"

Futile. My father was already striding ahead, and it was all Ned and I could do to keep up. We couldn't have made a very dignified entrance, skidding and lurching down the butte toward their camp. One of the Yalies spotted us first, shaded his eyes, and let out a loud cry.

"It's Professor Bolt! Everyone, Professor Bolt's here too!"

More and more people gathered at the edge of the camp, watching as we stomped across the grass. When we were close enough, I saw a smirk on Professor Cartland's face. And then my gaze found Rachel beside a tall officer, in the split skirt I'd seen her making on the train.

"Cartland!" my father called out. "How astounding to see you here!"

"Bolt, what do you make of these yes yes remarkable badlands?"

My father was hardly ten feet away, but he was still shouting as if from a great distance. I started to get even more worried.

"You must have passed our camp!" my father said.

"We did, and exchanged pleasantries with your man."

"Then you'll know we're prospecting here and plan to do so for some time. I hope you're not intending on setting up here."

I saw the journalist, Mr. Landry, his eyes bright, take out a notebook.

Cartland forced a laugh. "If I'm not mistaken, Bolt, you have no deed to this land."

"Surely we can be gentlemanly about this," said an officer—a lieutenant I think, by the chevrons on his jacket. "It seems to me there's plenty of rock for everyone."

"It is difficult to be gentlemanly," my father countered, "with a fellow who rides the coattails of another man's discovery."

"I believe we heard about these hunting grounds at the same time," said Cartland. "From your guide, Ned Plaskett." He pointed at Ned. "You *are* Mr. Plaskett, aren't you?"

Ned hung his head, looking thoroughly whipped.

"For simplicity's sake," said the lieutenant, "why don't we each take a side of the river, and then we won't be tripping each other up. The terrain seems just as interesting either side, yes?"

"I can agree to that, certainly," said Cartland.

"That might be a—" I began, but Father cut me off.

"No!" With his dusty hair spiking up, his clothes chalky and skin smudged, he looked like a crazed hobo. "I won't have my movements restricted by an interloper."

"Professor Bolt," said the lieutenant, "you might take a bit of comfort in our presence, being so close to Indian territory."

Father waved a hand. "I'm not at all worried about Indians."

"So your alternative is that yes yes we both have free run over these badlands?" Cartland said.

I could tell my father had just realized his mistake. But he was too pigheaded to backtrack. Cartland had a small army working for him.

My father conjured his smile and stood taller and spread his arms. "That suits me very well."

Cartland tilted his head. "We are bound to get in each other's way."

"We'll have a simple rule, then," said my father. "Lieutenant, I'll trust you to enforce honor in these matters. Whoever finds bone first, that site belongs to him alone. And the other party will keep well away."

"Agreed," said Cartland, unable to hide his smirk.

"The finder will claim it with a stake and flag. My color will be white."

"Ours blue," returned Cartland.

"Good!" shouted my father, turning. "We will leave you to your labors!"

"Found anything interesting yet, Bolt?" Cartland called after him.

"Not yet," he lied. "Early days yet."

I glanced quickly over at Rachel, and I never thought it could be so thrilling just to have your gaze met and held a few seconds. Then I followed my father back to where we'd picketed our horses.

We were silent until we were well out of earshot.

"After we quarry out the monoclonius," I said, "should we strike out farther upriver?"

"I'm not going anywhere," said my father.

I said, "He has twelve students—and dozens of soldiers."

"The soldiers wouldn't know fossilized timber from a femur. And I doubt his students know much more."

"He can be a lot more places at once. We should've split it up."

Silence from my father. There was as much chance of budging him as one of these massive buttes. It was a big blow, Cartland showing up so close at hand, but I couldn't help feeling glad. There would be so many more chances to see Rachel.

Plaskett mumbled, "Professor, I feel just terrible about this. This is my fault."

I felt sorry for him, he looked so miserable. I wished Father would show him some Quaker mercy. Or *any* kind of mercy. But he was oblivious, ranting inside his own head.

"It's not your fault, Mr. Plaskett," I said, giving my father a look. "If we'd replied to you faster, this wouldn't be happening."

"You mustn't chastise yourself a second longer, Ned," Father said magnanimously.

"I'll make it up to you in industry, sir."

"We'll need all of it," my father said. "The game's changed now. He's got the numbers, but we have speed on our side. Cartland's a plodder. He'll quarry out, crate them up, and send them back east. He won't write them up and name them out here." Father grinned. "But we will."

Even when standing, my father was in motion. Swaying from side to side, as if testing his center of gravity, hands thrust deep into his pockets, nodding, looking at the ground, peering into the sky. His mind a steam engine of activity.

Now his face took on a foxy look of mischief. It was impossible not to smile and be swept up in the tidal pull of his excitement.

"As of tomorrow we'll split up, claim as many sites as we can. Stake every bit of bone you see! Then we'll dig just enough so I can write them up. We name them, we *claim* them. You see? We'll telegraph our finds from Crowe to the *Transactions of the American Philosophical Society*."

"And they're ours!" I said, understanding.

"In print!"

"And it doesn't matter if Cartland finds the same creature back east in his crates. He's too late!"

My father nodded. "*That* is how we'll beat him."

11.
AT WORK IN THE
RUINS OF THE
WORLD

WHEN THE STONE HIT MY SKIRT, I turned and saw Samuel, and my first thought was: *Finally.*

I'd been working my way along the base of a butte, searching for bone shards. The ground was cluttered with an astonishing variety of rocks and bits of dead vegetation, but my eyes were patient. After years exploring the woods and hills of Connecticut, I was reasonably good at finding hidden things.

Samuel was leaning out from behind a stack of stone, waving at me to join him, before disappearing from sight. I turned and looked up at Daniel Simpson and Hugh Friar, my two chaperones—though I felt I was really chaperoning them, since their prospecting skills were very basic. They worked along a ledge higher up the butte. There was a soldier, too, who seemed content finding the highest point nearby and scanning the horizon.

"I'll be a few minutes," I called out.

Over the past couple days I'd learned this was the simplest way of letting them know I had to relieve myself and was going to disappear for a while.

Hugh glanced over his shoulder and gave a curt nod. Daniel told me, as usual, to watch out for rattlesnakes.

My pulse beat hard in my throat as I walked toward the out-cropping and rounded the corner. There was Samuel, his face now stubbled and deeply tanned, but the eager warmth in his eyes unchanged.

"Sorry about the rock," he said quietly, grinning. "I tried a bird whistle but you didn't notice. This is the first time I've seen you in a smaller group."

"You've seen me before?" I said, pleased. So this wasn't just a chance meeting.

He nodded. "I wanted to say hello, but I didn't think I'd be very welcome. There were so many of you, trailing after your father!"

I groaned. "He made us troop around in a big stupid clump the first five days, so he could teach everyone how to tell bone from rock and fossilized wood. Most of them are still having trouble."

He chuckled softly. This was probably welcome news to him.

"But then we started seeing your white flags staked everywhere, and Papa was fuming about how you were trying to claim the entire badlands for yourself. So yesterday he finally split us into smaller groups and told us to start hammering our own stakes."

"I've seen a few blue flags," he said. "I'm sure there'll be plenty more."

We looked at each other awkwardly.

"I didn't know about Plaskett," I said. "My father never told me that's why we came out here. But we certainly weren't following you—"

He held up his hands. "I know—"

"He didn't know about your expedition; he didn't think you had the money to mount one."

"It was my father's own fault," he said. "If he'd replied sooner to Ned, he wouldn't have written to your father at all. He heard about these badlands fair and square."

I'm not sure he really believed this, but it was kind of him to say. I realized I was angry—not at Samuel, but at my father because I doubted his motives. At the very least, he'd known Bolt had hired Plaskett to prospect for him here in these badlands. There was no law against Papa coming here too, but it seemed a bit sneaky. I was starting to wonder if part of his reason was simply to confound Bolt. Not that Bolt didn't want to do exactly the same. . . .

I looked carefully at Samuel. "We're not spying on each other anymore, are we?"

He shook his head emphatically. "You?"

"No."

"So it's all right to tell each other things? We won't tell our fathers?"

"Everything stays with us," I agreed. "What our fathers do has nothing to do with us."

I felt a secret delight saying these words; I felt like I was making, or at least choosing, a world for myself.

He smiled. "Good. I wasn't very good at spying anyway."

"I noticed. What about your *rex*?" For the past week, waiting and hoping for him to find me, I'd wanted to ask him about this.

He let out a big breath. "It wasn't the *rex*. It's a completely different kind of dinosaur. We're still quarrying it out. It's like a giant rhino. Horned! And"—he fanned his hands behind his head—"a big bony frill on its skull."

"Teeth?"

"Definitely an herbivore. I think the *rex* must've attacked it. That's why its tooth was there. It got broken off in the femur. Must've been quite a fight."

I couldn't wait any longer. "I found a tooth of my own."

His expression didn't disappoint me. He stared, then leaned toward me urgently.

"What kind? Where?"

"From a carnivore." And I described it and how I'd found it on the funeral platform.

His eyes widened, and I suddenly regretted telling him that last part. Maybe he'd think differently of me now. Maybe he'd be right to. For an uncomfortable moment he studied me. Was it shock? Admiration?

"I'd've done the same," he said. "Draw it for me!"

Relieved, I traced the outline in the earth.

"That's the actual size?"

"Very close."

"Incredible," he said, shaking his head. "Ours is a bit longer, and it's not silvery black, but— do you think?"

I'd wondered precisely the same thing. "From the same set of jaws as yours?"

Eagerly he nodded. "Say it attacked the other dinosaur, lost the tooth, maybe lived a long time afterward, and died somewhere else. Wherever it was the Sioux man found it."

"Our whole skeleton might be there."

Our. The word had come without any forethought. I'm not sure if he even noticed. His eyes were darting now, trying to keep up with his thoughts.

"If we could find out—" he began.

"Where the Sioux man got the tooth?" I was shaking my head. "The lieutenant won't go near them. Even without the army, the fact is we . . . well, we sawed off their heads."

"You *what*?"

"Not me personally! But my father did, to study them. I tried to stop him."

He exhaled. "Probably best not to bring it up with the Sioux. I wonder if they found the tooth here in the badlands. Or somewhere else entirely?"

"Imagine if we could find it," I said.

"That would be something." He looked at me, his eyes fierce with excitement.

I felt my cheeks heat up. "I've been wanting to tell you since the moment I found it."

"I want to kiss you," he said.

Surprise jolted through me. On the train I'd wondered if he'd wanted to—and decided no, he was just a little drunk, and naturally emphatic. And how could he want to kiss me right now? Right after I'd told him about chopping off heads and grave robbing?

Startling myself, I said, "Who's stopping you?"

We were in the middle of nowhere. All the rules we'd brought with us from the East had frayed like cobweb, mile by mile along the tracks.

And then he kissed me.

The entire world became the wide warmth of her mouth, the secret, thrilling taste of her. Heat galloped through my body.

She leaned back. "Is this how you kiss your other sweethearts?"

I liked the notion she might think me worldly, but I said, "You're my *only* sweetheart," and kissed her again.

Overwhelming: just the fact of being so close to her, all the things my eyes had been desiring from a distance. Her cheek and nose and brow all grazing mine. The smell of her skin and hair. I kept my eyes open. My hands touched her face, holding her close. Her cheeks were scalding.

"Gently," she murmured against my lips.

I wasn't aware of being rough, but I tried to kiss her more softly.

"I've wanted to do this for so long," I said.

"Gentler," she said again, and this time I was annoyed because she was making me feel like a slobbering dolt.

"As if you've been kissed a hundred times before!" I said, breaking off.

The fact was, my own experience was tragically small, even though I'd got the craving early. When I was seven I'd wanted to kiss girls. During a picnic I'd invited Abigail Sims into the bushes behind the gazebo. It was shady and hidden and smelled like dog pee. Without asking, I pushed my mouth against hers. But she clamped her teeth together, and I bruised my lips against them. It wasn't a pleasant experience, and she wouldn't sit near me anymore. After that, I had many flirtations—girls liked my sweet talk—but the only kisses I was allowed were on the cheek. Just this year, there was Rebecca, who was sleek and dark haired and said she was "exceedingly fond" of me, but she wouldn't even let me lift her hair so I could kiss the nape of her neck.

Rachel touched two fingers to her upper lip. "You've chafed me."

"Maybe you're too delicate."

She laughed. "I'm certainly not that. You're rough. And you smell like bacon grease."

I'd stopped noticing. "It keeps the bugs away. I've got some in my pocket if you'd like to try. Looks like you could use it."

"How kind of you. No thanks."

Even though her face was dotted by mosquito bites, her skin looked smooth and tanned—much nicer than when I'd first met her in Philadelphia. Altogether she looked less dowdy. Hair looser, dirt on her skirt and hands. It suited her.

Tentatively she stroked my stubbly jaw. I'd never been touched like this, and it was wonderful. She moved the pads of her fingers along my upper lip.

"I'd like to shave you."

I shook my head, laughing. "You really are odd."

She said, "I should be getting back, or they'll come looking."

"Yes," I said, and our lips found each other again. Her hands slid up my chest to my neck, and into my hair. I was trying to kiss her slower and more gently.

"I've got to go," she said, pulling away.

"Go then. But when will I see you again?"

"That's up to you."

"Father's got us quarrying in the morning, and prospecting afternoons. Tomorrow if I can get away!"

She laughed at my eagerness; it was the closest I'd come to seeing sheer delight in her expression.

"Where will you be?" I asked.

"The same general area, I think."

"I'll find you."

"Will we have a secret signal?" she asked teasingly.

"I'll try the bird whistle again."

"Let's hear it."

Softly I whistled. She grimaced. "No wonder I didn't hear it."

"Then I'll have to keep throwing stones at you!"

She closed her fingers briefly in my hair, and then walked back toward the Yale students.

I woke with the bird's dawn chorus, as if I couldn't wait to start thinking of him.

I went to the flaps of my tent and opened them to the still-dim sky. How I loved that promise of light in the east. I lay there on my stomach, watching, wondering what the day would bring.

My heart contained a double happiness. I was here in these badlands, getting to do what I'd always longed to do, and was eager to dress and eat and strike out into the buttes and ravines; and yesterday I'd had my first kiss.

I liked having my hands in his hair. It was thick, a bit coarse, but my fingers got deliciously tangled in it, and I could flex them and feel like I was holding all of him somehow. Best of all was the way he looked at me, his warm-eyed look that made me want to tell him everything.

I could still feel his skin, the small spikes of his stubble. His kissing was hurried and too hard. So his actual kisses did not please me much, but him wanting to give them to me did very much.

I'd never thought I'd get to hold something so warm and solid and good. I didn't even mind the bacon smell—

And at breakfast ate more than usual, grinning to myself.

My pony was saddled and ready before Hugh's or Daniel's, and I made sure Papa noticed. "Just waiting for Hugh and Daniel," I said casually.

And then, finally, we struck out. Papa had methodically assigned each group different areas to prospect, and every day we were responsible for making a map of what we'd covered.

So we set out in the same direction as yesterday, picketed our ponies near a pond, and walked into the ravines. After that, my entire concentration was focused on the rock, checking the ground for shards that might hint at something higher up, sweeping the rock faces for glints of bone.

An hour in, Hugh thought he found some.

"I think that might be limestone," I said. In fact I was sure it was glacial-erratic limestone but was trying to be polite. It was completely the wrong color and texture to be bone.

"No, that is definitely bone," Hugh said, not even glancing at me—which I found infuriating. He took a stake from his tool pouch, knocked it in, and tied a swath of blue cloth around it. "Done."

"We'll let the professor decide later," Daniel Simpson replied, trying to be diplomatic.

"Of course," I said. It would only look better for me when Papa glanced at it, sighed irritably, and told Hugh to remove his stake.

We worked on. Crossing a narrow ridge between two flat buttes, I caught sight of something sticking out from one of the steep slopes, about four feet down.

"Hold on," I said, crouching.

It protruded in a dark shallow V shape, which suggested to me a joint. And a joint meant articulated bone—two bones connected—which was what every fossil hunter wanted most to see. It meant it wasn't just some stray bit of bone. It was probably part of something much bigger, hidden inside the rock.

"It's wood," Hugh said, turning away.

"I don't think so. I want to take a closer look."

"Too steep," Daniel said.

"Wood," Hugh said again, and kept going. Daniel followed. They just assumed I'd fall in obediently behind them, like a little puppy.

The Sioux tooth was one thing, but I'd spent a week prospecting now, and I wanted to make a proper find, a full specimen. The slope wasn't so steep, by no means a vertical drop. But you certainly couldn't walk down safely, or even scramble down on your backside. So I got down on my stomach and stretched, thinking I might be able to reach out and tap the bone. It was still too far. I squirmed more of my body over the edge.

"What're you doing?" I heard Hugh call out.

The shadow my hat cast over the rock was making it hard for me to see the bone, and I still couldn't reach it.

"Stop!" Daniel shouted. "You're going to fall!"

"I'm not going to—"

I fell, or slid, fast, belly first, trying to slow myself with my hands. I clutched hold of the protruding bone and held tight. My body swung round, and my feet kicked and found a tiny little ledge that wasn't really a ledge, just a lip of sandstone. I was standing on my tiptoes, body pressed against the rock, fingernails dug into the bone—which I very quickly realized wasn't bone. It was petrified wood. I could see the grain all too clearly now.

I looked up. Hugh and Daniel were kneeling, peering down at me. Daniel looked terrified; Hugh looked more disgruntled.

"You were right," I said, mouth dry. "Wood."

I could hear bits of rock whispering and clicking down the slope from the disintegrating little ledge.

"We're going to get some rope from the ponies," Hugh said. "Don't move."

"I can't hold on that long."

"You've got to try."

I shifted my toes along the crumbling ledge. I wondered fleetingly if I was going to die and never see Samuel again.

"I might be able to go down on my backside." I risked a glance over my shoulder and fought a swell of vertigo. The stone was gray and coarse as elephant skin, but there were all sorts of corrugations and runnels that I might be able to jam my feet into. They'd slow me at least.

"I don't think that's a good idea," Daniel was saying.

But I didn't have any choice now anyway, because my left foot slipped altogether, and I just had time to turn myself round, back to the rock, as I started to slide. It was a terrible toboggan ride. I tried to dig in with my hands and boots, but I was mostly aware of going faster and faster and the heat on my palms and legs, and then I was sprawled in a big clump of sagebrush. It was very scratchy, but it had probably saved me from breaking a leg. I sat crumpled, feeling sick for a few moments, the breath knocked out of me. Dimly I heard the students shouting from above.

After a moment, I lifted an arm and called out hoarsely, "I'm all right."

I stood up. My tool pouch was still around my neck. My stockings were torn and bloodied, and my palms were lacerated and filled with splintered rock. But no other wounds. Nothing seemed broken.

"Stay there! We'll find a way down."

It took them a while. I leaned against the stone until my breathing slowed—and then stopped altogether for a second as I stared. And suddenly I was a young girl again, standing at dawn on a farmer's field, gazing at something miraculous and ancient in the earth.

12.
PTERODACTYLUS

LUCKILY, WHEN PAPA SAW ME LATER AT THE camp, I'd already had time to wash my cuts and have the army surgeon bandage them. I'd scrubbed the dust off my face and hair and changed into a clean skirt and blouse. Still, Papa was very angry.

"They tell me you were reckless," he said. "If this continues, I'll send you home; don't think I won't."

This was not the reaction I'd been hoping for. If I'd been a boy would he have praised me for my devotion, my initiative?

"You might have broken your leg, or your neck."

"Well, it was worth it," I said.

He grimaced. "How was it worth it?"

From my saddlebag, I took the hunk of rock I'd quarried out. I knew I shouldn't have done it—we were supposed to leave it in situ—but I'd been too excited. In any event, I'd been very careful. I handed the fossil to Papa.

"Now these," he said, "are very intriguing. Despite their length they look to me very much like cervical vertebrae."

"That's what I thought!"

"You staked the site?"

"I staked it."

He looked at the bones again. "Still yes yes, you must be more careful."

"I'm absolutely fine," I said, flexing my bandaged hands. "And look, I can still hold a geological hammer. Or a shovel, when we quarry it out!"

"But it's the arm bones that are really interesting," she told me, our backs to the rock, legs stretched out. It had been four days since I'd last seen her. "A humerus, a radius, and a long metacarpal bone. And radiating from that are three stubby fingers—and one extremely long one. It's much thicker then the others, and bent back at a strange angle. There are four phalanges, three of them very stubby, and the fourth one, it must be over three feet long!"

"A wing!" I said.

"Yes!" She grasped both my hands in hers. Her eyes were lively with the same excitement she must've felt when first seeing it. "It's a flier! And I wondered how it *could* have flown. It must be almost thirty feet across!"

"Hollow boned?" I said.

She nodded. "I looked inside a cracked bit of humerus. Paper thin. Bones light enough to fly! Imagine, they would've been soaring around up there!"

KENNETH OPPEL

I followed her gaze to the sky and pictured them: giant reptiles circling on a column of hot air from the earth.

"There would have been swamps and lakes then," I said. "Do you think they dived down and speared fish like the cape gannet?"

"Or they stood in the shallows and got them, like herons. I wish we had the skull."

"It might turn up."

"And we haven't found the other arm yet either."

"You never get the whole thing," I said. "That's what my father says. There's always some bit missing, maybe just a little bit, but you never get the complete skeleton."

I suppose I was a little jealous, too, that she'd found a winged reptile before me, because I said:

"They've already found some in Europe. Pterodactylus."

"I know, but none here yet. And most important, none anywhere near this big. This one's huge! A completely different species."

I had to smile at her enthusiasm. "The first American dragon."

"My father wouldn't approve of that term. Too showy, and inaccurate."

"Catchy, though," I said. "It's an amazing find. Congratulations. I can't believe you went over a cliff to get it!"

There was just the slightest space between us, and I felt a pull, like two magnets held very close. I closed the gap and kissed her. After a moment she pulled back.

"You still kiss me like you're afraid I'll run away."

I looked at her, indignant, but embarrassed, too. Because it was true. I felt like I was hurrying to convince her of something before she changed her mind.

"I won't run away," she said. "And I'm likely to stay even longer if you kiss me gently."

I think she meant it kindly, but I still felt exasperated. "Fine. You kiss me the way you like being kissed."

As I expected she looked hesitant.

"Go on," I said, triumphant. She'd be worried it was too forward or unladylike for her to initiate a kiss.

But suddenly she looked intrigued and then eager. She leaned forward, put her mouth to mine. I stayed still. It was a completely different experience, soft and unhurried. I felt every surface of her mouth. It was a kiss that took its time. It had its own pulse. Then her hands were in my hair, pulling me closer so the kiss became more urgent and it felt like we were desperate to reach each other.

"How was that?" she asked breathlessly when we broke off. She looked a little worried.

I felt strangely shy. "That was . . . excellent."

"I found it more satisfying," she said soberly.

I wondered how she could know so much about kissing. Had she been kissed before? Or had she just imagined the perfect kiss in her mind? Read about it? I felt ashamed of the ones I'd given before: She must have thought they were messy, careless things.

"I think I need more practice," I said.

Amusement brightened her eyes. "Do you now?"

After we kissed some more, sheer happiness made me mute.

"Look, you've already run out of things to say to me," she said with gentle mockery. "And I thought you found my mind scintillating."

"I do. I just like looking at you too."

"Well, stop it, please."

I was delighted to see her cheeks were actually red. "Are you blushing?"

"You're making me blush. And I hate it!"

"You're beautiful," I told her.

With a severity that surprised me she retorted, "I am *not* beautiful. At best I am striking—and only on account of my eyes."

I wasn't quite sure what to say to this. Should I rush in and insist she *was* beautiful, or would that only insult her? She seemed to have a very set view of her appearance. I kept quiet for a moment, then said:

"Well, you're beautiful to me, and there's nothing I'd rather do than look at you."

"You'd get bored very quickly."

I laughed. "You're supposed to say 'And there's nothing *I'd* rather do than look at *you*.'"

She let out a quick, exasperated breath. "It would be a lie. When the world has so many interesting things to look at."

I shook my head. "You really don't have a romantic bone in your body, do you?"

Solemnly she shook her head. "Not one. You should know this about me. Anyway, even if there's nothing better to look at, there are better things to talk about. You haven't told me about your finds."

"I've staked a bunch of things, but we've been spending mornings quarrying out one of Ned's finds."

I told her about the ancient reptile he'd found. Its skull was twice the size of an alligator. The fissured bone was mottled brown, the gaping eye socket filled with rock. Its long jaws and interlaced teeth were clenched shut, like it was gripping something it would never let go of.

I loved how Rachel listened to me properly—so different from a sour teacher, or my own father with his ten-second span of attention. Always in motion. Rachel didn't look distracted or move away to some other task or room. I felt like a child showing her all my prized cartons and boxes of specimens. As I talked, she lightly traced my knuckle with the tip of her index finger. It was distracting, and I liked it.

"It's really more like a giant monitor lizard than an alligator," I said. "It's probably a mosasaur. A Dutch surgeon found one about a hundred years ago near Maastricht. I think my father was disappointed he might not get to name it."

"It's still a great find," she said.

"Not as good as yours. That was an amazing bit of prospecting you did." I could tell she was pleased by her smile. She didn't care about compliments on her hairpins or appearance, but she cared about her fossil hunting. More than anything.

"I want to be a paleontologist," she said.

"You'll make a great one."

"Only if my father lets me go to university."

"He should," I said. "I would."

"Would you?" she asked, studying me, like she wasn't convinced.

"Of course. Then we could work together in the field."

She smiled at this, and then an angry clicking noise drew our attention. Twenty feet away, rising high from the scrub, were two rattlesnakes, necks tangled round each other. Their heads bobbed and feinted and twined. Both of us watched, fascinated. I wondered at first if they were fighting, but then understood this was a mating dance. They swayed together quite hypnotically. Bodies lifting higher and higher. Looping together until they'd formed a hoop—and started to roll straight toward us. I took Rachel's hand and pulled her out of the way, but the snakes never made it so far. Their hoop collapsed, and they were just a big tangle again on the ground, inseparable, and we were both laughing.

"They're not at all interested in us," I told her.

"Only each other."

"Like us." I kissed her again. "You don't have to go yet, do you?"

"Five more minutes," she said. "Any more and they'll think I've been kidnapped."

Back home none of this would have happened. Rachel and me. Meeting in secret. Kissing and holding each other tightly. But out here in the ruins of the world, there were no buildings or rooms to separate or contain us. No bookish laws and rules to manacle us. It seemed ridiculous out here, all that stuff made of brick and timbers and paper and people's stale breath. Out here the rock had no rules and the hills had no laws and the vast sky was everywhere and watching, but didn't care one bit.

Halfway back to camp, I dismounted to piss against a rock.

It wasn't a sound that made me turn, but something did. When I looked over my shoulder, I saw the boy sitting astride his pony. My first surprised thought was: *He belongs here*. Wearing only a breechclout that hung from his waist by a belt, he and his horse were all the colors of the landscape. He looked a bit younger than me. Muscles ridged his flat stomach and bronzed arms. Two braids of night-black hair, decorated with beads and feathers, hung past his shoulders. The illustrations in the magazines weren't enough.

Embarrassed, I quickly buttoned my trousers and turned to face him. He was about three yards away. He sat very tall in his saddle, stared down at me. How he'd gotten so close without my noticing, I had no idea. I saw the knife in his belt and the bow slung across the horse.

I thought he was Sioux but wasn't sure. I didn't know what to do, so I said, "Hello."

No reply, just a glare. He wasn't as big as me, or tall. But he had that knife, and I didn't want to cross him. Partly it was his confidence. He looked like he had every right to be here, and I had none. Like he would fight and win.

"What's your name?" I asked.

Nothing. Maybe he didn't understand; maybe he was just ignoring me.

He didn't come any closer, but he didn't go away. I didn't know what he wanted. What would happen next? If I got on my pony and started to ride away, would he follow me? If he wanted, he could probably shoot me with an arrow before I even got into the saddle.

My eyes strayed to my saddlebag. A geological hammer. An awl. Not much in the way of weapons. When I looked back to him, I could tell he'd been tracking my gaze. He raised his eyebrows. Mocking? Taunting? I stared back, frozen.

Then he clicked and turned his pony around and rode off. A leisurely pace. Didn't even look back once.

When I got up into my saddle, my legs felt watery. I kept watch over my shoulder the whole way back to camp, and when I got there, I told Ned and my father what had happened.

"A scout?" Father asked Ned.

"Sounds like he was too young," Ned said. "Maybe just a boy out on his own."

"It doesn't seem he meant you any harm," Father said easily. "He was probably as startled as you were."

"He didn't look one bit startled."

"Things have been pretty peaceful since the Laramie Treaty," Ned said. "Not to say there aren't still skirmishes. And with people getting interested in the Black Hills, that's only going to get worse."

I'd heard of the Black Hills but couldn't remember why. "What's special about them?"

"Well, they're sacred to the Sioux, and that land's supposed to be theirs forever, according to the treaty. But some prospectors found gold up there. And I heard a rumor the army's planning an expedition to see just how much."

"But what about the treaty?" I asked.

"Oh, I don't suppose the treaty will count for much if they find gold," my father said. "That land'll get taken."

He didn't seem very concerned about it one way or another, and it surprised me.

"It's a broken promise," I said. "It's unfair."

"I don't disagree," he replied. "But human history is the history of the conqueror and the conquered."

"Well, the Indians don't think of themselves as conquered," said Ned. "Not yet anyway. They got a lot of fight in them."

"Bows and arrows against rifles," said my father. "They might as well try to stop the tide, or the movement of the planets. In any event, their feud's with the army, not with people like us."

I wondered. If he'd seen that look in the Sioux boy's eyes, he might have felt differently.

13.
THE BARNUM MAN

RETURNING TO CAMP, THE SIXTH DAY AFTER I found the pterodactylus, I spotted an antelope drinking from the river.

"We need some fresh meat," Hugh Friar said, dismounting with his Springfield rifle and ammunition pouch. "We'll bring this one home with us."

The antelope saw us but showed no sign of fear, bending its graceful neck to the water once more. Even when the first shot rang out, and missed, the animal didn't bolt, just looked up and about curiously. Hugh loaded another cartridge into the breech and took aim. He missed the second time. The antelope looked directly at him now, as if unable to believe what a terrible shot Hugh was.

Unlike the Yalies, I hadn't bought myself a rifle in Omaha, so I swung myself off my pony and asked Daniel if I could borrow his.

"Are you sure, Miss Cartland?" he asked. "You know how to use one?"

"Oh, yes," I said as he handed it over. "I'll just need one cartridge, thanks."

I came to where Hugh was standing, just as he took his third try. This one hit, but it was a messy shot, in the antelope's hindquarters, and the poor animal staggered away from the river, one of its legs clearly broken. It made a piteous sound.

"Almost," muttered Hugh, reloading.

I took aim. The rifle had a satisfying heft and length, the stock hard and cool against my cheek.

I'd been shooting since I was twelve. Papa had taught me how to line the front bead up with the grooves; I discovered I had the most success if I kept the bead at the bottom of the target, so that when I pulled the trigger and the gun kicked, my shot didn't go too high but was usually just right. He'd always said I was a good shot. The first thing I'd hit was a partridge, and when it plunged to the ground, a heap of feather, I was stunned by what I had done. Beforehand I'd worried I would be ashamed or sickened, but I wasn't. I was exhilarated. My first thought in fact was: So this is how it feels to be powerful. Every creature on the earth is a hunter of one sort or another.

I squeezed the trigger and shot the antelope through both shoulders. It collapsed to the ground and was still. When I lowered my rifle, Hugh was looking at me, his expression both irritated and admiring.

"Good shot," he said.

It shamed me to admit how satisfying I found this, how I'd accomplished in one shot what he couldn't in three.

"Everything all right?" a voice shouted, and I looked over to see three men on saddle ponies riding quickly toward us, a single wagon in the distance. They certainly weren't from our party. "We heard gunshots."

"Just a bit of hunting," Hugh said, pointing at the fallen antelope in the grass.

"Thank goodness," said the lead rider, swinging himself a bit clumsily off his pony. "We worried there was an altercation." He was a tall fellow, not ten years older than me, shaggy hair tufting out beneath his slouch hat. Fine, sun-etched lines radiated from his smiling eyes. His cheeks were a little gaunt, but his teeth were surprisingly good, though slightly yellowed. He managed to look clean.

"Can you tell me if we're near Professor Cartland's camp?"

"You are," I said. "We're headed there ourselves. I'm his daughter, Rachel Cartland."

He looked surprised it was me addressing him and not one of the Yalies. "Ah! Very pleased to meet you, Miss Cartland. I had no idea he'd brought his daughter with him. I'm Ethan Withrow. They said in town your party was headed north. I was hoping to have a visit with your father."

Despite his weathered appearance, I had the sense Ethan Withrow wasn't from around here; he sounded like an Easterner. I'd never heard Papa mention his name, but I could only assume he was a scientist, or at least an amateur prospector. I took a good look at his companions. One of the other riders had red hair and a thick beard and looked like he was used to sunburn and horses. And the other rider, I was fairly sure, was Indian, though he had short hair and was dressed in regular clothes. Pawnee or Sioux, I couldn't tell. Was he their guide? The wagon was close enough now that I could see the teamster. He had a slightly treacherous look, and I wondered if I'd seen him on the streets of Crowe, maybe outside a saloon.

"Why don't we help get that fine antelope onto our wagon," said Withrow, "and we can ride into camp together."

There was nothing ominous about him, and Hugh and Daniel didn't seem to have any objections either, so we thanked him and rode the last mile or so to our camp. Not all the prospecting parties were back yet, but Papa was, and I introduced him to Withrow and his men.

"What brings you out here, Mr. Withrow?"

"Same thing as you, sir. Dinosaurs."

Could he actually imagine we'd be happy to hear this? No prospector wanted to share his bone fields. Probably Withrow didn't know Papa already had a wily competitor an hour down-river.

"Are you a hobbyist, or a scholar? I must confess I have not heard your name."

"I'm working for Mr. Barnum from New York City. He's a tireless man, as you know, and always looking for new wonders. I'm just one of his many lookers."

"He wants his very own dinosaur," I said.

KENNETH OPPEL

Withrow tipped his head at me. "Bigger the better, that's Mr. Barnum."

"Ah, I see," said Papa. I was impressed at his calm when he must have been roiling inside. I knew how he felt about ringmasters. He filled his pipe slowly and offered Withrow some tobacco. "How much experience do you have at hunting fossils, Mr. Withrow?"

He gave a good-natured smile. "A very little."

"Do you know, for instance, what this is?" He lifted my notebook from the crate and showed a drawing of an ilium.

"That is . . . a bone," said Withrow, chuckling with such self-deprecation it was impossible not to like him. I couldn't help wondering if he was as unskilled as he made out. "Don't ask me what part of the body it is, or what animal it came from."

"You seem somewhat ill-suited to your task," Papa remarked.

"I surely am, Professor. But I'm quick to learn, and I was hoping we might be of some use to each other. I've got some strong arms with me, and Thomas here"—he gestured to the Indian man—"is an excellent guide. But we don't know where to look, or *what* we're looking at if we get lucky. But if we were to work under your expert guidance, we'd be a lot more useful."

Papa chuckled. "You are proposing I help you become my competitor!"

"No, not at all," said Withrow. "I'm proposing we help you with *your* work. And if we should find something that Mr. Barnum might like, well, he would offer you a very attractive finder's fee."

"Well," said my father, waving his arm around our enormous camp, "as you can see, I have no shortage of help or resources."

"Clearly," said Withrow, "you're very well financed for this trip. But I'm sure there are future expeditions to think of. Science isn't as well funded as the circus business."

Maybe I had underestimated Withrow. He was a persuasive fellow and had a good point. Papa was a wealthy man, but not even a wealthy man wanted to spend his own money on expensive expeditions.

My father rocked on his heels, a prelude to a lecture. "How much do you know about me, Mr. Withrow?"

The Barnum man grinned. "Only that you're the most famous paleontologist in the nation, sir."

As a bit of flattery, it wasn't bad, and Papa did look slightly mollified, but not for long. "Then you should know I'm a scientist and not a circus entertainer. If I were to work in tandem with a showman like Mr. Barnum, it would discredit my work and the whole enterprise of science. I am not interested in entertaining the masses, only discovering the truth."

"I know, I know what you're thinking, Professor," said Withrow calmly, as though he'd anticipated just such a response. "'That Barnum, he's just after some new attraction.' And you're not entirely wrong. But Mr. Barnum does have a genuine interest in the natural sciences. He's even made charitable donations to universities and museums."

"Well, we scientists don't have his gift for making money," said Papa.

"No reason why money and science can't go together. All we need to do is *share* these things you're finding."

"We're doing that already," I said, "in the lobby of the Academy of Natural Sciences. Have you seen Joseph Leidy's hadrosaur?"

"That's a good start," said Withrow, "but we need to go further. In England, there's a fellow, Hawkins, who's created sculptures of dinosaurs, with skin and teeth and eyes, and put them on display in the Crystal Palace. There was even one you could eat dinner in. What was it called . . . a . . ."

"Iguanodon," I said, remembering the illustrated papers I'd seen.

"Mere spectacle!" my father said.

"A little spectacle's all right, surely, Professor, if it gets people interested in what you do."

"I like the idea of seeing them as they might have been," I admitted. "It's easy for us to imagine"—here I looked to Papa—"because we've spent so long with bones, but for most people it's just a jumble. I'm sure people would be more interested if we mounted more of them—I heard Leidy's hadrosaur brings a lot of people to the academy."

"And they started charging an entrance fee, didn't they?" said Withrow.

"Regrettable," Papa said.

"No. Just a measure of how important your work is. There's a lot of ignorance out there. You probably didn't hear about what Boss Tweed did in New York City just a couple weeks ago."

I shook my head. We'd had no news from back east since setting out from Crowe.

"Well, you probably knew that Hawkins came over here to make some life-size sculptures of English dinosaurs."

"For Central Park," I said. I remembered Papa telling me about it now, and naturally he hadn't approved of a British fellow bringing his artistic notions of dinosaurs to our country.

"Exactly," said Withrow. "Well, Boss Tweed thought the very notion of dinosaurs was blasphemous—there was no life on earth further back than the Bible, and the Bible had nothing to say about dinosaurs, so he had some fellows break into Hawkins's studio and smash up all his work."

"Despicable, to be sure," said my father. "Though of no great loss to science. Judging from his other work, his sculptures were wildly fanciful."

"Well, Professor, you'll also know that even in our own government and Senate, you don't have a lot of support for what you do. You've got people like the senator from Virginia saying we've no business digging these devil's scraps up in the first place."

"We've heard yes yes language like this before," said Papa, rolling his eyes at me.

"But these are the big boys who write the checks. They'll pay for a geological survey of the West. That's fine. They want to know where the land's good, where's water, where's coal and gold. That's important. But where are the dinosaur bones? The boys in Washington aren't very inclined to pay for your kind of work, or fund schools or museums that do."

Withrow seemed to have a good deal of information on hand. It was quite a speech he was making.

"All I'm saying is, Mr. Barnum might not be such a bad friend to have, looking ahead."

"So what exactly are you proposing, Mr. Withrow?" Papa said, sounding a bit weary. "That you get the biggest find we make? I just hand it over to Mr. Barnum?"

"There's one thing in particular we're eager to find." He nodded at his Indian guide. "Thomas grew up not far from here. He lost his people to the pox and would've starved if he hadn't been picked up by a traveling preacher. He still knows the Sioux language, and he hears things about his people from time to time. There's one story I was very taken with. Have either of you ever heard of the Black Beauty?"

I shook my head. The way he said it conjured the feeling of a legend, and in the cooling air I shivered. This was a story I definitely wanted to hear.

"I should let Thomas tell it."

When Thomas spoke, it was deliberately, with enough spaces between sentences to let each one have an echoing power. It was the story of a Sioux boy on something called a vision quest, a rite of passage from boy to man. Thomas drew the story with vivid, bold strokes. The boy wandered until he was delirious from lack of food and water and all night fought with some kind of monster that had a skull of black bones.

My pulse quickened. There was a hypnotic quality to the tale that increased second by second.

"When he woke, the sun was rising and he was walking, streaked with blood, a black tooth clutched in his fist. He called it the Black Beauty."

The shock of recognition was so strong, I had to work hard to compose my face. The black tooth. My tooth. I listened, rapt, as Thomas said the tooth had magical powers, could be shot like an arrow. Its owner became a great hunter and warrior.

"They buried him with the tooth," Thomas said, "and set his funeral platform apart from the others."

My eyes flicked from Thomas to Withrow to Papa. Like me, he must've known this was the story of our tooth, but he looked remarkably relaxed—amused, even.

"Extraordinary tale," he said pleasantly.

Withrow held up a hand. "I don't expect you to believe all of it. The supernatural properties of the tooth, shooting like an arrow, all that. But I can't help thinking that this fellow must've stumbled on a dinosaur fossil."

"Without seeing the tooth itself," Papa said bluffly, "it would be difficult to assess its true character. You've never seen this tooth yourself, I'm assuming?"

"I have not."

"The Plains Indians seem to have yes yes a great respect for visions, but this man might have brought back nothing more than an interestingly shaped stone."

"There are bones everywhere here," said Thomas placidly. "When I was young, I saw many. My people said they were the bones of sky and water monsters."

"Let's just say our boy was on one of their vision quests, and had an encounter with a dinosaur fossil," Withrow said, leaning forward. "That seems plausible to me. Are you aware, Professor, of any creature that has teeth that size? It must have been a real monster!"

"We're only just starting to see the full variety of these creatures, Mr. Withrow. Certainly I know of no creature with black bones!"

"Well, I was wondering if they might have been colored by the rock around it. Is that possible?"

It was completely possible, and my father and I both knew it.

"It's been known to happen," my father said. Maybe his professor's heart couldn't bear an outright lie.

"Maybe coal? I see the layers in the buttes all round here. Or shale? Limestone?"

Withrow was definitely more knowledgeable than he'd let on earlier. He watched my father intently.

"Possibly," Papa said.

"What do you think, Professor? An intriguing lead?"

"Are you saying your friend Thomas here knows where this tooth might have come from?"

I watched Withrow tensely and felt myself sag when he shook his head regretfully.

"No. No, we don't know that. But we're willing to work our hardest, and under your direction. With the understanding that if we found it, you'd be credited with the discovery. You'd get to name it, and study it—"

"But the bones would be yours."

"And the fame and finder's fee yours."

It didn't sound like such a bad bargain to me, but I knew Papa would never be parted from his fossils. He hoarded them in the locked basement of the university and was very choosy about whom he entrusted with the key.

"I wish you luck, Mr. Withrow. Alas, we already have enough work under way here to keep us busy all season. I ask only that you respect our quarries. You'll find the area quite crowded already. Professor Bolt from Philadelphia is also digging here."

Withrow's eyebrows lifted. "Is he?"

I was surprised at the pang I felt. I wished Papa hadn't told him that. Bolt might very well take Withrow up on his offer to get more prospectors and . . . have a better chance of finding their *rex*. For the first time I realized how much I wanted it too. Why should it belong to Samuel and his father any more than to me and mine? We each had a tooth—if that was any claim at all. I wished Samuel the best, but I didn't want him to have an advantage over me.

"Yes. Just downriver. You should go talk to him. Perhaps he'd be more amenable to your proposal."

"Maybe so," he said.

"I doubt you'll find him any more receptive," I said abruptly, and Papa gave me a curious look. "These scientists are very high-minded."

"Ha. Well, thank you for your time, Professor. Miss Cartland. Our paths may cross again in the badlands."

14.
WORDPLAY

HE CAME TO US, TOO," I SAID, WHEN SHE started telling me about her visit from Ethan Withrow.

"He said he would. Are you going to work with him?"

I shook my head and wondered if she looked relieved. "My father got all pigheaded about it."

"Did he tell you the legend of the Black Beauty?"

"Incredible, isn't it? Did you tell him you have the tooth?"

"Of course not!"

I grinned. "Have you noticed yourself having any strange powers yet?"

"I do feel invincible," she admitted with a smile.

"You always were," I said, and meant it. To me there was something indestructible about her, like deep down there was this core of confidence and conviction that nothing could harm. "I like the idea of the tooth shooting like an arrow."

"I'll have to try it," she said. "Maybe on one of the singing Yalies."

As usual I'd found her out prospecting with her little team, and she'd broken away to join me in a large rectangular opening at the base of the butte. The sides and ceiling were so square it looked like it had been chiseled out on purpose, a small stage for the dinosaurs to put on plays for one another. We had to keep our voices low because it was quite echoey inside.

"The Plains Indians," she said, "they must have come across so many fossils, weathered out, over the centuries. I wonder if that's what gave them the idea for their giants and monsters. They had proof right at their feet."

"That's what Withrow thinks. I didn't think it was a bad idea, working with him. We could've used the help, and the money. He even offered to advance us some to keep us in the field longer. That guide of his, Thomas, he might've been able to talk to the local Sioux. To get some information about where the tooth came from."

"That might not have gone well."

"Maybe not. I had a run in with a Sioux boy." I'd been waiting to tell her about it for days.

"Were you frightened?" she said, putting her hand on my arm.

I gave a manly shrug. "No. Well, a bit. He had a bow and a knife."

"I would've been petrified," she said, then added, almost disappointed, "We haven't seen anyone yet. Our scouts say they've seen campfire smoke from the prairie, which means a village.

Although . . ." She looked off, remembering. "I was almost certain I saw a rider on horseback when we were at those funeral platforms."

"I don't think they'd come anywhere near you, with half the army in tow."

Her gaze was still thoughtful. "I feel even guiltier about taking the tooth, now I know how important it was to the man."

"Sounds like they thought it was a mixed blessing by the end."

"But they still buried it with him."

"Maybe to get rid of it. Maybe they thought it was cursed."

All that was a myth, but I envied her having held it. "Now there's someone else looking."

"Could you really have given it away, your *rex*?" she asked me.

I breathed out. "That would've been hard, for sure. Finding it would've been the main thing. That moment. That would be a very big, shiny moment. And getting to name it."

"After you, of course!"

"Of course! I sure don't want anyone else to name it."

"It doesn't seem like Withrow's very experienced," she said, "and he has far fewer people than us."

"But not us," I reminded her.

"Would you rather *he* found it, or my father?" she asked.

"I'd rather *we* found it. You and me." I kissed her.

After a moment she pulled away suddenly. "What would we call it?"

"Something magnificent." I thought for a moment. "*Tyrannosaurus rex!* How's that?"

"Tyrant lizard king. Not bad. And what would you call *me*?"

I laughed. "For you . . . how about . . . *Magevofoterus tigris*?"

She frowned, then smiled. "Witch-eyed tiger?"

"I think so."

"I'm not sure about your Latin and Greek, but I like it."

"Me now."

She thought, then said, "*Callidosaurus vulpes*."

"I get the last part, but not the first."

"From *callidus*. Cunning. Shrewd."

"Oh, so I'm a clever fox lizard."

"Exactly."

"We could be fossil-hunting partners, you and me. Find the Black Beauty and sell it to Mr. Barnum ourselves."

She laughed. She didn't realize how serious I was.

"Why don't we just run away and join the circus?" she said.

"I will if you will." But I felt a little hurt by her lighthearted dismissal.

"I should get back," she said with a sigh.

I kicked at some rocks. "I hate saying good-bye to you. I never know what to say."

"You're ridiculous."

"I thought I was cunning and shrewd."

"Not about this. Just say good-bye."

In the soft dirt I drew a grid, four columns, four rows, like the game she'd taught me on the train. I wrote a letter in each space. I paid attention to the rules and made sure all the right letters touched.

KENNETH OPPEL

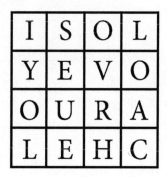

My pulse kicked hard. I felt like the sky had cracked open and I was naked to the sun and flying, as if on horseback, over the prairie. Fast and warm and scared.

She stared severely at the letters. "It's too easy."

I frowned, not understanding what she meant. "I knew that night," I said, "when we separated our fathers. I knew it would happen. I love you."

The three words were like a thunderclap in my head. I wanted to say them again and again.

Rachel looked down at her hands. Carefully she said, "Samuel, I am very *fond* of you. . . ."

"Don't," I said, wincing. "Please, just don't. I'd rather hear nothing."

Stupid. I'd supposed my love was so huge it would engulf her, and she couldn't help but feel the same about me. But I was an idiot.

"Let me ask you," she began. "How many other girls have you said this to?"

Her look demanded truthfulness. "One. All right, *two*—but I didn't mean it."

"So why should I think you mean it now?"

I struggled to untwist my thoughts. "I just *thought* I loved them. . . . It was childish. Not like this, how I feel about you."

And I meant it: It felt very different now, saying the words, a sick quaking in my stomach.

"I'm dubious," she said,

"You don't believe me?"

Brow creased, her eyes chiseling into me. "It's too soon. You don't know me well enough."

"I know you!" I said.

"Is everything all right, Miss Cartland?" called a voice—Daniel Simpson's, I thought.

I moved myself deeper into the niche. I didn't think we'd been heard. They were just checking on her.

"Coming!" Rachel called back. She stood and dusted off her skirt, pushed her hair back into place. And then she gave my hand a quick squeeze and walked away from me.

On the ride back to camp, my mind swarmed with thoughts.

He couldn't mean it. It was too much, too fast. How could anyone love so quickly? He was hotheaded, rash with everything, especially his feelings. I liked his heat, I did—but I didn't trust it.

Certainly I was attracted to him, much more than I'd ever imagined being attracted to anyone. What he'd said about me being a brilliant paleontologist—and how we could prospect together—that was very appealing. He'd said it so naturally, so easily, as though he didn't know how incredibly rare his opinions were. I liked that very much. But love? I wasn't even sure I knew what love would feel like.

Anything I'd known for sure came slowly—like drawing a fossil in painstaking detail. You got to know every curve and bump and notch. It took time. I had to look a great deal and think a great deal. They were momentous things, those three words "I love you," and I imagined they could only be uttered with total certainty, and to one person only.

Samuel was all impulse. But his face when he'd told me—so open, like a child's. And then the way it collapsed when I told him I was fond of him. But what else could I say? Should I have lied? I wouldn't. That wouldn't have been fair, not to him, and not to me.

I'd let him get the wrong impression, with all the kissing and touching. Those things would have heralded an engagement back east. But out here I'd been careless, and selfish, too. I liked being kissed and touched. I liked his eyes on me and all his words—even the ridiculous ones, though I suspect he'd told them to his other sweethearts. Sometimes I worried my own good sense might be swept away entirely, unless I anchored myself.

So careless! I would have to be smarter. If we were found out, Papa would certainly ship me back home. And I would have thrown away the thing I'd fought so hard for.

No one had ever told me they loved me. Not that I remembered anyhow. It was possible, I supposed, that my mother had whispered it to my newborn head. But I doubted it. She wasn't even able to nurse me; Father had said a wet nurse had to be brought in. My mother had always been weak, and my birth had only made her weaker. It was hard to imagine she'd had the energy to spare loving thoughts for me.

My father had certainly never said it to me. That was not his way. Then again, I wasn't sure I'd heard any father say it to his son. Honestly, they were not words you heard spoken very often, not in public anyway. They were big words. I saw them rising from the horizon like the pillars and arches of an ancient civilization.

I'd wanted to hear her say them. I imagined how her eyes would look. How her lips would move. How her breath would feel against my face.

Riding home at the end of the day, our last conversation echoed in my head, made me more lonesome and desperate. Why hadn't she said it back? There were not so many possibilities. The likeliest was that she simply didn't love me. But why not? What had I done or not done? Said or not said?

As a boy, when there was a specimen I wanted, I searched and searched harder until I found it. I'd never been happy until all the spaces in my collection box were filled.

I shouldn't have told her I loved her. That was too much. Should've kept my mouth shut. Maybe I'd wrecked things, and she thought I was foolish now. Maybe I'd scared her away.

I craved those three words more than anything.

15.
THE NAMING OF SPECIES

AT FIRST LIGHT WE WERE UP AND LOADING the crates onto the wagon.

Over the past five days we'd finished quarrying out the monoclonius and the mosasaur. Father had us working such long hours, I hadn't seen Rachel for nearly a week.

Five days, my hands carefully prizing bones from million-year-old rock. But my mind on Rachel's mouth. Or the small mole on her neck. Or the light beaming out from her eyes. Thoughts of her punctuated every tap of my awl and hammer, like the spaces between heartbeats. That bit of bone I'd quarried out, that was for Rachel, and the next bit too. Inside my head I was narrating my entire life for her, making lists of things I wanted to ask her, things I wanted to tell her. And always thinking ahead to the moment I'd next see her. That moment when, finally, I'd hear her say she loved me.

The night before, we'd packed the bulky bones in buffalo grass for the journey back to Philadelphia. I'd already helped Father label them and make diagrams of how they were found, so we'd have an easier time reassembling them when we got home.

As Hitch harnessed the team, Father gave Ned the note to be telegraphed to the *Transactions of the American Philosophical Society.*

"Can you read his handwriting?" I asked Ned.

"The professor's gone over it with me enough times."

"Our finds should appear in their next issue," Father said jovially, "before we're even home! This is how we do it, gentlemen. We may be outnumbered, but we work faster."

He looked grave, though, as he counted out money to Ned. After the cost of freight, the sizeable telegram, and another month of supplies and food, we'd be lucky to make it through the summer. And get ourselves home at the end of it. If we sold the team for a decent price, we'd be all right. Still, made me think again about Withrow and his offer.

Father winked at me. "We may have to play some more billiards in Crowe, eh?"

Which did nothing to ease my mind. He still thought I'd won all that money. Another thing he didn't know: I'd held back some of what Mrs. Cummins had returned to me. Partly I didn't think it was safe for my father to have it all. He might lose it or pack fossils with it or kindle a fire with it. Partly I just wanted to have some money of my own. All my life I'd been dependent on him, and it made me feel good to be more self-reliant.

After a hasty breakfast, Hitch and Ned loaded the last few items onto the wagon.

"I've left my revolver in your bedroll," Ned told me quietly. "I know your pa doesn't approve. Just between you and me, all right?"

"Thanks," I said.

"See you tomorrow."

I felt a bit nervous watching the wagon disappear. I was worried about their safety and also our own. I thought of the Sioux boy. I thought of wavery lines of smoke rising beyond the badlands. Yes, we were only an hour away from Cartland's cavalry, but still, our camp had just been cut in half.

In the last light of day, a group of soldiers arrived with a bag of mail from Crowe. To my surprise there was a letter for me from Aunt Berton. It was a single sheet of creamy paper, on which she urged me to return home and expressed her concern for my reputation as a lady, spending so much time among soldiers and savages and dead things. I laughed aloud and was about to read it to Papa, but he was engrossed in his own letter.

"Who's that from?" I asked.

"The postmaster yes yes in Crowe."

His eyes marched across the lines. "It seems our friend Bolt has been most active."

"What is it you're reading?"

Without looking up, he said, "I came to an arrangement with

the postmaster to let me know when Bolt was shipping freight or sending telegrams back east."

"Papa! That's private business!"

He glanced up irritably. "Not in Crowe it seems. He's been kind enough to send me a transcript here." He looked back down. "Bolt has a mosasaur, nothing new there . . . oh, and yes yes he's been *naming* species already . . . *Monoclonius crassus*, very nice . . ."

His voice was calm, but his high domed forehead was flushed, and I knew he was furious that his rival had claimed a new species before him.

". . . working in his usual slapdash way. I should have known this would be his modus operandi. Laying claim even before he left the field. It'll all have to be redone properly by others like myself at some point—"

When he stopped abruptly, brow furrowed, I knew something had upset him even more.

"What?" I demanded.

". . . partial skull, scapula, humerus, ulna, fourth metacarpal, four phalanges . . ." He looked up, his face suddenly drained of color. "He has a pterodactylus with a wingspan of possibly thirty feet. He has a wing *and* a head! And he has named it *Quetzalcoatlus* Bolt!"

"No." Samuel would've told me if they'd found a pterodactylus. Unless all this had happened in the last five days when I hadn't see him. Could they have found and quarried out an entire specimen in so few days?

In a clenched voice my father said, "He has *poached* my fossil!"

"What?" I said, still so bewildered I wasn't even sure what he meant. "Stolen it?"

"From our quarry."

"No one would do such a thing!"

"No? Perhaps this explains why we found no skull and only *one* arm."

"We would've noticed, wouldn't we?"

"Not if he came in the night yes yes. I wouldn't put it past Bolt. He's a skillful digger; we might not have noticed his workings. The Yalies kept the quarry so messy there was debris everywhere." He looked at me sharply. "Have you seen his boy? Told him anything?"

"Of course not!" I was shocked by his insinuation—and my own quick lie.

The doubt had always been there, dormant in my mind, and now it began to germinate and send out tendrils. Had everything I'd told Sam been relayed straight to his father? Was he just spying after all? What else had he lied about?

"Isn't it possible," I said hopefully, "they just found one of their own?"

My father paced. His head rode atop his shoulders like a fierce cannonball. "I find that very hard to believe. I'll confront him!"

"And admit you've been reading his telegrams? I think that's a crime."

"There are no Union laws out here yet," my father said evasively, but his temper seemed to cool. "Bolt's a thief, no question, but it's impossible to prove right now. No point pursuing it. In any event, he'll find all his rash haste is fruitless."

"Why's that?"

"Before we left Crowe, I telegraphed the editor of *American Philosophical*, and we came to an understanding he'd publish only *my* finds during this season. Bolt will have to secure publication elsewhere."

My face must have radiated my astonishment, for he said, "Don't worry, my dear. There's nothing nefarious in it. It's a perfectly yes yes legitimate arrangement. Bolt will have his finds published, only in some other journal, and later than he might like. Much later perhaps."

He walked off, leaving me tangled up in my own thoughts and wondering who was less trustworthy: my father or Samuel Bolt.

I'd barely said hello to her before she asked, "Did you find a pterodactylus?"

Her piercing look made me feel instantly guilty. "No. I would've told you!"

"And you didn't tell your father about ours?"

I shook my head. "What's wrong?"

She looked miserable. "I don't know if you're telling the truth."

"I am! What's going on?"

Suddenly *she* seemed like the guilty one. "My father . . ." Her eyes dropped, and she tried again. "He's paid the postmaster in Crowe to show him your father's telegrams."

"What!" I'd always thought my father was exaggerating, the way he raged about Cartland's scheming. But this was despicable! Before I could say anything else, Rachel was lifting her hand, beseeching.

"I know, it's terrible, but please listen. In the telegram your father says he found a new species of pterodactylus. It sounds exactly like ours, except he has the head and left wing—the parts *we're* missing."

I felt a hot rush of outrage. "And you think my father *stole* from your quarry?"

"Why didn't he tell you he found a flying reptile?"

"The only thief's your father!" I countered. "Has he ever told you what he did at the New Jersey marl pits? No? Going behind my father's back with the pit owner to sneak out the best fossils?"

"I don't know anything about that."

Both of us went silent. My head raged. Was Cartland inventing some crime of my father's? To explain his incomplete skeleton? If yes, it was a wicked lie to hammer together and tell his own daughter.

"Some of the students say they saw him from a distance," she said.

"All right, let's say my father saw the quarry. How could he dig it up with your people there all the time?"

"At night."

It stung me, her assumption my father was guilty. But already I was rummaging through my memories. And came to those nights I'd woken and Father hadn't been beside me in our tent. That one time especially I'd found him poking at the campfire, bedraggled and dusty, before even Hitch was awake. He was always an early riser, and a restless sleeper, and I'd just assumed he was getting some fresh air.

"I don't believe it," I said, furious at the possibility. "The only thing we know for sure is your father's breaking the law to spy on my father. Because he's *jealous* we'll claim things faster. And that's exactly what we're doing!"

She looked away. Haltingly she said, "There's something else," and told me how Cartland had fixed things with the journal before he'd left Crowe.

"This is too much!" I said. "I've got to tell my father."

She stared at me balefully. "Go ahead. And you can ask him where he got his pterodactylus."

Again we fell silent. She was right. If I told my father, everything would come spilling out. My meetings with Rachel. All our traded secrets.

"Our fathers . . . ," I began, and trailed off.

"It's awful what mine did," she said. "I'm ashamed of him. But yours—you have to admit, it looks suspicious."

Miserably I nodded. I knew my father was rash, but the idea of him stealing outright was too painful.

She was quiet a moment, then looked me square in the eye. "You really didn't know anything about this?"

I squinted. "You're asking if I *helped* him now?"

She took her time. "Did you?"

"No! How can I prove it?" I asked, feeling helpless. "Whatever my father did, or didn't do, I had nothing to do with it."

I felt like she was watching me from a long way away, and I wanted to bring her back to me. I needed to fix things but didn't know how.

"I have to go," she said abruptly. "I think they're getting suspicious."

Desolate, I said, "Not yet, not like this."

"I have to," she said, and left.

That evening Father was in high spirits. He'd found articulated bone, and so had Ned, who'd returned from Crowe in the early afternoon. As we washed up by the river before dinner, the two of them eagerly traded details, debated which one we should quarry out first. I said nothing, still deep in the rabbit warren of my own thoughts—until I heard my father say:

"At this rate, we'll have another three to claim soon."

Another three. Monoclonius. Mosasaur. And . . .

With a sick feeling I asked, "What was the third?"

My father's smile contracted. Then he chuckled. "I was thinking about our *rex* tooth, I suppose."

"You mentioned the tooth to the journal?" I asked. "A bit early, isn't it?"

I shot a look at Ned. He looked like he had a big greasy meal sliding around inside him. He said nothing.

"So what was the third?" I persisted.

Ned's head drooped like a whipped dog. He was too honest to hide a lie.

"I found a partial skeleton of a pterodactylus," Father said, "and shipped it off last minute. I forgot to tell you."

This lie hurt me almost the worst. So half hearted. Did he think I was an idiot? Everything we found we talked about. At night we made measurements, imagined anatomy and function. He would *never* forget to tell me about a find—unless he was hiding it on purpose.

"Where'd you find it?" I demanded. If he was going to drag this out, I wanted to make it as painful as possible.

Father buttoned his shirt, pulled his suspenders up over his shoulders.

"Ned?" I asked.

"Professor," he said miserably, "I'd feel better if you answered this."

Father swiped water droplets from his eyebrows. "I found it in one of Cartland's quarries. They'd made a mess of it. They'd scrounged out a wing and the rear limbs, a fragment of pelvic girdle, but it was obvious they weren't going to find anything more. Ned and I just had a poke around and caught what they'd missed. We got the skull and another wing."

"At night."

"Certainly at night. I wanted to see how he was making out, just have a look. I wasn't planning on touching anything—but that pterodactyl. It was huge. Nothing like the European ones."

"What about the agreement? No interfering with each other's quarries?"

Far from apologetic, his expression was almost pugnacious. "I didn't tamper with what they'd already uncovered. He's welcome to his find."

"I'm sure they would've found the skull on their own!"

A dismissive wave of his hand. "Likely I saved those pieces from being forgotten, or mashed to chalk by his ham-fisted students."

He was a talker, my father. Could spin a story any which way. But even by his standards, this was a stupendous performance.

"You wanted a flier, so you stole his," I insisted.

"He *owed* me a specimen after the New Jersey marl pits!"

"Ah, here we go."

"At least one! I'm setting things *right*. He wouldn't even be here if it weren't for me—and Ned's lead. He's brought more men and money than I could ever muster, and there shouldn't be any doubt, Samuel, in your mind about his intentions. He means to strip me of as many finds as possible. No, I'll go further. He means to *destroy* me."

I thought of Cartland humiliating him onstage in Philadelphia. Spying on him through the postmaster. Blocking my father's publications. The word "destroy" didn't seem so far-fetched right now.

I could tell my father what I knew. If I did, he'd at least find another journal and get his finds published faster. But everything else would come out about me and Rachel. And right now I wasn't even sure I wanted to help him. I was angry and disgusted by what he'd done, how he was trying to justify it. Even angrier that he'd bashed up things with Rachel. His greed had pushed her away from me. She didn't even love me, and now she doubted my honesty.

"It's not right," I said to him. "It's shameful!"

He turned to me, such fury in his eyes.

"Watch how you speak to me," he said coldly. "This has nothing to do with you. This affects only me and my future."

Heat pulsed at my temples. "Maybe having a thief for a father affects my future too!"

His shoulders tensed. For a second I thought he'd strike me. Instead he turned and walked off. As if *I'd* done something that needed punishing.

I wasn't telling him anything about Cartland. I wouldn't help him. Like he said, it had nothing to do with me. He and Cartland could fight their own battles. Let the best scoundrel win.

16.
PROSPECTING

I SET OUT EARLY, THE EARTH AND GRASS STILL sleepy, exhaling their night sweetness into the air before the heat came. The sun sent its light long, changing everything. The dullest tree trunk, the plainest leaves, the pebbly ground, even my own skin became luminous and charged with beauty. It never lasted long enough, this amazing light.

I was trying hard not to think about Samuel, which only meant that his face and voice flickered constantly in the background of my mind. I'd slept poorly.

On a rise I spotted some figures on a distant butte and was quite certain it was Ethan Withrow and his men. I raised a hand to them, and one of them waved back. I wondered how much luck they'd been having.

Then we were back down into the defiles and onto a new stretch of badlands we hadn't prospected yet. Two soldiers were with us now, because we were farther from camp. In the saddle, Daniel Simpson made jerky map notations and took compass readings as we went along. Would Sam be able to find me this far out?

We picketed our horses near some grass and went on by foot, scrabbling up a hill to get our bearings. Once you were out of the maze of defiles, the badlands looked almost orderly. I caught myself looking for him.

On the butte's flat top we discussed how to divide up the terrain for prospecting. I walked off toward the east side and started looking for the easiest place to scramble down into the narrow valley. Sunlight was spreading down the slope, making the sage and the stone glow.

There was a chain of massive, clumped boulders that would make good steps. And then I just stopped, because I realized I wasn't looking at boulders but at the biggest vertebrae I'd ever seen.

It was four days before I found her, she was so far out. I wondered if she was trying to avoid me. There were more people with her than usual, including soldiers. I'd found a good hiding place atop a nearby butte. The narrow valley made it impossible for me to sneak close enough to toss a pebble at her. She was crouched down with her hammer and awl. Hadn't looked up once in the whole time I'd been watching.

And the bones—

Magnificent. So big you couldn't miss them. Great hunks

KENNETH OPPEL

weathered out, definitely vertebrae, and a couple massive thigh bones. I felt weak with desire. The Black Beauty? Had they found it? Crickets settled near me and deafened me. Mosquitoes feasted on me despite the bacon grease. I didn't care. Their bites didn't itch as much anymore. I waited almost an hour before Rachel walked away from the others, in search of privacy.

I scrambled backward down the far side of the slope. I stood, realized too late my right foot had fallen asleep. Staggered, fell, and rolled down the hill. Got up streaked with dust and lurched on like a hunchback. When I found her, she was seated primly on a rock, about to pull down her underpants. She gasped when she saw me.

"Just me," I said.

"I thought you were some crazy hermit."

I brushed myself off a bit. "You've got quite a find there."

She looked wary. Did she think I was here to spy?

"My father did it," I blurted, eager to get all this out of the way. "He stole from your quarry."

She nodded silently. No surprise, but no gloating.

"I had nothing to do with it. I've been trying to figure out some way of proving it to you, but I can't. So I just hope you believe me."

"I do," she said.

My head tipped forward in surprise. "Really?"

"Yes. I'm choosing to trust you."

She made it sound like a cool, unemotional decision. I felt a bit uneasy, but I figured I should be grateful.

She said, "I really do need to have some privacy."

"Oh. Right." I walked off a bit, back turned.

"Could you go a bit farther, please?"

"Should I find myself a little hermit cave?"

I walked on, and that seemed to satisfy her.

"Did you have a good look at the quarry?" she asked. She didn't sound suspicious, just excited.

"It's incredible," I said. "They're huge!"

"The vertebrae were just sitting there! They're not in the best of condition, but just *seeing* them! You can come back now."

I turned to see her eyes bright and lively. "The femur was the size of my father. Stand it on end and you'd think it was a tree trunk!"

She told me what else they'd uncovered. In my imagination the creature grew and grew—and my relief grew too. This dinosaur was too big for the *rex* my father had calculated. So maybe this thing wasn't the *rex*, just . . . My spirits sagged. Just the *biggest* dinosaur yet. And it belonged to Cartland.

"Tell me what you've found," she said.

"Do you think you could love me?" I blurted.

The light in her eyes dimmed. She came close and put her hands lightly on my shoulders. "I don't know what I feel. Things take a long time for me, and I'm confused. I just want to dig right now and give my full attention to that."

"Can you actually do that?"

She nodded. "Mostly, yes. When I'm working, I don't think of much else."

I nodded, dejected. "I can't. I've been a terrible fossil hunter this past week. If I found the *rex*'s skull, I'd probably just trip over it and keep going. Too distracted."

She smiled faintly. "You are a veritable fount of emotion."

I felt like I was being mocked. I stepped away from her. "At least I *have* emotions."

"I can't say what I don't feel."

It hurt me so much to hear this, I barely knew what I was saying next.

"I would've thought you'd be grateful—"

"Grateful?" she said, eyebrows lifting. "You mean because you're so charming and handsome and I'm so plain?"

"Yes!" I wanted to see her eyes brim. I wanted to see that I could hurt her.

"I know I'm plain," she said. "This is hardly new or upsetting to me."

She was like a fortress. Impenetrable. It made me even more furious.

"Your heart's made of the same substance as your teeth!"

She stared back at me, and I wondered if she was going to lash out finally.

"And yet," she said, "you've managed to burrow your way inside like a clever fox."

This stopped me. "Was that romantic?"

"My heart is *not* made of enamel," she said, frowning.

"You said something romantic to me!"

"Not really."

But she couldn't stop her smile, and there was color deepening in her cheeks.

"You're ridiculous," she said. "You look like you've won some huge victory."

That was exactly how I felt. I went to her and kissed her. After a moment she drew back and said, "Listen, I meant what I said. I just want to concentrate on this dig for a while. It's really exciting."

I nodded, said nothing.

"You'd be excited too. It's a new species! Isn't that why we both came? To pursue our passions? When I saw those bones . . . my heart *thrilled* at it."

Thrilled. I was jealous of her find, of everything that pulled her attention away from me.

"And that's what I want to think of," she said. "I worked hard to get here, Samuel—"

"Me too!"

"I know. So let's make the most of it. We're only here for a couple of months. Let's not waste it."

She was right. Of course she was right. Didn't make me feel one bit better. Just like a scolded child.

"I'm not going to waste it," I told her.

"This expedition might convince my father to let me go to university."

I grimaced. "My father wants me to go, and I don't even want to."

"Then you're an idiot," she said, her anger startling me. *Now* she was angry. "How lucky you can just throw away an opportunity

I might never get. All you care about is whether *I'm* thinking enough about *you*!"

I stared at her furious face and felt frozen. Didn't know what to do or say. I must've looked pathetic, because her expression softened and she came close and put her arms around me.

"I care about a lot of things," I said to the top of her head. "I've wanted to find the *rex* since the moment I touched its tooth. I've got a lot of fire in me for that. I just care about you more."

She kissed me. "If you care about me, it's probably best you don't come round for a bit. Father thinks this could take us weeks to dig out, and starting tomorrow, practically everyone's working here."

"I don't want to go that long without seeing you."

"Me neither," she said. "But it'll be too risky."

"I'm still going to try," I said stubbornly.

"All right. But just don't be hurt if I can't get away safely to meet you."

I shrugged and lied. "I won't be."

"I can't get caught, Sam. He'll send me back home."

"I don't want that to happen to you. I'll be careful."

We kissed again, and she told me she had to go. I wanted to tell her I loved her, but I didn't. Maybe I didn't have the courage. Maybe I still wanted to hurt her. I watched her as she walked away without looking back.

Thunder woke me.

I poked my head from the tent. Lightning made blinding

fissures in the night. The thunder tolled like colossal church bells that had burst from their towers and were cartwheeling straight for us—no buildings or streets or trees to stop them. In the flashes of lightning, the rain writhed like twisting serpents.

It was terrifying, and I loved it. The calamity of it. I completely understood how the Pawnee could believe their great spirit had sent a flood to wash away the world. The wind pummeled the tent, and I heard the pegs straining.

It had been over a week since I'd seen Sam. When I was at work, my mind was focused, but on my way to and from the quarry, I'd look for him in the hills and ravines.

He hadn't called me plain—but he didn't disagree when I had. That night I'd cried in my tent and told myself he was a conceited ass. I'd wanted to put him inside one of my killing jars. I'd keep him all bottled up, perfectly preserved so I could look at his beautiful face and body, and he'd never say anything hurtful or stupid again.

Could I ever love him? He made being in love look so miserable, and like so much *work*. Such a distraction from what I wanted most to be doing right now.

The storm was still directly overhead, its claps so loud I had to put my hands over my ears. The horses neighed, and I heard the shouts of soldiers, lashing things down and telling one another to stay low. I heard Papa bellowing at his students to get back inside. There was a searing crack, and I saw a great cottonwood near the river cleaved in two.

My face and the collar of my nightgown were soaked. I was

KENNETH OPPEL

more frightened and thrilled than ever before in my life.

And I realized that, more than anything, I wanted to be seeing this with Samuel. To have him beside me, his shoulder against mine, peering out into this wild world, where everything was being broken down, and built anew.

It was still drizzling the next morning. Too wet to prospect or quarry. The clay in the rock made it slippery as soap.

We cleared space inside the covered wagon so we could work out of the rain. We had a couple bones from our latest quarry, and I got busy chipping away the matrix, working like I always worked these days, which meant thinking about Rachel.

"He's made a big find," Father was saying. "I saw it two days ago in passing. They've got enough vertebrae for the keel of a schooner."

"Wouldn't be surprised if Cartland set a night sentry," I said. Scoundrel that he was, I didn't want my father getting shot in the dark.

"I have no designs on it." Glumly he added, "He'll have to build a new hall at his university to house it. No doubt named after him."

"It's not the rex," I said. "Sounds too big."

"Yes," he agreed, "something that size couldn't be a predator. Too slow. Ours is a predator."

It could still be ours. Even though Cartland might have the upper hand right now. Even though there were only three of us, looking in a sea of surfaces. I'd find it. Despite everything, that fire had not gone out.

I worked on mechanically. I'd tried to see her again. Once I'd waited for hours and had to leave without getting a chance; another time I couldn't even get close to the quarry, there were so many people and horses coming and going.

After lunch it stopped raining. Hitch tended to the horses. In the soft dirt near our cookstove I took a stick and made a four-by-four grid. Wrote some random letters inside the boxes. I hoped to quiet my mind, have a few minutes without her. Foolish. Every word led me back to her.

Dear. My dear Rachel. I'm sorry I called you plain. You aren't.

Head. I sometimes think your head is firmly, resolutely above your heart.

Order. Something I cannot do with my mind at the moment.

Her. A pronoun I use all the time now.

17.
BRONTOSAURUS

AS WE NEARED THE QUARRY, MY EXCITE-ment built, just like it did every day. I'd found the biggest dinosaur in history, Papa had said. A quadruped of massive proportions, it had a thick tail and a long tapering neck, and a small head with teeth for mashing plants. My father had already gone so far as to suggest a name. It was completely unlike him to be so bold and spontaneous. Maybe he'd been truly swept up by the excitement of discovery, or maybe he was just impatient to catch up with Bolt. But yesterday, as we'd stood surveying the giant bones, I'd said, "Imagine the noise it would have made, just walking. It would shake the earth."

And he'd said, "Brontosaurus. Thunder lizard."

"I think that suits it very well," I'd said, and he'd put a hand on my shoulder.

I could only hope that this find, along with the pterodactylus, would convince Papa that I was more than suited for a life as a fossil hunter—and win me his blessing for university. I wouldn't bring it up just yet, though. I'd wait a bit longer.

Our large party made its final turn into the valley. I gazed at the quarry and didn't understand what I was seeing. Utter devastation. I swung myself off my pony. Every step brought me closer to the wreckage of bones. Spiny vertebrae hacked to bits, ribs snapped like kindling, limb bones smashed to shards, the skull unrecognizable except for a few scattered teeth on the lower jaw. Our own picks and shovels had been the weapons of destruction, and they lay scattered among the ruins, their blades and points dented and dulled, handles snapped in two.

"Bolt," my father said beside me.

"No . . ." Even though he'd stolen from our last quarry, I couldn't believe a paleontologist would destroy something so valuable. It was too much.

Students and soldiers were fanning out, stunned, through the wreckage. It was like the graveyard of some terrible massacre.

"Don't touch anything!" Papa called out. "We may be able yes yes to salvage. Bones can be glued."

"Bolt saw the site," Daniel Simpson was saying. "Just a few days ago we saw him go by."

"No one person could've done all this," my father said. "His boy and Plaskett and their half-wit teamster must've helped."

"Samuel wouldn't do this," I murmured.

"No?" Papa said angrily. "I think we've already seen what that

KENNETH OPPEL

family's capable of. If they can steal, they can destroy."

I felt a deep cramping pain in my belly, worse than the ones that came before my monthlies. All those beautiful ancient bones, fragile as newborn things. My eyes welled, and I turned away so Papa wouldn't see and think me too emotional. I doubted we could repair much. It was too broken, too scattered, all our bones and all our work. *My* work.

"Look who's come to admire his handiwork!"

The shout was Hugh Friar's, and we looked to where he stood on a butte, clenching the shirt collar of Samuel Bolt.

You idiot, I thought. *What are you doing here?*

I cried out as Hugh gave him a shove and sent him staggering down the steep slope into the valley. He tried to keep his balance but fell, tumbling. Carefully, Hugh skidded down after him.

Shakily Samuel stood, hands bleeding, sleeves torn at the elbows. I wanted to run to him, but forced myself to walk at the same pace as Papa and the others.

Hugh got there first and shoved him down again. I could see the fury in Sam's face as he stood and faced Hugh.

"What was that for?" he demanded.

"You know exactly, you little bastard."

It was only then Samuel turned and looked at the quarry, and I saw the honest shock in his face.

"I didn't do this," he said, his eyes finding mine.

Hugh pushed him. "Liar!"

Samuel flew at him and landed a punch on Hugh's big handsome face. Hugh was solid and a bit taller, and he didn't move much. He came at Sam hard. Fists, knees, heads, they struck and butted each other.

"You two, stop it!" My voice was strangled. I hurried forward and grabbed Hugh's arm and tried to pull him away, but then I felt myself being forcefully removed, and saw two blue-coated soldiers dragging Samuel back. No one had their hands on Hugh, and he punched Samuel in the stomach while his arms were pinned. He pitched forward, retching and gasping.

"Hugh!" I shouted. "Leave him alone! He didn't do it!"

"Like hell!"

"Hugh," my father said calmly, and the Yalie turned with a curse and walked off.

A bruise was already darkening around Sam's right eye, and his lip was split.

"You can let him go," I told the soldiers.

They looked at my father first and, when he nodded, released Samuel.

"You were very thorough," my father said to him.

"This wasn't us," Samuel replied hoarsely.

"I suspected you'd stolen from one of my quarries, but this is something altogether more atrocious. You've destroyed an entire specimen—you've deprived me and the world of a treasure!"

"I didn't do this!"

Papa laughed coldly. "Not alone, certainly. This was a great deal of work. I gather all of you came yesterday in the rain."

"We were at our camp all day."

"At night, then."

Samuel's eyes came to me, pleading—and there was something else in them now, a terrible uncertainty, as if he himself was wondering if his own father was capable of this terrible thing.

I believe you, I tried to tell him with my eyes.

"How do we know it wasn't Ethan Withrow and his men?" I said rashly. "Or Indians. There's a village nearby."

My father just shook his head with a bitter smile. "You go tell your father he has gone too far. I will publish this widely, in both the popular and academic press, and he will find himself a very despised and lonely man. His career, whatever career he had, is utterly finished."

He did not shout. His face was calm, but I could sense a malicious pleasure in him, and it chilled me.

"Go give your father my message."

Samuel shot me one last look, and I had to look away. I felt cowardly, like I was abandoning him, but I didn't know how to help him right now, and I didn't want Papa to suspect anything. If he did, more than our dinosaur bones would be destroyed.

Head throbbing with every step my pony took, I made my way back to camp. I touched my face, spat to see how much blood was left in my mouth. My father, could he have done such a thing? He'd already stolen, but would he *destroy*? It was against everything he upheld as a scientist. It was also idiotic. Who else did he think Cartland would blame?

At least Rachel didn't think it was me. I'd heard her shout it out to Hugh, before we began fighting. Would she think I'd started it? I hit first, but only after I'd been pushed down a hill. And shoved. And barked at and called a liar. What a coward he was, punching me when the soldiers had me.

I came out onto the river and saw our wagon—and four unfamiliar ponies tied up, cropping. They didn't have saddles. Their tails were braided. I felt icy through to my toes.

I jerked the reins and hurried my pony behind some tall brush. I hopped off. My hand was shaky as I rifled through my saddlebag and grabbed the hammer. I walked closer to the camp. I spotted four Indians. The tallest held a bow in his right hand and had a quiver of arrows slung over his shoulder. They all had their backs to me, standing shoulder to shoulder, heads angled. Like they were looking intently at something. Or interrogating someone. I heard my father's voice, but he was blocked from view by the Indians.

Off to one side Ned stood frozen, watching. In the middle of the camp, Hitch squatted by the cookstove. Everything was so still, it felt like only something terrible could follow.

I moved a little closer. I was pretty sure they were Sioux. I felt a strange numbness inflate inside me, like I was about to float free of my body.

I could ride for Cartland's camp, get the army. Two hours it would take. Anything could happen by then. The hammer was slippery in my fist. Ned kept a rifle under the seat of the wagon. If I could somehow get to it.

Ned saw me first, grinned uneasily, tilted his head in my

father's direction. I had no idea what he meant. That everything was going to be okay? That my father was already dead? That this was my chance to get the rifle when their backs were turned?

The choice was taken from me. All the Indians turned at once, their faces surprised. I fixed on one. The boy I'd run into in the badlands. The Indians had parted enough so I could finally catch a glimpse of my father, seated on a camp chair.

Impossibly, he was smiling. With a shock I saw that two of his front teeth were missing. Had they beaten him already? And then I saw he held them in his hand, attached to the dental bridge he'd had made several years ago.

He saw me and said cheerfully, "Samuel. Put down the hammer."

I let it slip from my fingers. The Indians lost interest in me and turned back to Father. Who, with a theatrical flourish, held his fake teeth high and then reinserted them deftly inside his mouth.

After a moment of stunned silence, the shortest of the Indians made an eager circling motion with his hand. Again.

Twice more my father obligingly removed and inserted his false teeth before the boy said something to the other Sioux. He sounded irritable. Like he'd had enough of this nonsense. To my amazement, the three men nodded deferentially.

"Ned," said my father carefully, "maybe we can offer our guests here some dinner. Hitch, what are we eating tonight?"

From the cookstove, Hitch began, in his methodical way, to count off what he'd prepared. He was frightened and stammered a bit. His hands fluttered and kept patting his trousers. He had a gun too, and was an excellent shot. I didn't know where his gun was right now, but I was worried if he started shooting, it would be all over for us. The Sioux all had knives.

"That sounds like a wonderful meal," my father told Hitch. "Ned, you said you knew some Sioux."

"Not much, but I'll try." He said a few words, which won snorts from the Indians. He ended up miming eating with his fingers.

They ignored this and instead started looking around our camp. The second tallest Sioux had a face ravaged by the pox. Peering inside our tents, rummaging through our clothing. They didn't take anything, though they looked for a while at Father's shaving kit.

My eyes passed over their ponies. A pick was strung over the back of one. Unlikely thing for a Sioux to have, wasn't it? Its blade was powdered gray.

"What happened to you?" Ned asked.

"Run in with the Yalies."

"Your face looks pretty bad, son." Ned seemed more concerned about me than my own father, who was busy watching the Sioux as they strutted around our tents.

"They destroyed Cartland's big quarry," I whispered.

This got my father's attention. "What's this?"

"They smashed it all up," I said. "Unless you did."

"Don't be absurd," my father hissed.

The Sioux went into the wagon, rummaged around our food-stuffs, but came out without anything. On the ground we had a couple crates we'd been packing, their lids off. The Indians started sifting through the buffalo grass, lifting out the flour sacks we'd packed a few bones in.

"Careful. Please," Father said, unable to restrain himself. He walked closer, one hand held up beseechingly.

They looked over at him severely. "Gold?" the pockmarked one said, jabbing his finger at the sack.

"Gold? No, no." My father shook his head.

Was that what they were after? I remembered Ned talking about gold in the Black Hills, but that was a long way away. Did the Sioux think we'd found some here?

"Bones," my father told them, looking at Ned to see if he knew the word in Sioux. Ned shook his head helplessly.

My father walked closer to the crate, his hand extended toward the Indian for the flour sack, smiling helpfully. "May I? I'll show you."

After a tense hesitation, the Sioux handed the sack to my father. He quickly untied it, reached in, and brought out a partial rib.

"Bone," he said again, tracing his own rib. "From a big animal." He got down on all fours and lumbered around like a rhinoceros. "Big animal!" he said encouragingly.

It was such a ridiculous sight, I might've laughed if I hadn't felt so queasy with fear. The Sioux looked at him like he was a madman, and then the short one began to laugh, and the other two men followed. The boy looked at him disapprovingly. He said something sharply to the men, and they stopped laughing. I was amazed by how he treated them.

The boy came and stood over my father, still on the ground. I

EVERY HIDDEN THING

worried he was about to kick him. There was an anger in this boy I didn't understand. He said something to Father, and then, with both hands, gripped his own head below the chin and gave a jerk as if he meant to pull it right off his neck. He looked crazy.

Slowly Father stood, frowning. "There is a head, yes," he said, pointing at one of the crates. He touched his hands to his temples, turned his index fingers to horns. "Animal head!"

"No." The Sioux boy pointed at my father's head.

My guts churned coldly. I saw Ned's eyes stray to the wagon, where his rifle waited. The Sioux boy looked at the other Indians and said something to the tallest. He sounded angry but also frustrated.

"You take heads," the tall Indian said to Father. "Our heads."

I understood now. The heads that Cartland had sawed off at the Sioux burial platforms.

"No," I said, shaking my head with slow emphasis.

The Sioux glanced at me with scorn, like I'd spoken out of turn, and turned back to Father.

"We did not take any heads." He opened his hands invitingly to the crates. "You can look. Ned, Sam, let's unpack these crates so they can see."

We set to it as the Indians watched. Sack after sack was laid carefully on the ground and opened. Wood shavings spilled out as we extracted the vertebrae and ribs and femurs and tibiae. I noticed that the three Sioux men kept their distance as the bones were revealed. Like standing downwind from a foul smell. Only the boy seemed not to be afraid. All the while I thought about the heads they were looking for—and who had them—and worried there was something else they wanted back too. When we were halfway through the second crate, the tallest Indian held out his hand to stop us. Enough.

"No head," he said.

"No heads," father told him.

The Sioux boy seemed a bit forlorn. The other men looked at him with a mix of pity and annoyance. I might've felt sorry for him if I hadn't also been terrified. Of all the Indians he'd been most intent as we'd unpacked the crates. He bent down now and picked up a fossil toe and closed his fist around it while staring defiantly at my father.

"Yes, of course," said Father, smiling. "Keep it."

Ned said, "Hitch, is our meal ready?"

"Ready," said Hitch from the cookstove, which had been producing a distracting medley of smells.

"Will you eat?" my father asked the Sioux.

They said nothing, but looked at one another, and then, in agreement, sat down on the ground. Ned and I hurried about, bringing them plates of food and utensils, which they ignored in favor of their fingers.

My stomach was all clenched up. I picked at my food. The Sioux seemed to enjoy theirs. They finished what was on their plates and let us give them seconds. It was a very quiet meal. Occasionally Hitch would say something to himself, like he did sometimes, and the Sioux would look over at him, startled, then back at us, and we'd smile tensely, and they'd go back to eating. When they were done, Plaskett offered them tobacco. They took it and chewed meditatively, spitting once in a while. Finally they stood, mounted their ponies, and left—in the opposite direction from the Cartland camp, I was glad to see.

"I won't lie," said Plaskett. "I had some very gloomy thoughts back there."

"I thought we were done for," I said. "Where will they go now?"

"They're likely scouts," said Ned. "They'll go back to their camp or village and tell them what they've found. What's all this about heads?"

"Cartland's group found some burial platforms on their way out. He cut off the heads to study them."

Father looked at me sharply. "How do you know this?"

"Rachel Cartland told me. I ran into her, a few weeks ago."

Ned frowned. "How'd the Indians find out?"

"Must've seen them do it," I said. Had they seen Rachel take the tooth, too? Maybe it was more than just heads they were looking for.

"That was a bad mistake," said Ned. "Burial's sacred to them. You don't just saw up their dead."

"So they thought we were the culprits," said Father.

"Good thing we didn't have those heads," Ned said, "or they might've taken ours."

It was a horrible thought that came to me suddenly. "You think they'll go to Cartland's camp?"

Father was already packing up the uncrated bones. "They wouldn't risk it, not with so many soldiers."

"We'd better tell them," I said.

"They'll be fine, Sam. They've got thirty-five cavalrymen!"

"Still. They should know there's Sioux around."

"They have their own scouts."

"And someone's got to tell them it was the Indians who smashed their fossil. One of the Sioux had a pickax on his pony, all covered in bone dust. Maybe they were getting even with Cartland for taking the heads. Anyhow, someone's got to clear your name. And it might come better from me."

I waited anxiously for his answer. I was much more worried about Rachel's safety than Father's reputation. For the first time he seemed to notice my bruised face.

"Who gave you that beating?"

"One of the Yalies when I was riding past their quarry."

"I hope you blackened his eye too."

"Might've. Cartland said he's going to finish you. Publish it all over the place. We better tell him before he sends a telegraph."

"Not safe," he said. "Those Sioux seem pretty agitated."

"If they wanted to hurt me, they'd have already done it," I pointed out. "They just ate our food. Chewed our tobacco. They can't have any grudge against us."

"Sam's right," Ned said. "We should tell them. But it'll be dark in a couple hours. I'll go with him."

Finally Father nodded. "Keep your eyes open in their camp. See if they have anything interesting."

"Sure," I lied. I didn't care why he was letting me go. I just wanted the chance to make sure Rachel was safe. And get the chance to talk to her.

As I saddled my pony, Plaskett sauntered over and pressed a pistol into my hand. "You don't have the same aversion as your pa, I think."

"No."

"This can't hurt then."

He showed me how to use it, and put a holster on me. I'd never fired a gun, rarely even held one. With the pistol against my hip, we headed toward Cartland's camp, a plan for thievery taking shape in my mind.

18.
THE THIEF

AT TWILIGHT TWO SOLDIERS DRAGGED HIM into camp, his face bloody. He couldn't have been more than fifteen.

"Found him by the river, sir, hiding in the grass," one of the soldiers told the lieutenant. "He's Sioux. Had an eye on our horses."

They'd already bound the Indian boy's hands behind his back and now forced him down against the side of a wagon and tied him to the sturdy axle. His bruised, bloodied face made me think of Samuel, and I felt a sorrowful squeeze inside my throat.

Lieutenant Frye looked the boy over without a flicker of compassion. "Were there any others?" he asked his two men.

"Not that we saw."

"Does he speak English?" the lieutenant asked.

One of the soldiers shook his head. "Or won't."

"Bring Duellist here," the lieutenant said.

The top of a distant butte held the sun's last light, like a beacon. When Duellist saw the Sioux boy, his normally genial face hardened into a mask. He squatted down and said a few words. The boy glared mutely, then spat on him. Duellist wiped away the spittle, then struck the boy hard across the face.

I gasped. "Was that necessary?"

"You shouldn't watch this, my dear," my father said, trying to usher me away, but I shook off his hand with a scowl.

"Don't feel sorry for him, Miss Cartland," said the lieutenant. "We're going easy on him, compared to what his own people do to horse thieves. I knew a trapper who traded with the Sioux. One night they caught a Crow Indian in their corral. First they shot him off his horse, then the braves came and counted coup on him—are you familiar with that practice? They gain honor from striking their enemy with a stick before scalping him. And then the women came with axes and chopped him up and scattered the pieces hither and thither."

He made a motion with his hand like sowing seed in a field. It made the carnage he described all the more revolting. I was tired of Lieutenant Frye and his instructive little stories about the Indians.

Duellist turned to us. "He says he didn't come to steal horses."

"Lying," said one of the soldiers who'd dragged him in. "Horses are like gold to them."

Quite a crowd had gathered. I was amazed at the change the Sioux boy's presence made in the men. Not just the soldiers but the Yalies. They stood taller. They talked louder. Their jaws hardened. They were ridiculous.

Duellist and the boy had another exchange. The Pawnee scout turned to my father.

"He says you took the heads of the dead. He saw it."

"Ah," Papa said.

I'd never forgotten that mirage-like horse and rider I'd spied on the ridge. We *had* been watched. Guiltily I wondered exactly how much he'd seen.

Duellist said, "He wants them back."

The Sioux boy was speaking more fiercely now.

"One of the dead was his father," Duellist said.

Papa must have seen my stricken face, because he said, "'Father' may be a rather vague term for these people. A term for a relative, or even an elder."

"We should return them," I said.

He frowned. "We have no proof any of these men were truly related to him."

From a distance Mr. Landry jotted notes.

The boy was speaking again to Duellist. The Pawnee scout grunted, turned to us.

"He says you also took something from his father's body—a tooth."

My father and I glanced at each other, and I felt sickened by our complicity. I'd stood by as bodies were decapitated—maybe even the body of this boy's father. Yes, I'd objected, but maybe not strongly enough. And then I'd made everything much worse by stealing from the body. With a twist of self-loathing, I knew I would do it again, for that tooth.

"He can tell us," Papa whispered to me, and his expression was nakedly covetous. "He can tell us where he found it."

Before I could react, he hurried off. I saw him duck into his tent. He came back with the black tooth in his hand. He crouched close to the Sioux boy and put the tooth on the earth. The boy's eyes blazed. It was obviously an object he knew well.

Papa said, "Duellist, will you translate for me, please? Now, where did your father find this?"

Duellist relayed the question, but the boy just stared defiantly into the distance.

Duellist cuffed him on the side of the head.

"No, no!" said my father. "That's not necessary, please."

From his pocket, my father pulled a silver dollar. "Tell him if he tells me, I will give him this." He put it on the ground.

With his foot, the boy kicked the coin away and unleashed a torrent of angry words.

I admired his defiance very much, when he was surrounded by dozens of soldiers, defenseless.

Duellist said, "He says the tooth should be with the body, and you are thieves, and they will smash any bones you find, just like the big ones they broke yesterday."

Triumphantly I looked at my father. "The Bolts had nothing to do with it!"

"That's of no concern yes yes to me right now," he said. He showed no signs of remorse. If anything his face had hardened, and I could tell from his mouth, the forward jut of his neck, how very angry he was.

Pensively he stood, hands clasped behind his back, and stepped over to the lieutenant. "I know this boy is your prisoner, and you will deal with him as you see fit. But to know where that tooth came from would be a very good bit of information. The skeleton of that creature would be a great prize for me and our nation. Can you think of any way we could . . . *induce* him to talk?"

"They're stubborn," the lieutenant said, "and they're proud."

"We could give him a good thrashing," said Daniel Simpson.

I looked at him in revulsion; at the same moment my father sternly said, "That won't be necessary. We're not savages. What you can do is fetch the heads. They're in the storage wagon."

Was he planning on returning them after all? But I felt a slithering unease. Papa crouched down once more, staring at the boy. The boy stared back. If he was intimidated or frightened he did not show it.

Daniel returned with the burlap sacks, and my father motioned for him to unwrap them. One by one, the three heads were set before the boy. I watched his reaction, saw where his eyes rested. When I glanced at Papa, I saw he'd noticed too. Far right. The boy's father.

"If you tell me where the tooth was found, I'll give you back the heads and the tooth."

I wasn't at all certain my father was sincere, but the boy had no doubts.

"He says he doesn't trust you," Duellist said. "He thinks you are a liar, like all the other *Wasicu*."

Wasicu. This was what the Indians called us, according to the lieutenant. The word actually meant fat-taker—the person who was selfish enough to take the finest part of the animal for himself.

My father chuckled coldly. "Very good. Well, yes yes tell him, please, Duellist, that he's destroyed something very important to me. Those bones were my property, and he needs to give me something in return. A trade. He needs to tell me where I can find the bones belonging to that tooth. That's fair."

He spoke with measured calm, but I sensed a terrible undercurrent beneath his words.

Once again Duellist translated; the Indian boy said nothing. I didn't see what more my father could do, but he went and picked up a shovel leaning against the wagon.

"Professor Cartland," said Mr. Landry, "I urge you not to hurt this boy."

I looked at the journalist in surprise and gratitude. I didn't feel quite so alone anymore.

"You are a journalist, Mr. Landry, are you not?" my father said quietly. "Then I suggest yes yes that you *observe*, and not *participate*."

"Papa," I said, taking a step toward him. I put my hand on his arm, could feel his muscles tensed.

"Don't worry, my dear; I'm not going to harm him."

He let the tip of the shovel rest very lightly atop each skull in turn, like he was playing a counting game.

"These are, after all, just bones."

His knuckles whitened as he drove the shovel down into the head on the far left, again and again, shattering the skull and upper jaw. Horrified, I stared, not at the mangled remains, but at my own father, who was suddenly unrecognizable to me, his face so clenched, eyes narrowed and furious.

"Now," he said, his voice strained, "I will not ask you again. I want to know where that tooth came from." He let the shovel rest on the head of the Sioux boy's father, the blade tip-tapping the forehead, the nose, the hole of the ravaged mouth.

He looked at the silent boy—"No?"—and lifted the shovel high.

"Stop it!" I cried.

The Indian boy strained forward, shouting, and my father pulled back.

Duellist began translating haltingly, cutting the Sioux boy short to ask questions of his own. "He says the place is almost a full day's ride up the river. There is a butte taller than all the rest. At its base is a coulee with several big rocks like . . ." He made a curving shape with his hands, as though describing a toadstool.

"A hoodoo," said Lieutenant Frye.

I'd seen them. They sprouted plentifully from the ground here: a pillar of rock supporting a large stone cap, sometimes very teetery.

"Near these," Duellist went on, "is where the tooth was found."

"Is he telling the truth?" my father asked Duellist.

Duellist looked at the boy hard and then said, "I don't know."

The Sioux boy spoke again.

"What's he saying?" I asked.

"He wants to be released now, with the heads and the tooth."

"Tell him tomorrow," my father said. "After he's led us to the place."

"You *lied* to him!" I protested.

"Only so he doesn't lie to us," he replied patiently.

The lieutenant said, "I don't want to keep him any longer than that, Professor. His people will come looking, and I'd rather avoid a fight, especially with you and your daughter here. It's not something you'd want to see."

"I understand, Lieutenant. Would you be willing to send a detail with us?"

"Professor, we're at your disposal. But you realize he might be leading you into an ambush—or straight into an Indian camp."

"It did yes yes occur to me."

"But it shouldn't be anything my boys can't handle," the lieutenant said. His grin was confident. "We'll send Duellist and Best-One-of-All with you too."

The Sioux boy was shouting his outrage. I heard the word *Wasicu* again.

I rounded on Papa. "Are you even planning on returning the heads and tooth?"

"We'll see what tomorrow holds."

He bent down and picked up the tooth; he nodded at Daniel

Simpson to bundle the heads back up. The Sioux boy bellowed louder, and Duellist gave him another clout across his face.

"Stop hitting him!" I shouted.

The boy's manacled hands made it impossible for him to wipe away his tears, so he set his face into a fierce mask. He'd been caught. He'd lost his horse. And now he was humiliated and tied up before a Pawnee, one of his sworn enemies.

I looked over at Landry, still writing notes with a grim face. I wondered how much of this would make it into print.

"My dear, don't look so forlorn," my father told me. "This time tomorrow we might be standing before the bones. Imagine that yes yes. There they'll be, all curled up in the rock like a slumbering giant."

I pulled away from him. I didn't want him calling me "my dear." The way he'd treated that boy was monstrous.

But I must have been monstrous too, because even now, even after all I'd seen tonight, when Papa mentioned the slumbering giant, I'd felt a pulse of excitement and thought: *We can wake him.*

The rifle's crack gave me such a jolt I almost spilled off my pony. It sidestepped nervously, nickering.

"Stop there!" a voice shouted.

As we approached Cartland's camp, it was properly dusk, and I hadn't seen the soldier's blue uniform until he stepped away from one of the wagons.

"It's Sam Bolt!" I shouted. "From Professor Bolt's camp!"

"Just making sure," he added when I came closer. "Wasn't aiming at you."

After the treatment I'd had at their quarry, I wasn't so sure. I wondered what kind of reception I was going to get from Cartland.

"We caught a Sioux trying to steal horses," the soldier said.

I glanced at Ned. Our Sioux? I was amazed the Indians had dared come so close. They must've seen there were dozens of soldiers.

"Just one?" Ned asked.

"There might be more of them around. Lieutenant's put a double guard on tonight."

Why would he risk getting caught? Unless he was acting on his own, maybe ignoring the others. I thought: *The boy.*

"Four of them paid us a visit earlier," Ned said.

"That's why we came," I said. "To warn you."

"Bit late. But tell the lieutenant."

Ned and I picketed our ponies and made our way into the camp. Orderly rows of tents, some round, some rectangular, were enclosed within the perimeter of their wagons. A simple corral had been created. They'd dug a proper privy. A chimney jutted from their cookhouse tent. Some men were hammering together crates, tending horses, cleaning tack. I saw one of the students, Simpson, carrying a burlap sack into one of the wagons. I glimpsed the inside and spotted plenty of small open boxes and a little desk.

I was relieved to find everything so safe and orderly. On the way here I'd had terrible images of a burning camp, massacred bodies strewn everywhere.

I stopped when I saw the Indian boy tied against a wagon. An officer with a doctor's case knelt in front of him, trying to clean the ugly wound on the boy's face. But he kept jerking his head from side to side, shouting and spitting. Eventually the doctor gave up. Closing his case, he stood and gave me a nod.

"Proud people," he said. "Won't let himself be helped."

The Indian boy stared at me scornfully for a moment, then back down at the earth. I wondered what he thought of me. A liar? Part of Cartland's crew? I wanted to explain but didn't know how. I was shocked at how bloodied and swollen he was. He seemed a lot smaller down on the ground, arms yanked back.

"I owe you a sincere apology, Samuel."

I looked up to see Professor Cartland strolling over with the lieutenant.

"We have the real vandal here, as you see. I hope Friar wasn't too hard on you—though from what I saw, you punch above your weight. Your father's son to be sure."

His words were friendly enough, but his smile was forced.

"He visited us first," I said, nodding at the boy, "with three others. They went through our things pretty thoroughly. I think they were looking for heads."

I didn't say any more; I wanted the rest to come from him. He didn't disappoint me.

"So they were." He told a breezy version of how they'd collected the heads. He didn't mention the tooth. "I suppose smashing our quarry was their way of getting back at us."

"Do you think it might be an idea," said Ned, "to give back the heads and let the boy go? Might make a more peaceable atmosphere for all of us out here."

"Thank you for your advice, Mr. Plaskett," the professor replied stiffly. "We'll be releasing him tomorrow."

"We just came to warn you," I said.

"And we're much obliged," said the lieutenant. "You'll stay the night. Not a good idea to be out after dark tonight. There should be dinner before long."

"We've already eaten, but thank you," said Ned.

"Have a second dinner," said the lieutenant affably.

By Cartland's sour expression I could tell he wasn't happy about this. Maybe he was worried we'd sneak around and peek at his finds—which was exactly what my father wanted us to do.

"That's very hospitable," Ned said.

When I saw Rachel, I kept my face tight because I worried it would betray the sheer happiness of seeing her again.

"Miss Cartland, hello," I said. I watched her eyes as they traveled across my bruised face.

"I hope your face isn't too badly off," she said.

"I'm fine, thank you. Ned and I just came over to let you know there were Indians around. But you've already figured that out."

"Yes, but thank you very much."

"I'm sorry about what they did to your quarry."

"There's a few things to salvage, I hope."

It was hard to think very well, because I was so hungry to look at her and try to breathe in her scent, but she was too far away. She was very good at this pretend formality.

After dinner I went to get my bedroll from my horse. And as I was coming back through the shadowed camp, Rachel appeared suddenly at my side.

"I'm so sorry about what happened," she said.

There were a few soldiers and students around, but as long as we walked cordially side by side, no one was paying any attention.

"I'm all right. It made me sick to see those bones. After all the work you did."

"Well. There are more fossils out there."

"And you'll find them. You're like a divining rod."

She grazed my fingers with hers. How simple a touch was. Heat coursed from my ears and cheeks. I wanted to take her and kiss her.

"I've missed you," I said quietly, but my heart beat loud in my ears. I felt like I was running too fast down a hill. Could only go faster to keep from falling over. "I'm sorry for the mean things I said last time. I'm an idiot. Did you know that since meeting you, there hasn't been a single day—not even a single hour—when I didn't think of you?"

Looking straight ahead, she said quietly, "You make regular appearances in my thoughts too."

"I played that word game with myself. It was terrible."

This made her laugh. "Well, you're not very good at it."

"No, I meant every word just reminded me of you."

"Every word?"

"*Every* word!"

She shook her head. "You're absurd."

"I missed your smell. That place at the base of your neck."

I glanced over and even in the twilight saw the dark bloom in her cheeks.

"Don't make me blush," she said.

"I'd wake up in the middle of the night and not be able to get back to sleep. It was like you were haunting me. Once I begged you to let me sleep, and you did."

"Ridiculous," she said. "Listen. The tooth I took, it belonged to the Sioux boy's father. That was his body we beheaded. His own *father* was the one who found the Black Beauty."

I was so startled I had to force myself not to turn to her. This very boy was the son of the man who'd owned the Black Beauty and ridden it into battle. "He told you all this?"

She nodded. "Papa's making him take us to the place it was found."

"When?"

"Tomorrow."

I kept walking, looking straight ahead. On my way here I'd made a plan—a bold and crazy one. Now I saw it crinkling up like a scrap of paper in a bonfire.

"Why would he help you?" I asked.

"Papa says he'll give him back the tooth and heads."

"Will he?"

"I don't think so."

It was a physical pain, a clenching up below my ribs, to think of the Black Beauty going to Cartland. And this, too: I'd always imagined Rachel and me finding it together.

"Did he say where it was?" I asked.

"He described a place upriver, near some hoodoos."

"Which are everywhere. It's probably a lie—I don't see why he'd help you."

"That's why Papa's making him come with us."

I hesitated a moment, then said, "Better hope he doesn't get free tonight and steal the heads and tooth."

She nodded toward a covered wagon. "Even if he found the specimen wagon, he'd have trouble getting the tooth from Papa's tent."

"He keeps it inside his tent?"

Professor Cartland himself came into view and stared at me in a way I didn't like. I said good night to Rachel and found Ned. We settled down around the fire with some of the Yalies and listened to them sing, and even joined in on a few songs. But all the singing was just background noise in my head as I made my own plans.

19.
A PROPOSAL

THE NIGHT COOLED. THE FIRE CRACKLED down to embers. Gradually the camp went to sleep, leaving only the distant murmur of the sentries.

Ned's snores came and went. I would not let myself doze off. My mind was busy, body tingling with hot panic at what I was about to do. A breeze came up, and the moon's glow was shuttered by brisk clouds. From where I lay, there was just enough light to see the form of the Sioux boy against the wagon. I couldn't tell if he was awake or asleep. There was no one guarding him. They must've been pretty confident in their knots.

I waited for the sentry to change and the camp to go silent again. Barefoot, I slid from my bedroll. I made my way toward the wagon Rachel had pointed out, the same place Daniel Simpson had taken the burlap sack. I was pretty sure this was where they kept the specimens. If I was spotted, I'd say I was on my way to the latrine and gotten lost.

Inside the wagon I shut the flaps. Dug in my pocket for matches and candle. I cupped the flame with my palm. Shelves were filled with small crates and open boxes with rock-encrusted bones. Burlap sacks were everywhere, and I had to look through several before I found the heads.

Back outside I moved quickly. No way of explaining this if I was stopped. *What's in the sack, boy?* Nothing much, just a change of clothes and a shaving kit and bar of soap. Oh, and a couple heads.

I reached Professor Cartland's large tent, set down the sack of heads. The flap hung shut but wasn't buttoned. I crouched and listened, then folded back the tent flap so that a little moonlight spilled inside. I took a silent step. I dared not light the candle in case the smell roused him. He was a dark shape at the back of the tent. There was a little folding chair where he'd laid out his clothes. I saw his jacket and patted the pockets. Nothing. My neck and armpits prickled hotly. Several stacked suitcases made a dressing table. On top was a shaving kit. I took a step closer and opened it up. Razor, strop, soap, mirror. I lifted the tray and underneath saw the silhouette of something long and pointed.

"Yes yes," the professor said, sitting up.

My flexed hand froze above his shaving kit. I couldn't see his eyes, just the outline of his cannonball head. The light was behind me. I was just a shadow to him—I could run for it, dive into my bedroll, and fake sleep before he raised hell. But I just stood.

"Yes yes," he said again, and lay back down. He began to snore lightly. Heart clattering, I stood for a few moments longer, then lifted the tooth from the shaving kit.

I backed out and closed the flap, feeling like I was about to suffocate. I wouldn't let myself take a breath until I was several paces from the tent. Then I gasped air into my lungs.

When I padded closer to the Sioux boy, his eyes opened in surprise, then went straight to the small knife I'd taken from my pocket. I put my finger to my lips. Mimed what I meant to do. He stayed quiet.

I opened the sack with the heads so he could look inside. Crouching beside him, I started cutting the rope around his wrists. I worried about the sound. The boy kept looking back impatiently. Maybe wondering how I could take so long, maybe planning on attacking me when he was free. I sawed through the last cord and moved away. Knife ready in case he tried anything.

He looked at me uncertainly. From my pocket I pulled out the tooth, held it out to him. When he took it, I turned my palms upward, swept a hand out across the dark horizon, asking the question with my eyes. I'd pinned all my hopes on this. That he'd be grateful. That he'd tell me where the tooth was found. Assuming he even knew.

He began drawing in the dirt. An undulating line, which I assumed was the badlands river. He made a mark nested in one deep bend and looked up at me, making sure I understood.

Cartland's camp. I nodded. He continued drawing. I marveled that he knew the river's path so well. He drew a tight S curve and then, off to the east, far from the river, he deftly outlined three steep slopes. They looked like shrouded nuns.

"There?" I breathed. "That's where this came from?" I touched the tooth.

He looked at me, gave a single nod, then stood in a crouch. He looked toward the edges of the camp, where, at intervals, you could see a dim spill of lantern light from the sentries. Without a backward look at me, he took the sack and the tooth and started off toward the river. He disappeared among the shadows. I didn't know what more I could do for him.

I waited a moment more. Half expecting to hear a shout, or worse, a shot fired. All was quiet. He must be clear by now. How long, though, would it be before he was noticed missing?

I stared hard at the map he'd drawn, at those three hills. I couldn't remember seeing anything like them. Who knew how large or small they were? Who knew whether they existed at all? I memorized each turn of the river. With my finger, I drew the map myself and compared it to the original. I was good at shapes. Then I erased both maps with my palm. But I wanted to commit it to paper as quickly as possible. I had a pencil in my sleeping roll.

I couldn't sleep. My mind raced with all that had happened. I went to unbutton my tent flaps to let in some cooler air, when I heard footsteps. They weren't the steady tread of a soldier—they were the sneaky steps of someone trying to be very quiet. My first thought was: *the Sioux boy.* I felt a quick squeeze of fear but crawled forward and parted the flaps to peek out.

I caught the familiar outline of Samuel, head hanging even lower than usual as he tiptoed past.

"What are you doing?" I whispered.

He started and looked down at me.

"Latrine," he said in the most unconvincing way a person could.

"No, you're not."

He squinted. "How would you know?"

He looked so guilty. "What have you done?"

"Shhhh," he said, looking frantically over his shoulder.

I heard the footsteps too. It was instinct: I grabbed him by the sleeve and pulled him inside the tent. He tumbled down onto the blankets, and the pale moonlight was cut off as I closed the flaps and did up the buttons. I hoped it smelled all right inside.

The footsteps—certainly a soldier coming on or off duty— passed by, and then the only sound was me trying not to breathe. I sat very still, my fingers resting lightly on the blankets, afraid of touching anything in the dark. I felt his presence acutely. I thought, *He is inside the tent with me.*

Very softly, I heard him move, felt his hand find my leg. I reached for his face, gingerly touched the raised welt around his eye, the rough split in his lip. The darkness was hypnotic. It was like the entire world had now contracted to the pads of my fingers, all my senses reaching out like the tendrils of an anemone. It was private as the inside of a dream. I wanted him to kiss me more than anything.

His breath against my cheek. "I set him free."

I pulled back my hand. "What?"

"The Sioux boy. I let him go."

I was barraged by a volley of thoughts. Of course it was right he was set free; I'd told Papa to do it myself. A boy beaten and tied up—it was disgusting. But the Black Beauty—he was supposed to guide us there.

"Why?" I demanded. "To sabotage my father?"

"The boy wasn't going to help you anyway! He hates you all. You sawed off his father's head—"

"*I* didn't—"

" —stole his father's sacred tooth. Beat him. Why would he tell your father anything? He probably wanted to lead you all into an ambush so they could kill you. I might've saved your lives!"

We were both angry, whispering directly into each other's ears. His lips grazed my lobe, and for a moment I lost track of what I meant to say. I pulled my head back.

"Stop making excuses. You just don't want my father to find it!"

"That's right," he said fiercely. "I *don't* want him to find it. I want *us* to find it."

"What do you mean?" This was just like all the other rash, ridiculous things he said.

"The boy told *me* where it was."

"Just like that?"

"Yep. After I cut him loose. Do you have paper and pencil? I want to get it down before I forget."

I heard him rooting around in his pockets and then a match strike. His eyes shone bright. I held the wick of my candle to his flame.

"Listen," he said, "the map he drew for me was nothing like the route he told your father."

"How do you know he's not lying to you?"

"Well, I gave him the heads back." He paused, then winced. "And your tooth."

"You wretch!" It was like a slap. Even though I'd urged my father to do exactly the same thing. That tooth was my first find. On its own it was incredibly valuable, and he'd just bargained it away. "You had no right to do that!"

"I know. But it got us a map!"

Another thought careened into my head. "You went *inside* my father's tent?"

He nodded. In the fluttering light he saw the notebook beside my bedroll and pointed to it hopefully.

"Can I just draw it, please?"

I handed the book to him, along with a pencil. For the next few minutes I watched as he traced out a map, erasing little bits, redoing them.

"I think that's right," he murmured. "I think so." He closed the book and gave it to me. "I want this to be ours. I want us to find it."

I shook my head. "You keep saying that. But how?"

"We don't need our fathers' help. Or permission. We'll strike out on our own."

I got the sense he was making this up on the spot. It was too outlandish to take seriously. "You don't have a practical bone in your body. We have no equipment."

He leaned closer and whispered his plan to me: how we could team up with the Barnum man, Ethan Withrow. He had the manpower, and we had the know-how. We'd make a deal with him and lead him to the site, and together we'd excavate the Black Beauty. And claim the finder's fee.

So he *had* given this some thought, quite a lot. For a moment I let the plan hang there, wavering like a mirage. Then I scowled at his naivete. "And the scandal we'd create, running off together? You haven't taken that into account."

"We'd already be married," he said, looking straight at me. His warm eyes.

"You're not serious."

"We'll find the skeleton together as man and wife. Will you marry me?"

It was like a gunpowder explosion in my head, my thoughts little bits of shrapnel.

"You look horrified," he said.

I blew out the candle. The darkness was calming, but I still couldn't think properly.

"This is abrupt" was all I could say.

"You've never thought about it?" he asked. *"Never?"*

Of course I had, idly, fleetingly, especially in those drifting moments before sleep, or when I imagined how a man's touch might feel. But in the morning such thoughts seemed flimsy and illogical as dreams.

"How would we get married?" I demanded. It was the first coherent thought that came to me.

I heard him exhale in exasperation. *"How?"*

"Where?" It was hardly the most important issue, but it bought me time to think.

"Well, Crowe. It would have to be Crowe."

"We'd elope?"

"Yes. We'd get the justice of the peace to marry us. Are you saying yes?"

I said nothing. My eyes cast about frantically in the darkness.

"Yes" meant my father cutting me off. "Yes" meant he would most definitely *not* pay for me to go to university—and right now there was still a chance he would. "Yes" meant good-bye to my comfortable home, to my lovely library, where I sketched Father's specimens.

But I would always be a mere helper, while his own fossils and articles multiplied like treasure. Meanwhile my own frustration and loneliness would divide and subdivide until they filled me like a cancer. At best I would teach school and become the odd lady who collected fossils around New Haven.

"Yes" meant Sam's curly hair and his fine body and his big feet and slouch and his improved kissing and his bacon smell. But . . .

"Would you let me go to university?" I demanded.

"Of course! You deserve it."

"And you'd pay for it?"

"Even if it were my last penny."

"And let me work in the field?

"Well. Only if it was with me."

If anything was likely to make me swoon, it was talk like this. But before I could say anything at all, people outside were shouting, "Fire! Fire on the hill!"

20.
THE BLAZE

I **BURST FROM HER TENT TO SEE FIRE SPIKED** across the hilltops. Over a week without rain, and the grass was parched as paper. Flaring in the sagebrush, the flames crackled down the slopes toward the camp. On all other sides, we were cut off by the river.

People were hollering and running around. I was about to hurry away from Rachel's tent when I noticed Professor Cartland standing outside his own, one suspender hitched up. He stared directly at me, then at his daughter, kneeling at the flaps.

Lieutenant Frye ran up and said, "It's the Indians."

Flickering on the hills, in the growing light from the blaze, were the shapes of horses and riders. They set up a cry that curdled my blood, made it almost impossible to hear or think. Then: a sudden spatter of gunshots.

"Are we under attack?" Cartland demanded furiously, like this was some personal insult.

"Those rifles are ours," said Frye. "I'm more worried about the flames."

Ned Plaskett was suddenly at my side. "The flames might not reach us," he said. "You've already cut down most of the nearby grass for forage; the rest looks pretty trampled. We've got a good buffer."

"We still need to douse it," said the lieutenant. To Cartland he said, "Organize your students into a bucket brigade," and he was off, shouting orders to his soldiers.

Cartland looked at me, then told Rachel, "Stay in your tent," before heading off to gather his students.

"Come on, " Ned said to me.

Hurrying through camp, grabbing buckets from the cookhouse and stables. Rachel, hastily dressed, rushed to help us. With our empty buckets we headed to the river. From the far side I heard more violent whooping from the buttes, and it made my knees weak to know we were surrounded. How many Indians were out there?

The three of us were the only people at the riverbank right now. We each filled two buckets and staggered them to the front of the camp. We passed Yalies and shouted at them to form a line. Everyone was up now. I saw Landry the journalist in his underpants, looking petrified. Panicked words ricocheted everywhere.

"—got us hemmed right in!"

"—attack any second!"

"—if the camp catches fire—"

"—damn savages—"

"—the horses—"

"—how deep's the river—"

"—can swim them across—"

"—exterminate 'em's the only way—"

"—move supplies?"

"—no time—"

Soldiers were hunkered down by the outer wagons, taking wild shots into the darkness. Then I heard Lieutenant Frye shout:

"Hold your fire!"

There were no more gunshots—just the wild hollering of the Indians and the nervous snorting of our own ponies.

"They ain't firing," Ned told me. "Just trying to scare us. They want their boy back."

"Boy's gone," the lieutenant snapped. "Got himself free, or someone came and did it under our noses."

I'd set that boy free, and this was how he thanked me? Trying to burn us alive? I guessed the flames were about sixty yards from the wagons and jumping closer.

Before we could advance with our buckets, the lieutenant stopped us.

"Let my men take them. You keep supplying."

I admit I was relieved. I didn't want to go into the open, within range of gunfire or arrows. But the soldiers did, crouched low, dumping bucket after bucket onto the grass after first trampling it with their boots. By then more full buckets were arriving from the brigade, and we were busy passing back the empty ones.

Despite the flames, it suddenly got darker. I glanced up. We'd lost the moon entirely. Clouds blotted the sky. The wind came stronger against my face, hastening the fire. A cottonwood tree, scalded too long, suddenly went up like a torch. From its dry branches and leaves, embers floated over our heads like fireflies.

"No," I breathed, following the sparks as they shimmied into camp. A cluster landed on a tent and started to smolder.

"Fire in the camp!" I shouted. I took the full bucket just handed to me, rushed to the tent, and doused it.

Everything was built on grass. Trampled as it was, it would still burn. We were backed against the river. We wouldn't die, but the camp would be destroyed.

Moon gone now, the campsite was flickering shadow and smoke and complete mayhem. I rushed back to my post in the bucket brigade, but the line was busted now, everyone rushing to put out the little fires starting all over.

"Sluice the wagons!" someone shouted. I think it might've been the lieutenant but wasn't sure. "Start with the ammunition!"

"Keep the bucket brigade going!" another voice shouted.

No hope of that now. The wind built. My eyes streamed from the smoke. Where was Ned? Rachel? Some empty buckets were coming back to me, but I had no one to pass them to, so I ran for the river, handing them out to whoever reached for one. People loomed out of the smoke and darkness, intent and fierce, and I was suddenly afraid I'd see an Indian burst toward me, club raised. I got a lung full of smoke and hacked. *Rachel, where are you?*

Someone seized my arm, and I whirled to see Ned, his face

tilted ecstatically heavenward. For a second I worried he was having a religious vision.

"Listen!" he shouted.

Above the din came a tectonic rumble, and then the wind kicked up from a new direction. Pushing back the smoke. Rain spattered my face, then came good and steady until it was a downpour. Beating on the tents and wagon covers. The grass blaze dwindled, smoking furiously. Embers kept coming, but even those that landed were extinguished fast enough by the rain. We were all of us soaked, still working to douse any last struggling fires. The rain had saved us.

I spotted Rachel and rushed to her, knowing we wouldn't have much time together. Her blouse and skirt were sodden, hair a tangled mess. I wanted to wrap her up in my arms, but there were too many people around.

"Say yes," I said.

In the rain it took me a moment to realize she was crying.

"He saw you coming out of my tent! He knows."

"It doesn't matter."

Her face crumpled. Anguish and anger. "Of course it matters! Everything's ruined! He'll send me home. It's all ruined."

At first light Papa woke me and told me to get dressed; he wanted to speak to me in his tent. I'd only had a few hours sleep, and my arms ached from carrying the water buckets. My hair reeked of smoke. As I hurriedly pulled and hooked and buttoned my clothes, my hands trembled. I knew what was to come. The camp was still quiet as I crossed to this tent, and inside I was surprised to see Sam already there, looking bleary eyed and disheveled and damp.

Papa sat in the camp chair, and we two stood before him, like schoolchildren about to receive their punishment.

"I must know exactly what transpired yes yes inside that tent."

"We spoke," I told him.

His gaze moved to Sam. "And that is all?"

"That's all," he said.

"I have a strong inclination to buggy-whip you."

At this I saw Sam stand up taller, and I hurriedly said, "We're telling the truth."

Papa inhaled, tilted his head higher. "A man does not typically end up inside a lady's tent without some kind of prior acquaintance."

"We've become friends," I admitted. "We spoke on the train journey, and our paths crossed sometimes in the badlands."

"I see. You never mentioned it to me. And you thought to continue your *friendship* in the middle of the night."

"I was returning from the latrine," Sam said, "and saw her outside her tent, getting a breath of air. We were talking. We only went inside because a soldier was coming, and we didn't want him spreading any wild rumors."

My father's eyes widened. "And you think entering a young lady's tent is less likely to encourage wild rumors?"

Sam had the good sense to keep quiet. I could see Papa was stoking a good temper, and anything we said would just be fuel. His speech was measured, every word a tight little bundle of

EVERY HIDDEN THING

255

fury. "It is fortunate, Samuel Bolt, that we are far from civilization and I was the only one to see this outrage. Or else my daughter's reputation would be irreparably damaged."

"Yes, sir," Sam said. "It was very reckless of me. I'm sorry."

I was grateful he didn't say it was me who'd dragged him inside, and I had no intention of setting the record straight now.

"But what offends me almost as much," Papa went on, his cold eyes fixed on Sam, "is that you've no doubt been spying on us—"

Sam tried to protest but was harshly cut off.

"—and *pretended* you have feelings for my daughter, in the hopes of gaining information about our work. Do you deny it?"

I was terrified by what he might say next. Deny it or admit it—I didn't know which was worse.

He hung his head, his voice so low it was difficult to hear. "You're right," he said. "I was pretending. I wanted to find out all I could." He glanced guiltily at me. "But your daughter never told me anything useful. Nothing."

I knew he was lying but was surprised by the ache in my throat. A ghost of all my previous doubts flitted through my head. Were his feelings false? Was he really just spying on me? But no, he was playacting, and he'd made the right choice just now. If he'd confessed how close we really were, the fury of my father would have been limitless. This way, there was some small hope Papa might feel sorry for me and let me stay on.

"You've told the truth yes yes at least," my father said to him, then shook his head. "You are certainly your father's son. I don't want to see you anywhere near this camp, or any of our quarries, ever again. Understood? Now wake Ned, and be on your way."

Samuel didn't even glance at me as he left the tent.

"Would you like to take a little walk?" Papa asked me. I felt like a prisoner being asked if I'd like to look at the gallows.

We strolled around the periphery of the camp, just the two of us. On all sides the grass was charred to stubble. In the daylight it was shocking to see how close we'd come to being consumed by the flames. I was too afraid to speak first. When he stopped and put his hand on my arm, I was even more worried.

"I am sorry, my dear, that you were taken in by that scoundrel. A little surprised, too, I must admit. You're far too intelligent to assume his affections were genuine."

I pulled my arm free. Did he think I was so unworthy of affection?

"What makes you think I was taken in?" I replied coolly. I was not a liar, but I was surprised how easily it came. "My feelings for him were friendly at best. We share some interests, and he was the only person of my age in a hundred miles."

Papa nodded but looked doubtful. "I am glad to hear it. I would hate to think yes yes that he had trifled with your heart."

"Not at all," I said.

"I wish only for your happiness. That boy imposed himself on you most dishonorably. You must try to banish him from your thoughts. It will be easier once you've left."

I'd been expecting this moment, dreading it like a hangman's noose, but when it came, I felt curiously numb. My eyes rested

EVERY HIDDEN THING

257

on a cottonwood tree, still smoldering in its highest branches.

"You want to send me back home."

"Fort Crowe first, and then home when a suitable chaperone can be found."

My anger caught up with me. "I don't want to go home! There's too much work here."

"Who knows what else the Sioux might do. I was a fool to allow you on this expedition. It's no longer safe for you. That's what I have told the lieutenant yes yes, and that is what Commander Collins and his wife will be told. No one needs to know the other reasons, or else you will be ruined."

I sighed wearily. "What of it? Hasn't everyone decided I'll never marry because I'm too plain? What's there to ruin?"

His chest swelled. "There is my *name* to think of, my professional standing. And I won't have a harlot for a daughter."

My cheeks burned as though I'd been slapped. I'd rather have been.

He looked away. "I am thinking of you yes yes." He cleared his throat. "And I am saving you from yourself. I very much doubt you're being honest with me. You do have feelings for that boy. You have risked scandal for him. And I suspect you may have told him things. Our pterodactylus perhaps? Our latest quarry?"

"You know it was the Indians who smashed it up!" I said evasively.

"My mind is made up. We have a shipment of fossils ready for tomorrow, and you will go with it."

KENNETH OPPEL

"This isn't fair!" I said. "I've found *so many* things on this expedition."

"The pterodactylus was a good find, I grant you. But I wonder if we'd have *all* of it to ourselves, if you hadn't been friendly with Samuel Bolt. As for the brontosaurus, anyone would have found that. You were just lucky enough to stumble over it."

For a moment I was speechless with hurt at how easily he belittled my contributions. It was as if he wasn't at all proud of me, not one bit. And despite my anger, no matter how hard I tried not to, I began to cry at the sheer injustice of it.

"There, there, my dear," he said, putting a hand on my shoulder. "Don't be so distressed."

"I am *not* distressed!" I said. "I am furious!"

"This is entirely my fault," he said. "This is no fit occupation for a young woman."

"It's the occupation I want more than anything," I said, swiping the last tears from my cheeks and glaring at him. "And I am very good at it."

"I was wrong to be so encouraging when you were little; I can see that now. I've in no way helped you prepare for the life ahead."

"My life ahead includes university," I said. "You can send me home, but you can't take university away from me."

"I never agreed to university, my dear. And recent events have made me realize you're not fit for a scholarly life."

I swallowed, mute with shock.

"Your judgment on this expedition has been very poor. You nearly broke your neck when prospecting."

"And discovered the pterodactylus!"

"You've allowed yourself to be manipulated by a young man who was only interested in spying on us."

"Nothing I told him had any bad effect on us!"

He wasn't listening to me. "You've shown yourself to be sentimental about the Indians. I fear you lack the necessary objectivity for serious study of the sciences. You are far too emotional."

"And what about you?" I retorted. "Didn't you come out here to defeat a rival? You've stolen his telegrams, blocked his publications. Isn't that emotional?"

"You are very vocal in your criticism, young lady, and I have tolerated it in good humor thus far—even in front of my students. But no longer. At a university, a student learns to respect and accept the teachings of his superiors—something you clearly are unable to do. You will stay at the camp today, and ready your things. Tomorrow, you're going back to Fort Crowe."

Infuriatingly, he just walked off without giving me a chance to defend myself or protest. I seethed. I paced, fists clenched, fingernails digging into my palms. It was so unjust. I was going to be packed up and shipped back like a sack of fossils. If my father had his way, I'd *become* a fossil, petrified in his library.

I stopped pacing and stood looking at the sun clearing the buttes. It didn't have to be this way. I had a map to the Black Beauty. I had a young man who'd asked me to marry him. He had a plan—and together the two of us could make a good team.

Mind churning, I was stomping back to my tent when Mr. Landry approached and tipped his hat to me.

KENNETH OPPEL

"Good morning, Miss Cartland, I've come to say good-bye."

I blinked. "You're leaving?"

"The encounter with the Sioux has left me shaken, I'll confess."

"It was very frightening."

"Oh, the fire certainly. I was talking more about the treatment of the boy they caught."

I looked at him anew. I'd been too quick to assume he was just a toady of my father, obediently chronicling his triumphs.

"I meant to thank you, for speaking out the way you did," I said. "I thought I was the only one who was shocked."

He smiled and shook his head.

"Well, you must certainly have enough material for your article. I'm afraid we may not come off looking very well."

"I think *you* will come off just fine."

"I'm sorry to see you go, Mr. Landry."

"Well, to be honest, your father *encouraged* me to leave today."

I sniffed. "So we've both been expelled."

His eyes telegraphed his surprise.

"Yes. I'm being sent home for my own safety."

"That's a great shame. You have a fire for this kind of work."

"Thank you." I smiled, not just at the compliment, but because a critical piece of my plan had just come together like meshing gears. "I imagine you'll be riding past the Bolt camp this morning on your way back to Crowe."

"I think so, yes."

"Mr. Landry, could you please deliver a letter for me?"

• • •

When Ned and I made it back to camp, Father and Hitch were just settling down to breakfast. They'd both slept through the fire and gunshots—they were too far away to see or hear. They listened in amazement when we told them what had happened last night.

"I'm thinking we might want to stick together from now on," Ned said.

Father frowned. "We'll cover much less ground that way. Do you really think the Sioux bear us any ill will?"

"Yesterday I didn't think so," said Ned. "But after last night, I'm not sure they care if we're wearing army coats. It was a terrible mistake for them to capture that boy and beat him. Not to mention sawing off those heads in the first place."

I was dead tired, chilled from sleeping in soggy bedclothes under a wagon. My black eye throbbed. My head throbbed. How was I going to see Rachel again? I needed my proposal answered. I went to the tent to change into some dry clothes and only meant to lie down for a minute, but I must've fallen asleep. When I woke, the sun was high, and Hitch was making lunch on the cookstove.

"Saved you some," he said.

"Thanks, Hitch." I went and sat with him and gratefully ate the stew he put on a tin plate.

"Did Ned and my father head off?"

He nodded. "Ned said don't wake you."

Not my father, but Ned. He wanted me to get enough sleep. I felt pretty crestfallen as I sat there. But Hitch was a very comforting presence. He was so calm and orderly. When he ate, he just ate. When he cleaned up, that's all he did, methodically. When he took out one of his favorite books to read, his attention was focused on that and nothing else. He always seemed to be living completely in the moment, without any distracting chatter in his head. I envied him.

My head was *all* chatter. What had happened between Rachel and her father after I was sent off? Would he really send her home? Would he confine her to camp? When Ned and I had left, I over-heard two soldiers saying they might have to move camp, because all the nearby forage for the horses had been burned. There was no way I could get near her in the camp. Her father had probably given orders for the soldiers to shoot at me—maybe without warn-ing shots this time.

But there was a small chance her father had let her stay on. If yes, would she be at the brontosaurus quarry today? I might be able to get to her there. I'd have to be a lot more careful. But I needed to see her. Needed her answer, one way or another. I wasn't hopeful. Last night in the rain she'd seemed almost angry with me.

I was getting my pony ready to head out when Hitch came up to me, looking apologetic. He held out a crumpled envelope.

"The man gave this to me. Mr. Laundry."

"When?"

"This morning. You were sleeping."

I ripped open the envelope, pulled out the single piece of paper. It was quite a long letter, with Rachel's name at the bottom. And at the top, the first word was "Yes."

21.
AT THE PIONEER

IT TOOK MOST OF THE AFTERNOON TO FIND them. I rode to the place Rachel described in her letter, the place she'd last seen them working, and kept looking from there. Finally I saw Withrow and one of his men, working a coal seam high on a slope. I trudged up. They glistened with soot.

"Not much luck," said Withrow, loosening his neckerchief, swiping his grimy face. He'd been using a trowel, loosening the soft coal in the hopes of revealing bone.

"You won't find much there," I said. "Not what you're looking for anyway."

"That right?" He laughed a little and took a pull from his canteen, then offered it to me.

I drank. "I know where you should be looking."

He sat down with his back to the rock, removed his slouch hat, and rubbed at his damp hair. "Tell me more."

"We need to settle a few things first," I said. "I can lead you to the Black Beauty, but I need to know what I'll be paid."

His eyebrows lifted only slightly. "Your father know you're here?"

"This has nothing to do with my father. I'm striking out on my own."

He didn't laugh as I'd expected, just nodded, his eyes on me. "So it'll just be you—no helpers, no equipment, no great professor."

I knew he was trying to make me feel like I wasn't much of a bargain.

"I can find bones as fast as my father, and I'm faster at piecing them together. Also, I have a map."

I told him about the tooth and the Sioux boy.

Withrow looked over at Thomas, his Sioux guide, who'd been listening in. "The boy may not have told the truth."

"He was already cut free. He could've run. He didn't have to draw me a map."

"Still," said Withrow. "A big if."

I waited, saying nothing.

"So we'd be fronting you food and supplies and labor."

"For me and my partner."

"Who's your partner? Ned Plaskett?"

"No."

"Why do you need a partner? Why do *I* need your partner?"

"It belongs to both of us. And I left the map with her."

Withrow grinned. "Her?"

I pressed on. "So how much is the Black Beauty worth to you?"

He named a figure, and I mentioned another figure and then we hemmed and hawed and talked a bit and juggled some other figures and eventually shook hands.

"So. Lead the way," Withrow said.

"Yep," I said. "I just need to get married first."

He nodded, like this was unsurprising to him. "That Cartland girl by any chance?"

I couldn't help grinning, I felt so happy and proud. "Yes. Tomorrow."

"Well, congratulations. I think you're headed for a world of trouble, but maybe we can help out."

Daniel Simpson deposited me in the parlor of the Scots Hotel—one of the very few appropriate places for an unescorted young lady to wait, I supposed—while he and the soldiers went to the train station to arrange shipment for our crates and get our mail. I sat in a lumpy chair, where the hotel clerk could keep an eye on me. In an hour or so I'd be collected, taken on to the fort, and transferred—like a convict!—into the custody of the commander and his wife.

It had been a dry little good-bye between me and Papa early this morning. I think he was surprised I didn't put up more of a fuss, shout, and refuse to climb aboard the wagon, which I might have done, if I hadn't had a different plan in my head.

A fly battered itself against the glass, over and over, and all I could think about was all the possible mishaps. Had Mr. Landry

KENNETH OPPEL

actually delivered the letter? Had he given it to the right person? Had Professor Bolt opened it instead and tied Samuel to the wagon to stop him meeting me? Had Samuel got the letter, but something stopped him from coming? Had he fallen on the way and broken his leg? Had he been attacked by the Sioux? Had he changed his mind altogether and was, right now, looking for the Black Beauty on his own?

I stopped myself here. What I knew for certain was this: If he was coming, I needed to give him more time. Simpson and the soldiers would come back for me soon, and once I was at the fort, there was no way Samuel could reach me.

I watched the hotel clerk. His eyes swung from his ledger to me with the regularity of a metronome. He even gave me a rather roguish smile at one point. I walked to the counter.

"I will be taking a room for the night," I announced.

He tilted his head in confusion. "I thought you were waiting here for your friends, miss."

"I have changed my plans," I said with what I hoped was the right amount of haughtiness. "I've decided to spend the night and have a bath before continuing on."

From my pocket I pulled a dollar bill and placed it on the counter, to show I wasn't making an idle request.

"Very good." He consulted his ledger. "I do have a room."

"Does it look onto the main street?" I asked.

"It does. Just the one night?"

I told him yes and took the key and fifty cents change.

"Do you need any help with your luggage, Miss Cartland?"

It was all on the wagon. All I had with me was the map Samuel had drawn and his promise to marry me. "They'll bring it later," I said, and proceeded upstairs.

Inside the room I bolted the door and sat down on the edge of the bed. The mattress was soggy. The smell of floor soap was so cloying it must have been covering some other noxious scent that haunted the room. My heart pounded. After a few moments I opened the window wide. The air that came in was fetid with manure, but at least it didn't smell like soap. I positioned a chair so I could watch the comings and goings on the street. I would see him if he came. *When* he came.

It felt like I was watching a rehearsal for some kind of amateur play: people coming and going, shards of inaudible conversation, shouts of anger that were cut short by the clatter of hooves and a wagon, the windblown sound of hammering from offstage. I was waiting for my real life to begin.

The knock on my door came later than I'd expected. I'd planned what to say.

I opened the door to Daniel Simpson, who looked perplexed and distinctly uncomfortable, his hat in his hands.

"Miss Cartland, are you unwell?"

"I am, yes. I wanted to lie down, and it seemed simplest to take a room. I'd like to stay the night before carrying on."

He nodded, looking at me a bit more closely, maybe trying to diagnose my affliction.

"Should I send for the doctor?"

"No, no. I think it's just the heat. A good night's rest will fix

KENNETH OPPEL

things. I'm sorry to be a nuisance. Did the crates get off all right?"

"Yes. It's just . . . the soldiers are anxious to get you to the fort. It's not two hours' journey. You don't think you could manage it?"

He was suspicious. He'd seen me work full days in the badlands with no ill effects.

"I'm so sorry; I really can't."

He nodded some more. "All right, we'll make arrangements. Shall I have your luggage brought up?"

"Oh, yes, the small case, please, thank you very much."

I resumed my watch at the window and tried not to think words like "foolhardy" and "disastrous" and "madness." Simpson knocked again timidly and said through the door that he'd left my suitcase outside. Three o'clock and I watched the street. Four o'clock and I watched the street.

I was hungry, so decided to go downstairs to see if they were serving dinner. I was relieved to find the dining room nearly deserted—no sign of Simpson or the soldiers—and I asked for a table near the window. I had never sat in a restaurant alone before. I stared at my menu without reading a single line, my eyes pulled constantly to the street. I ordered the thing that seemed least likely to be disgusting. It came—and was disgusting.

Suddenly the hotel clerk was standing over me with a folded piece of paper.

"Excuse me, Miss Cartland. This message was left for you."

I waited till he left before I opened it. The message was

written with the terseness of a telegram. "Abandon meal. (Looks disgusting.) Cross street to the Pioneer. I'll be waiting inside. I love you. Sam."

Through the window, I watched her cross the road. My heart hammered away. I thought: *This is her walking down the aisle. This is her coming to marry me.* My heart did another run. She squinted in the harsh light, looked furtively left and right, then back over her shoulder. Like she was afraid she'd be followed or stopped. I was afraid too. With every step she took closer to me, my fear grew. Someone would come and snatch her away. Or no one would stop her, and she would cross the threshold of the saloon and we would do this mad, momentous thing.

I went to the door so I was right there when she came in. She gave her slightly wary smile, and I laughed with sheer happiness.

"Why are we meeting here?" she whispered, looking at the bar, at the gaming tables.

"Well, it turns out Mr. Murchison, the proprietor, is also the justice of the peace." The last time I'd seen him, he'd been standing on top of the bar with a smoking shotgun, telling us to clear out. "So he'll be marrying us."

"In a saloon?"

"The cathedral wasn't available. Are you ready?"

"Don't we need witnesses?"

I wondered if she was having second thoughts. Possibly third. "Murchison's getting a couple from the barber."

At that moment he walked in with a man who still had a daub

of shaving cream on his prominent Adam's apple.

"Just need one more," Murchison said to me. "I'll get someone in back. This way."

He lead us to the door beside the bar.

I took Rachel's hand. "Are you ready?"

She gave the smallest nod I'd ever seen. We followed Murchison down a narrow hallway to a cramped office. There was barely room for us around his surprisingly fancy desk. Reassuringly large and official tomes sagged on a shelf. The open top drawer of a filing cabinet bristled with ledgers that promised legality.

Which was good, because Murchison himself looked none too reputable. He was heavyset with gopher eyes and a torso that sagged like a discouraged letter *b*. Teeth mottled brown. One tooth on top seemed to bob up and down and sometimes even switch places with its neighbor. I couldn't be sure. He kept his left hand buried in his trouser pockets and jingled some coins for emphasis. First off he asked if we had the license fee. I counted out two dollars. Then he asked our names and ages and places of birth and wrote them down on a form with a fancy insignia on top.

I was just about to ask where the other witness was when the door opened and Mrs. Cummins came in, made-up and brightly dressed. When her eyes met mine, she registered no surprise. No recognition.

"How sweet," she said, turning to Rachel. "So young."

"Weren't you on the train with us?" Rachel asked her.

"I can't recall," she replied.

Murchison jingled his change. "Let's get started. Do you, Samuel, um . . ."

"Bolt," I told him helpfully.

"Bolt"—jingle jingle—"take Rachel Cartland as your lawful"— jingly jingly—"wedded"—jingledy-jingly—"wife?"

I tried not to smile.

"Yes, I do."

And then it was Rachel's turn. I watched her, wanting to see her mouth form the words.

I waited, and then waited some more.

It was one thing to write "yes" in a letter. But to say it aloud, in public, here in a saloon, a woman of ill repute as a witness, the sounds of carousing beyond the walls, with four expectant sets of eyes on me. . . . The whole thing seemed lunacy. All my good sense told me: wait. The decision was too extreme.

When I looked at Samuel's face, I was frightened—of his intensity, and what he was asking me. He had no idea how different I was from him. He burned so fiercely; but wasn't that a sign of his love? But everything that burned fiercely died all the faster. If he could fall in love so easily, couldn't he fall *out* just as easily? And what if I couldn't love him properly? I was difficult and prickly and unused to loving.

Would it really be so bad to keep my cloistered life so long as I had my books and my magnifying glass and trips to explore and materials to draw? Would it be so bad to keep on like before?

But *before*, I hadn't met Samuel Bolt. And he'd changed

everything with his charm and eyes and curly hair and promises of love—and university and a fulfillment of my dream to be a paleontologist.

And what if his love didn't last? What if it faded?

But I couldn't predict that. I had love before me, right now, and I didn't think anyone could ever love me as much as Samuel. Or hunt with me for fossils as a true partner.

I thought: *If not now, when?*

I said, "Yes. I do."

22.
A WEDDING NIGHT

BEFORE WE LEFT MURCHISON'S OFFICE, Mrs. Cummins touched my arm and pressed ten dollars into my hand.

"A small wedding gift," she said.

"That's too kind of you," Rachel said, blushing, "really, we can't—"

"Sure we can," I said.

"I know how hard it can be for young people starting out," Mrs. Cummins said. I think her eyes might have been moist.

"Thank you," I said.

Marriage certificate clutched in one hand, I lead Rachel out through the saloon. I felt like I was moving without taking steps.

"She was certainly on the train with us," Rachel whispered. "She was very friendly with your father."

"Yes," I said.

"It was very generous of her to give us a gift."

"Not really. It's a fraction of what she stole from us."

"*What?*"

I told her the story as we crossed the street to the hotel. It seemed like the most hilarious thing in the world right now, and we were both laughing when someone called out, "Miss Cartland!" I looked and saw Daniel Simpson up the street, waving.

"I was hoping we'd have a little more time," Rachel said.

We hurried into the hotel and went upstairs. The clerk watched us disapprovingly but said nothing.

Inside her room—*our* room—we locked the door, giggling like naughty schoolchildren. I was in a hotel room, alone with a woman. I put my arms around her and kissed her. We were both trembling. I felt slightly feverish.

"We did it," she said.

"Yes."

"Are we crazy?"

There was a knocking on the door.

"Who is it?" Rachel asked.

"Miss Cartland, it's Daniel. Are you all right?"

"Just resting, thank you."

"I saw you outside on the street."

I looked at her, wondering what her response would be.

"Just getting a breath of fresh air."

"The clerk says he saw you with a young man. It looked to me like Samuel Bolt. Are you sure you're all right?"

"Absolutely fine, Mr. Simpson."

"Could you open the door, please, just so I can be sure you're all right?"

"Honestly, I'd like some peace and quiet."

"The clerk is concerned as well. He's offered to unlock the door if you won't."

With an irritable sigh, she opened the door to reveal the both of us to Simpson.

His face paled. He swallowed and said, "Miss Cartland, my instructions were to take you to the fort."

He was looking at me the whole time he spoke.

"I won't be going to the fort. You can tell my father I'm staying here. And I am not Miss Cartland anymore. I am Mrs. Bolt."

I think I must have looked as shocked as Simpson; it was the first time I'd heard those words myself. Mrs. Bolt.

Simpson's dry mouth clicked as he spoke. "You're married?"

"We are."

"Your father will want to hear this."

"I doubt that," she said, "but you can tell him if you like."

She closed the door in his stunned face. We stood, holding our breaths until we heard his boots clapping down the stairs.

"His face," she said. For a bit neither of us could speak, we were laughing so hard. Nothing seemed real. The chair, the chest of drawers. The bed.

"He won't leave till tomorrow, will he?" she asked.

"Not unless they want to travel in the dark."

"Papa won't get here till noon tomorrow, then."

"There's nothing they can do anyway," I said. "We're married.

They'll just have to accept it. And by the time they get here we'll already have left town."

"Yes."

Awkwardly we regarded each other.

I said, "We belong to each other now."

I was surprised to see her bristle. "I'm not sure I like the idea of belonging to anyone. It makes me think of what I just escaped, being kept in a series of rooms, and allowed out from time to time."

"I didn't mean it like . . ." I shook my head. "You really aren't one bit romantic, are you?"

"You know I'm not. But I *am* your wife now."

Standing beside the bed, we kissed. Our hands and mouths became more urgent. She released her hair and let it fall about her face and over her shoulders, and I touched it and held it to my face so I could breathe it in. There was no part of her I wasn't allowed to touch now. We traced each other's contours and pulled each other closer. She asked me to draw the curtains. I was glad of the simple request, because a kind of frenzy was stealing over me, and I was mute with desire.

When I turned, she said, "Undress me."

There were so many buttons and hooks and eyes. Every bit of new skin I uncovered I had to break off to kiss. I'd never imagined such a warm, supple creature could spring from all those stiff layers. Still it was an absorbing business and required some attention. She laughed as I removed her boots and her stockings and blouse and said it tickled. She got quieter when I reached her last layer of undergarments. I paused, and she stepped back against the bed and removed the final things herself. She did it practically, without any fanfare, and stood before me.

I'd never seen a woman naked. There was a great deal to look at.

"You're beautiful," I said. I wanted to touch everything.

"You now," she said with a gesture that was both playful and impatient. "Come on."

Hurriedly I stripped off my sweaty trousers and shirt and vest and underpants. In dismay I looked down to see myself—that part which had always been so lively and troublesome in the past—suddenly and completely withered.

"It's . . . ," I mumbled, tensing my thigh muscles and urging it to lift, "suddenly defective. I don't know what to do with the fellow."

"Let him alone for now," she said. "Lie down beside me." Pulling back the covers, she climbed into bed and shifted over for me to join her. "This bed has had many visitors," she said as the springs creaked.

"Do you think it's seen a wedding night?"

"I think it's seen many," she laughed, bouncing on the saggy mattress.

We each bounced a bit, seeing who could make the longest and most tortured squeak. The sheets, though clean enough, couldn't quite conceal the mildew of the mattress. And a faint whiff of urine that came and went when one moved around. But our door was bolted, and the window curtained, and this little room was ours alone.

We turned to face each other. I was aware of the heat of her body, all the length of it. I loved it. When I touched her cheek, it was scalding. I kissed her and whispered that hers was the most beautiful body I'd ever seen, and she told me it was the *only* body I'd ever seen and anyway that it was just a regular body. Then she took my hand and placed it upon her and showed me how best to touch her.

And then, even if I'd counted down from a thousand, and had Mrs. Shaw perched on our bed, nothing could have withered me.

"You're not one bit defective," Rachel whispered to me.

When I moved myself on top of her, it took a bit of fumbling to find the right place. But after that it felt like her body and mine, all our parts, were designed to fit perfectly together.

She winced. Her eyes were wide, and we watched each other, mesmerized. I felt a huge heat and urgency flooding me, but her face flinched with my movements. Then her eyes closed tight and her eyelids crinkled and water beaded from their edges.

"I'm hurting you," I said, stopping, though it was the last thing I wanted to do.

She began to cry. "I'm sorry. I didn't think it would be so painful."

"We don't have to," I said.

"Keep going," she said.

I shook my head, mortified, wondering what I was doing wrong.

"Maybe it's meant to hurt," she said.

"Is it?"

"I'm not sure. No one ever told me."

No one had told me anything either. A house filled with books and not one to tell me what I should be doing now.

"We can wait," I said. Her tears had made me wither anyway.

"Is there blood? There's supposed to be blood the first time."

I looked at the sheets and shook my head.

"Hold me for a while?" she said.

I brought her close, and she put her head on my chest, her arm across me.

"You're kind," she said, pressing closer. "I feel safe with you."

I stroked her hair and inhaled her scent and stared at the ceiling. I couldn't quite believe anything right now. I felt exultant and terrified. I felt like a conquering hero, and like a soldier shot and waiting for death. I felt that I'd never sleep again, but I did. We both did.

When I woke, it was dark but close to dawn. Light made a pale line between the curtains. Our bodies had parted during the night, and you were turned away from me on your side, still asleep.

I'm not sure why I didn't wake you. My body wanted more of you, but you were sleeping, and I'd never seen you like that. I liked seeing your hair fanned across the pillow. I propped myself on an elbow and looked at your ear, your cheek, your nose. You had a small raised mole on your neck. I stared at your face, and you didn't wake up. I felt like you were completely mine.

And then I didn't want to be alone any longer, so I kissed your mole, traced its shape with the tip of my tongue. I pressed my nose into the nape of your neck and inhaled you, and nudged and nuzzled you until you turned yourself to me with a sleepy smile.

"Did you sleep too?"

"Not at all," I said. "I just watched over you all night, stunned by your beauty."

She snorted. "Not a romantic bone in my body, remember?"

"Maybe I can find one," I said, kissing her throat.

The rapping at the door was sharp enough to send us both sitting ramrod straight.

"What time is it?" I whispered pointlessly. My pocket watch was in my clothing, scattered across the floor.

Sternly, from beyond our door: "Rachel. It's your father."

I couldn't imagine four more horrifying words. "Don't get it," I whispered. I'd known that, sooner or later, we'd have to contend with her father. But I hadn't thought it would come so fast. Simpson must've ridden through the night with the soldiers to deliver his news.

"Samuel!"

I jolted again. That was *my* father's voice. They were both there. On the other side of the door.

"It's too early," Rachel said with impressive command. I was filled with admiration. "Come back later, please."

The sound of a key in the lock. The doorknob turning. Rachel clutched the sheets to her throat. The door swung open. I caught sight of the hotel clerk, sneaking a peek inside before backing up so Cartland and my father could enter. They strode with such purpose—like emissaries from a great power—and I almost laughed.

Seeing them side by side, united, was almost as shocking as

having them at the foot of my bed. With me naked beneath the covers beside my new, equally naked wife. They were both grimy from the long ride, exhausted-looking, and stern.

"Get up," Cartland told his daughter.

"I can't," she retorted. "I'm not wearing anything."

In mute fury Cartland turned to my father, like this was all his fault.

"We're married now," I said, as steadily as I could.

"This marriage never took place," Cartland said.

I told him it was done in front of witnesses and the justice of the peace.

"Fortunately," said Cartland, "out here in the territories, a marriage leaves very little fossil record. Mr. Murchison has been most cooperative."

From a pocket he produced a sheet of paper and held it before us long enough for me to see it was the original copy of our marriage certificate, torn from the justice's ledger.

"I imagine the witnesses can be made forgetful for a few dollars," he added, and proceeded to rip the certificate into tiny and tinier pieces.

"That doesn't change anything," said Rachel. "We have our own copy."

"Ah, this one," her father said, spotting the certificate we'd giddily placed on the chest of drawers last night.

"Put that down," I said. "We're married. You'll have to accept it."

"I'll do no such thing. You are two children who did a rash thing without consent—"

"We don't need your consent!" I told him. "Give me that!"

I could tell he was going to rip it, and I leaped out of bed naked.

Cartland tore it down the middle. Let the halves flutter to the floor. I charged at him, murderous, but my own father stepped out and punched me in the stomach.

"Have you known her?" Father demanded as I gasped, sagging to one knee. I hated him. I spluttered upright and punched him as hard as I could in the face. He staggered back, and I moved to hit him again when Cartland flicked his knuckles across my privates. I fell to my knees, gagging.

"How dare you!" I heard Rachel yell. "Don't you dare touch him! You can rip up the certificates. It doesn't change a thing. We've spent a night together as man and wife."

"I see," said my father, dabbing blood from his split lip.

"We're married," I said, standing. My voice didn't shake. "You know this can't be undone. God's witnessed it."

Father's fury was instant. "Do not invoke God's name. What happened has nothing to do with God. This was not a considered thing you did. She is *not* a Friend. This marriage *never* happened."

I'd anticipated their rage, but not this—their total refusal to acknowledge the marriage. I felt completely upended. They'd destroyed the evidence. They'd bribe the witnesses. They'd lie. They wanted to separate us forever.

"And what if I'm with child?" Rachel demanded from the bed.

I looked at her, stunned by her boldness—but also by the stark reminder I could easily become a father. Not from last night, but from this day forward. When I turned back to our two fathers, I caught them glancing at each other, momentarily at a loss. Cartland spoke first.

"Unlikely. But you're going back east, and then yes yes we shall see. If you are with child, it's simple enough to confine you to the house until it's born. And then place it in an orphanage. Bolt, do you concur?"

I watched in horror as my father nodded.

"You are monstrous!" Rachel said. "Both of you!"

"Get dressed," her father said, distastefully picking her clothes off the floor and depositing them behind the embroidered screen.

Rachel glared. I looked at her and nodded. I could see the play of confusion in her eyes and forehead, but I nodded again, asking her to trust me. She pulled the sheet around her and disappeared behind the screen.

I stood taller. I'd once read that the Sioux rode naked into battle, and thought it was insanity to be so vulnerable. But there was a strange liberation to it, to be stripped down, nothing between me and my anger. They wanted to humiliate me. But I had something neither of them did: a wife.

"Get out," I said. "You're not welcome here."

Cartland snorted. "I'm not leaving without my daughter."

"You'll have to fight me, then."

"Just like his father," said Cartland. "So be it."

From his belt he pulled a pair of army manacles.

I could tell my father was as stunned as me. "You're not serious, Cartland."

"We agreed our first course of action yes yes was to separate them. This will expedite the matter. Help me, Bolt."

"You'll not shackle my son like a common criminal!"

"Come here, boy!" Cartland commanded me.

My father grasped Cartland's arm. "No!"

Cartland quickly snapped one of the manacles around my father's wrist. "I suspected you'd become a problem, Bolt." He grabbed for my father's other hand, but Father delivered a punch that sent Cartland staggering to the floor. A second pair of manacles, and a ring of keys, spun from his belt toward me. I snatched them up. How many people was he planning on shackling?

Cartland launched himself at me, just as my father threw himself at Cartland.

Rachel leaned out from behind the screen in astonishment. "What's going—"

"Keep getting dressed!" I said.

Our fathers were a writhing mess. Punching and kicking and trying to get atop the other. I took my manacles and closed one loop around Cartland's kicking ankle, then grabbed my father's leg and did the same. Before the two men realized I'd shackled them together, I threw myself into their flailing midst, getting punched right and left. I grabbed the loose end of the manacles attached to my father's hand and tried to snap it around Cartland's wrist. He was on to me by now and fought like a fiend. I gave him a quick punch to the side of his big noggin and stunned him.

"I hope," I grunted, as I snapped the clasp shut, "that you two will be very happy together."

I jumped clear. They thrashed there together on the floor, bound hand and foot. They shouted to be unlocked and couldn't cooperate enough to get themselves to their feet. I started dressing fast. When it looked like they were about to stand, I charged and crashed them over again. They scrambled like overturned beetles, cursing me and each other.

Rachel emerged from behind the screen, fully clothed.

"We're going," she said.

"You don't know what you're doing," Cartland told his daughter. He wasn't shouting anymore, his voice cold and venomous. "Bolt seduced my fiancée—the woman who became your mother."

"What?" my father cried.

My eyes darted between them, not knowing where to settle. This was a story I'd never heard. Cartland continued, eyes locked on Rachel's.

"Bolt and I met as students in Europe. I gave him letters to take home and deliver to my fiancée, but he courted her himself. He is a scoundrel! And his son will be the same. He will abandon you!"

My father cuffed Cartland's head. "This is a lie!"

"You know it's true, Bolt. There are letters!"

I looked at Rachel, her face expressionless.

"We've got to go!" I said desperately. I went to the window, parted the curtains slightly. "There's soldiers out front."

"Do not do this!" Cartland implored his daughter.

"Samuel, do not leave this room!" my father roared.

KENNETH OPPEL

I snatched up the ripped halves of our marriage certificate, then grabbed Rachel's hand. She scooped up her suitcase. At the end of the hall there was a back door that opened onto a rickety set of stairs. Out we went, full tilt down to the alley. I took a moment to remember the fastest way to the stable and ran.

Near the stable was a covered wagon, already harnessed, with Ethan Withrow kicked back in the seat, snoozing.

"Withrow!" I said, slapping his foot.

He jerked his head. "Ah! Good morning, Mr. and Mrs. Bolt."

"We've got to go. Now!"

"Hop up."

We clambered into the back with all the supplies, closed the flaps, the wagon already moving. We went right down the main street, past the soldiers and the hotel. I peeked through a hole in the duck cloth. In the upstairs window I saw Cartland and my father—still manacled together—trying to bellow instructions at the soldiers but mostly just shouting at each other. I waited in tense silence until we were on the outskirts of town. Then Ethan Withrow leaned back and parted the flap.

"Must've been one hell of a wedding," he said.

PART III

THE BLACK BEAUTY

IN THE MOON WHEN THE CHERRIES TURN BLACK, *smallpox came to the village, and the Black Beauty wasn't enough to keep him safe. When the man died, some were shocked. Others said it was no surprise: Since he'd been using the power of the horned serpent, it was only a matter of time before he was defeated like the serpent.*

He was buried with it, though placed apart from the other platforms, out of both respect and fear.

Still, many boys hoped that when they went searching for their vision, they would find the horned serpent and win a tooth of their own. But the man had never talked much about where he'd found his gift. He said he couldn't remember exactly. After all, he'd woken up walking.

The only person he'd told was his own son, and even he hadn't been able to locate the exact place where his father had found the Black Beauty.

23.
THE HONEYMOON

'D READ BOOKS WHERE HONEYMOONS BEGAN with a glamorous send-off and a voyage to Europe. Ours started in the back of a musty, rocking wagon, among crates of rice and shovels and tarps and clods of dirt—and a heated discussion.

"Do you believe it?" I asked Samuel. "What my father said."

"I knew *my* father was in Europe," he replied, "but he didn't mention your father at all, or any of that other stuff."

"Of course not. It's too shameful."

"If it's even true. Your father's not exactly trustworthy!"

"Neither is yours. He steals."

"And you think he stole your father's fiancée too?"

"'Seduced' was the word he used."

The word had a distracting shape and shimmer to it; it swayed there between us, and for a moment we both stared at it in silence.

Samuel cleared his throat. "That word can have many meanings. It doesn't have to mean he . . . well, had intimate relations with her."

"My *mother*!"

"She wasn't your mother *yet*. And remember, your father also used the word 'courted.' 'Courted' is very different from 'seduced.' That's just wooing. Anyway, you're assuming it's all true! My father denied it, and we never heard his side!"

"Well," I said, "*something* happened between our fathers—at least it helps explain why they hate each other so much."

"They have plenty of other reasons to hate each other," he replied, sensibly enough.

His fingers prodded at his bruised stomach, and he winced, then looked off, his eyes sad.

"I hit him. My own father."

I put my arm around him. "He richly deserved it."

He nodded but looked unconsoled.

"You're a fiery pair," I told him. "You'll reconcile. Do you think our fathers ever will?"

It hadn't occurred to me before this moment. Up till now, every thought had been on what kind of husband Sam would be and whether he'd give me what my father never would. But right now I couldn't help wondering what our lives would be like if we could never bring our families together.

Savagely Sam said, "I don't care. I'm disgusted with both of them."

"Me too, but . . . it would be sad if they never accepted it. *Us*."

He shrugged, like he didn't want to consider it anymore.

"We were motherless," I said, "and now we're fatherless, too. We're like orphans."

He pulled me close, just as I'd wanted him to.

"Can we be orphans," he asked, "if we have each other?"

"Yes," I said.

"So here's what we're looking for," I told them. "Twenty, maybe thirty years ago, a man found a huge tooth in the rock. The story makes it sound like there might've been a jaw, maybe a bit of skull. Every year the rock crumbles, and the bones weather out, so we should have even more to see now. Rachel's a better drawer than me, so she's going to sketch out what the skull might look like."

The light was low. It had taken us most of the day to reach the three buttes on the Sioux boy's map. Outside of Crowe we'd met up with the rest of Barnum's men and traveled north over rolling grassland, keeping the sunken badlands to our left. From our high vantage point I watched the turns of the brown winding river, matching them to the map. The prairie became rockier. It looked parched and underfed. When I finally saw those three tall buttes, crowded together like a trio of nuns, I felt my shoulders relax and realized how tightly my fears had been clenched up inside me. The buttes were real. The Sioux boy hadn't lied about that.

We were far from the river now, but Thomas found a nearby creek, and we pitched camp there. With only a half hour of light left, there was no point prospecting, but I'd gathered everyone

KENNETH OPPEL

around for a talk. They were all crouched in front of me and Rachel like I was giving a class. Like I was the professor. This was my quarry, my dig. I was giving the orders to men much older than me, and it took some doing. I wanted to appear strong. I couldn't falter, or the men would smell it and lose faith in me.

I looked now at Rachel, who had a stick and was ready to draw on the parched earth. "Do you remember the *Laelaps* skull?" I asked her.

She nodded. "I'll make it a bigger version." And as she drew, she narrated. She was very skilled. "So here's the mandible, the lower jaw. There might be teeth still in the jaw. The teeth are big, remember, almost a foot, banana shaped, but some will be smaller, some broken into pieces. Teeth are pretty easy to spot; they're enameled, smooth, with a shine to them. Now, the rest of the skull . . . there'll be gaps, do you see? That's the orbit, the big hole where the eye was, and then below that several other gaps. Fenestra they're called. That's just Latin for 'windows,' one here, and here, and a smaller one for the nostrils at the very front."

She probably could have laid off with the Latin, but the men seemed to be paying attention fine. The fellow with the scary eyes, Hobart, spent a little too much time looking at her instead of her drawing, which worried me.

"How big's the skull?" Withrow wanted to know.

"Five feet across, give or take," I said.

He gave a slow whistle of appreciation.

"You might also find some bits of the spine near the skull. Rachel, can you sketch those, too? See, they're weird-looking things, lots of spiky bits jutting off from the ring. You probably won't see any of this all neat and tidy. It might be busted up and scrambled. If the bones have been exposed for a while, they might be bleached white. But other ones might be dark. Silvery black is what we're hoping for, just like the Black Beauty's tooth. Just keep your eyes open, and if you see something on the ground, look up, because there's something higher up the slope."

"How do we tell them from rocks?" asked Withrow's other man, Browne. He had a bushy red beard, and there was a bit of food stuck in it, maybe the same bit I'd seen all day. "I've been staring at stuff for weeks, and half of it looks like rock or old wood. Only way I can tell for sure is if the thing looks like a big chicken drumstick."

I made myself chuckle, even though it worried me they were still so inexperienced. "If it's bone weathered out," I said, "it might have lichen on it, usually yellow. It might look a bit like wood—you're right, it's hard to tell—but bone's got a darker, purply color sometimes. Also, bone's porous. You can put your tongue to it. If it sticks for a second, it's bone. Rock won't do that. You see anything and you're not sure, just call out."

Thomas said, "We should keep a lookout for the Sioux, too."

"A very good point," Withrow said. "Thomas tells me we're close to Indian territory."

"How close?" I asked.

"A couple of miles to the north," Thomas said.

I glanced at Rachel. I hadn't realized we were so close.

"Well, at least we're on the safe side," I said.

Thomas shrugged. "I don't think lines on a map mean anything anymore. They get scribbled out and moved around too much."

"We put some space between our tents and yours," Mr. Withrow told me and Samuel.

I was glad it was dark, so my blush wouldn't show.

"And, Sam," said Hobart, "check for rattlesnakes first, boy. One snake in a tent's enough." He laughed at his own vulgar joke.

We'd finished cleaning up the dinner, and I was glad when Sam and I made our way to the tent. And I did check for snakes. I'd been doing it every night since we reached the badlands. During the day they'd sometimes slither inside for the shade, and at night they liked the heat of human bodies—even Aunt Berton's wizened armpit.

Inside our tent there was just room for our two bedrolls, squished side by side. I set our lantern wick low. Samuel buttoned the flaps and then kissed me ardently. We fell back together onto the bedclothes.

"I've been waiting to kiss you all day," he said.

"Really?" Most of the day he'd seemed so intent on his map, scanning the horizon for our buttes. I'd wondered if I was in his thoughts at all.

"Yes!" he said.

"It occurred to me once or twice, I suppose." I was playing at being coy, something I'd never done before, but it made him smile.

"Is the ground hard enough for you?" he inquired, thumping

the bedroll with his fist. "Or would you like it a little bit harder?"

"At least it doesn't squeak," I said. The thought of the four men milling about mere yards away did make me feel a bit self-conscious. "You were good with Withrow and his men," I told him.

"Was I?"

His uncertainty was genuine, and it touched me. I thought his natural charm and confidence would float him through everything like a magic carpet. I nodded my reassurance, but then wished I hadn't mentioned it at all, because his eyes were suddenly distracted.

"Will your father come looking for you?" he asked.

"I think so, yes."

"He'll want to separate us."

"But he can't. We're married. You have the certificate."

"Ripped in half. You never told him about our map?"

"Of course not!"

"If he's got the army scouts looking, we've got a week, prob- ably less, before they spot us. He'll want to take over our site."

"Well, he can't. He doesn't own the badlands."

"Neither do we. He could plonk himself down nearby and start prospecting. We've got to work fast."

I put my hand on the back of his neck and felt the cords of his muscles soften. His shoulders relaxed. "We don't need to think about that now," I said. "We're on our honeymoon."

He grinned and let out a long breath. We kissed and touched each other and moved the lantern off to one side so we wouldn't kick it over as we undressed. His body was still so new to me, but it already felt surprisingly natural to see it naked. I was very curious about it. Under the blanket I felt his hardness against me, and even though I wanted to be as close to him as possible, I was nervous, remembering last time.

I did like his weight upon me; it made me feel safe. I knew the mechanics of how mammals mated—I'd seen them do it—and I knew where the parts went. But I'd never had a mother to tell me how it would *feel*. Asking Papa had never for one second occurred to me. As for Aunt Berton, the idea was simply too horrifying. I don't think she'd ever known a man's touch. I'd never known about the pain—and maybe there wasn't even supposed to be pain. I was not some squeamish girl; I'd broken my arm when I was eight and not cried at all, even when the doctor was clumsy setting the bones. But now I was afraid I was abnormal.

When he came into me, I felt myself tense. It hurt, but not quite as much as last time.

"Should I stop?" he whispered in my ear.

I held him tight, bit my lip. "No."

"Are you sure?"

"Yes. Keep going."

Because now the pain was fading, and I was beginning to recognize the pleasurable tightening, the spreading heat I sometimes gave myself, only this time it was more urgent, and much, much better.

• • •

EVERY HIDDEN THING

Rock like elephant hide. Rock cut deep with fissures. Rock sculpted into melting ice cream humps. The entire landscape looked like a giant wet cloth had been thrown over it, hanging saggy and furrowed and gray.

The sun high in the sky, my hair plastered inside my hat.

My mouth tasted like her mouth. My skin smelled like her skin.

Keep looking. Always be looking.

Underfoot: desperate little cacti, a sloughed snakeskin, dead grass, tiny rabbit skulls that would be fossils in a million years. And rocks, hundreds of rocks, a colorful mess a million years in the making. Sinkholes everywhere—some just big enough to pull in your leg and break it, others deep and wide enough to fit a man or two.

The deep curve of her waist where I'd gripped tight, the damp hair of her underarms.

It was much more desolate and scraggly up here than down by the river. Thomas had said these three buttes had a name. The Sisters. They had broad bases, ledges higher up, crooked peaks. It might take weeks to scour all their surfaces properly.

I'd split us up into two groups for now. I made sure Hobart, the scary-looking one, was in my group, along with Thomas, whom I sensed would have a good eye for spotting bone. Rachel was heading up the other group with Ethan Withrow and Browne. When people got a little better at telling rock from bone, I was hoping we could split off a third group, maybe even a fourth.

If the Sioux man had stumbled on the Black Beauty two or three decades ago, it must be much more exposed now. I imagined the skull jutting from the rock like a ship's figurehead. I wanted to hear a shout from someone any moment now.

But all we'd spotted this morning was the bleached heap of a bison skeleton.

Evening came on, and we didn't find anything more.

That night I dreamed the *rex* rose from the earth. Its scattered bones found one another, snapped themselves into place. I watched, jubilant. There it was! I'd found it! It became bigger and more fearsome by the second, and I began to feel afraid. What had I done? It snuffled the dirt for its missing teeth, and they lodged themselves into its jawbones. But it was still missing one tooth. It snorted. It stood to its full height and looked at me. It wanted the missing tooth. There was no chance of outrunning it. It stood taller and taller on the plain, looking down at me in fury.

24.
ALWAYS SOMETHING MISSING

SAMUEL WAS THE LAST BACK TO CAMP, JUST like the past four days. He'd prospect until the sun fell below the horizon, and only then trudge back to camp, clothes damp with sweat, face pale with grit.

"Early days yet," I said as he sank wearily down beside me. I took his hand, and he squeezed back absentmindedly and forced his lips into a smile, but his eyes were focused inward.

For me, each day began with an excited thrum in my head. I walked eager and alert among the ancient rock with my geological hammer, hat shading my eyes, looking. I still felt the same delight I had as a girl in Connecticut. But I knew it wasn't like that for Sam. With every day I saw him get quieter and more intent.

He barely touched his dinner. He just talked about how

much ground we'd covered, how much there was left. And he talked about the Black Beauty itself, what it must have looked like when alive, making size comparisons with nearby boulders and hills and buttes.

He reminded me of his father in Philadelphia. Samuel was the same masterful showman, but with a hint of desperation, so eager to impress. He was inventing, adding imaginative flourishes to the *rex*, as if he wanted to keep Withrow and his men keen. It made me sad to see him trying so hard but also kindled a protectiveness in me.

"I saw a rider today," Thomas said.

Browne picked a baked bean from his beard. "Army?"

"Too far away. Might've been anyone—Sioux, army, trapper."

"Did he see you?" Withrow asked.

Thomas shrugged.

I knew what Samuel was thinking; my father was looking for us. I did not know what he'd try to do if he found us.

Later, in our tent, trying to distract him, I asked, "Where will we live? Back east, or out west?"

I wanted to remind him of how we'd talked about being a great scientific couple, working side by side in the field, being beholden to no one.

"Nowhere," he said, "if we can't find the *rex*."

"We'll need a place to live regardless."

"Hard to find a place if we're penniless," he muttered.

"I was thinking," I said, "about my father. I can't believe he'd cut me off entirely. And even if he does, there's my aunt—"

"I don't want your family's money," he snapped.

"Even just at first, before—"

"I'll find this *rex*," he said. "If the map isn't a lie, I'll find it."

"*We'll* find it, you mean." My words came out harsher than I'd intended. I'd meant to reassure him, but it made me angry, the way he talked about finding it alone.

"Yes, I meant we," he said wearily.

"We're partners. And our team's not so bad. Withrow's pretty good, and Browne's coming along."

"That's good," he said.

And he turned onto his side, away from me—the way he always slept—and was silent. He hadn't made love to me yesterday, either, and I missed it. I wanted his weight on me; I wanted to be inundated by our heat.

I touched the coarse curls at the back of his head, then the fine hairs on his nape, but he was already asleep. I pressed myself against him a little bit, but he did not stir. I hoped it was truly sleep; I couldn't bear the idea of him lying there in the dark, ignoring me.

It was as though he'd sealed himself away from me, like a barnacle. I felt forlorn. I stole his heat like a wary cat. Was he tired of me already? Now that he'd seen me, known my body, was he already regretting it?

"Samuel?" I whispered.

She said my name, but my thoughts were tangled as sagebrush. Here's what I had: a map that might or might not be truthful, sixteen dollars and fifty-nine cents, the clothing and boots on my body. And a wife.

It was craziness. Without the rex, how could I support a wife, a family? I had no money. I hadn't even finished school. And I'd promised to send Rachel to university—how could I afford the tuition? Our fathers wouldn't help—the opposite. They'd try to separate us. I was entirely alone. All day I'd glared at rock, desperate to see something. Every passing hour was another failure, stacking up atop the others. There was still so much rock to cover. Who knew how much time I had before Cartland and the army found us and tried to separate us, or poached on our site? I'd promised Withrow something I might not be able to deliver. I was a boy pretending to be a man.

I felt a hopelessness all through me, wanted to snuff it out like the lantern wick. I wanted the oblivion of sleep.

"Samuel," she said again, then eventually moved away.

I didn't want her to see my fear. My thoughts began their little wander before sleep, and I thought about how there had never been a complete fossil found. Not ever. There was always something missing. A phalanx or a tiny rib joint or, even more often, the skull itself. You'd never have everything. Over millions of years things got scattered and crushed and lost. But I bet there wasn't a single paleontologist who didn't hope that, one day, he'd get every bone accounted for. The perfect specimen to complete the collection. The one thing that would finally make you say, *There now, yes, it's done.*

• • •

Throughout the night he muttered like he was having a prolonged nightmare. Once he thrashed and pulled the blankets off me; I gingerly tried to pull them back, but they were pinched beneath his body. I wasn't standing for it, so I gave a sharp yank and got my share back. Later he snored; once he passed wind quite musically. I hadn't imagined what it would be like to share a bed with a man—especially one so active and greedy in his sleep.

I slept poorly, dozing, waking suddenly, reaching out to make sure Samuel was still beside me. It was so dark I had to remind myself where I was, all that had happened to me in the past few days. I had to imagine there was still a world outside the tent, and the sun that would bring the day.

When I next woke, Samuel had dressed and left the tent, without even a hello.

I turned away from the rock face, massaged my sore neck. Mosquitoes seemed to have given up on me altogether. My skin was baked like clay from a kiln.

Nothing, and more nothing—except my thoughts echoing inside my skull:

The map was a lie, or—

The map wasn't a lie, but the Black Beauty had been weathered out too long. The elements had destroyed its bones. Sun had bleached them; ice had cracked them; rain had washed away the chalky remains; or—

The Sioux man, all those years ago, had just discovered a lone tooth, like the one Plaskett had found. And that was all. The rest of the Black Beauty was elsewhere.

Back to work, back to the rock.

And then, wafting crookedly through the air between the buttes:

"We got something! Something over here!"

When I reached them, Rachel and Withrow were peering at a spot about seven feet up the rock face.

Definitely bone.

"I think it might be part of a mandible," Rachel said. Her eyes were bright with excitement.

More than anything I wanted it to be the mandible—I wanted to see exactly what the Sioux man had seen. I rose up on my toes. There were several large, fractured bits of bone, buried at an oblique angle, but the shape of them made me think it might be the dentary bone of the lower jaw. Couldn't see any teeth, but the stone was sharply ridged just off to one side, and I wondered if there might be something underneath. It was hard to get a sense of its overall size. What was showing, how much was still hidden.

When you saw a fossil laid out all orderly, or in an illustration, the parts seemed obvious. But in the rock all the pieces were broken and jumbled and lying on top of one another, and it could take a long time to figure them out.

"I wouldn't call it exactly black," Withrow remarked.

That bothered me, too. Fossil teeth were often blacker than the other bones, but in the legend, the entire skeleton was described as black. But that was legend. The Sioux man who had found the tooth couldn't have seen much of the skeleton at all; he might've found the tooth on the ground and never glanced up.

All I said to Withrow was "Can we get some crates and lumber for a platform? It'll be easier to work."

After we set up our simple scaffold, Withrow asked, "What do the rest of us do?"

"Just wait," I said. "I want to see what we have here."

"Why can't we just start digging and dragging out bones?"

"We'd probably butcher them," I said. "We'll need to dig down from above, remove all the overburden, prepare a proper quarry."

"And that way," Rachel added, "we get to see how the bones lie and how they might fit together."

"All right," Withrow said, with a grudging nod. "You're the experts. Get to work. We'll have lunch."

Rachel and I stood side by side with our awls and hammers. I turned to her, and she grinned.

"This is how I imagined it," she said.

For the first time in days I felt like things were going to be all right. We went to work. I should have been slower, more careful. I burrowed deeper. Splitting apart stone. Too impatient. We worked out from the dentary bones, exploring. Like patting your clumsy hand into a dark closet. I wanted to get a sense of how big the skull was. I wanted to find teeth.

"Big jaw," she said. "I think I might have the maxilla here."

I looked. "Maybe. If its jaws are shut. But where are the teeth?"

We whisked away the silt with a broom, rubbed our watering eyes, kept going. We were making quite a hole in the slope, and

KENNETH OPPEL

I didn't know much deeper we could burrow without having to remove some of the overburden. A bit longer yet. I didn't want to break off. My world became very small, all edges and textures. The point of a blade. Tip of an awl.

Working back along the dentary bone, I uncovered a grooved stretch of darker bone. Its surface was smooth.

"Here we go, here we go . . . ," I breathed.

"What is it?" she said, looking over.

"Teeth, I'm pretty sure. . . ."

I worked around them, guessing at the edges, teasing them from the stone. Then I stepped back. Stared.

"This isn't it," I said.

She came closer, swiping dust and sweat from around her eyes.

"The teeth are wrong," I said.

I was aware of Withrow coming closer, hopping up on the boards to get a look.

"What's the matter?" he asked.

"How do you know?" Rachel asked me.

"Look at them!" They jutted from the big jaw like narrow leaves. "Right off they're too small."

"But you haven't cleared them all yet."

"Don't need to. Can't you tell?"

She stared harder. "Maybe they're juvenile teeth. . . ."

"They aren't even carnivore teeth! These are a completely different shape. You've seen herbivore teeth, haven't you?"

"Yes, I *am* familiar with teeth, thank you," she said.

"These ones chew plants, not meat. It's an herbivore."

"So this isn't our Black Beauty?" Withrow asked.

I took a good long look at the front end of the jaw Rachel had been working. "That's a beak," I said, pointing.

She frowned, trying to see it. "Are you sure?"

It was so clear to me. "Positive," I said impatiently. "This is not our *rex*."

Withrow licked his dry lips. "But you've never seen a *rex*, so how can you be absolutely sure?"

"This thing's like a giant cow," I said. "Look how far back the teeth start. Carnivore teeth start right up front and run the length of the dentary bone."

"Don't you think we should stick with it a bit longer?" she asked.

I could tell she wasn't convinced by what I was saying. She didn't trust me. All my life I'd puzzled and pieced together bones, and I was better at it than my father. And she didn't even trust me.

"It's not nearly big enough!"

"Those calculations of your father's—"

"Don't argue! It's not our *rex*!"

She glared at me, and I could see a wet shine in her eyes.

"There's no point quarrying it out," I muttered. She shouldn't have contradicted me.

"Well," she said coldly, "what does Mr. Withrow have to say, since he is our employer."

I bristled. An employee. But it was the truth.

"If you're sure," Withrow said to me, "let's keep looking elsewhere. The Black Beauty's the prize. This one isn't going anywhere.

But if it's not even a predator, I can't see Mr. Barnum caring much about it."

"We've still got a few hours of daylight," I said, checking the western sky. "Let's just carry on."

"Sounds good, boss," said Withrow. I think he was trying to make me feel better.

As the others headed back to their prospecting routes, I stayed put. I tightened my grip on my hammer. Watched my knuckles whiten. My mind felt empty, but in a dangerous way.

"You didn't need to be so rude to me," she said behind me, and I started. I thought she'd gone too.

I said, "You were arguing with me in front of Withrow."

"We're partners. That's what you said. It was going to be *our* find."

"*I* made the deal with Withrow; it's me he has to have faith in."

"My father never humiliated me publicly like that."

"Go back to him, then!" I shouted, and raised the hammer's sharp end and smashed it into the bone. She cried out for me to stop, but again and again I drove the hammer, rock and bone fragments flying until I'd crushed a foot-long section of it. Panting hard, I let my arm drop to my side.

When I turned to Rachel, she looked shocked. And afraid.

Maybe I should have tried to comfort him, touched his back and told him we would find it, everything would be all right. Would that have made things better? But anger held me back. He was no different from his fist-fighting father, a volatile bundle of temper. Even after his outburst, his grip on the hammer had been tight.

We didn't speak much that night, and when he turned away from me, I turned away too. I was furious with him, for treating me like a dim-witted student, for ignoring my body. Where was all his passion now, all his beautiful words?

In the middle of the night, when I felt my monthly bleeding start, I was glad I wasn't pregnant.

KENNETH OPPEL

25.
A FATHERLY VISIT

PAPA WAS WAITING FOR ME WHEN I RETURNED to camp.

He sat on a crate near our cookstove, his saddlebag near his feet. Aside from his slouch hat, he looked like he might have just given a lecture. Leaning against the shady side of our wagon was the Pawnee scout, Duellist. I couldn't see any soldiers. Their two horses were cropping nearby.

"Where is Samuel?" he asked, standing. His gaze flicked over Withrow and Browne.

"Still out prospecting. Why are you here?"

"To ensure the welfare of my daughter."

I was surprised at the pang I felt, the sheer familiarity of his sturdy shape, the shining curve of his forehead. My whole life, with scarcely an exception, he'd been the one person I'd seen every day.

"We knew you hadn't taken the train, and Samuel abandoned his horse in Crowe. I had a hunch you meant to continue prospecting on your own, but you'd need some help."

"We're helping each other," said Withrow. "Your daughter is a fine fossil hunter."

Father glanced at Withrow with barely veiled disdain, and then returned his gaze to me.

"I am absolutely fine," I told him. "I'm sorry you worried. I would've written a note if there hadn't been such a scene in the hotel."

He lifted his chin, as if he was too dignified to think about it. "Shall we walk a bit?" he asked.

"Are there handcuffs clipped to your belt?"

"Ha," he said, and pulled back his jacket. "No handcuffs, you see."

I looked at Ethan Withrow, and he tipped his head gently. *Go.* Papa and I walked to the edge of the camp; I made sure the others were in plain view. Ethan kept his eye on us.

"My dear," Papa said, and lifted his hands in entreaty. His fleshy hands had handled geological hammers and picks and shovels. They'd held pens and written journals and lectures. They'd hefted me up into a wagon when I was little, helped me shape my first letters. "You can't mean to continue like this. Come back with me."

I said nothing.

"You don't need to ruin the rest of your life because of one youthful misadventure."

"You're saying I should abandon my marriage?"

At the word he winced as though someone had put something unpleasant into his mouth. I saw his eyes counting the tents. "Whether you're married yes yes is debatable."

"We are *married*," I said, "in every sense of the word."

"That being as it may, I simply want you to come back with us and think things through. You may find some time alone will be clarifying."

I almost smiled at his attempts to be cunning. But I was ashamed at the pull I felt. Even for the most mundane things: a softer bedroll, a tent to myself, my clothes, a better washbasin. I wished Samuel were here. Where was he?

I inhaled. The words were surprisingly hard to say. "I'm not leaving."

"That boy can't offer you a respectable home. He's had too poor an example from his father. A known philanderer."

"So you say."

"The stories of his womanizing are numerous. He makes a mockery of his faith."

I thought of the woman on the train. "Samuel is not his father."

He sniffed. "You will come to grief if you stay with him. You will most certainly be very poor."

"Is that a threat?"

He sidestepped. "My dear, he cannot support you."

"We've hired our services to Mr. Barnum. If we make a find, we will be paid."

"Samuel's plan no doubt. He shows the same poor judgment as his father. I'm not hopeful of your prospects with this lot." He tilted his head toward camp. "They look about as skilled as grave diggers"

"We'll find something." Where was he? Why wasn't he here to stand beside me?

"He will not love you, my dear."

"How can you dare say that?" I retorted, and then realized I'd just asked a question.

"He's only a boy. A rash boy from a rash, obsessive father who will soon ruin himself. All I'm asking is for you to come back with me and think it over, and *then* make your decision when you're clearheaded."

"I'm perfectly clearheaded."

"I would take care of you."

My voice was hoarse with anger. "So I can be your helpmate?"

"So you can go to university and become a paleontologist."

I faltered a moment, then sniffed. "Last time we spoke you said I was unsuited for university."

"I did say that, and I was mistaken. I was speaking out of anger, and concern for you. But I've given it a great deal of thought since. And I think the world of science would be the poorer if you were not properly trained."

I watched him like he was an unfamiliar reptile. "I want to make sure I understand you. You're offering to send me to university *if*..."

"Yes, *if* you choose to put this foolishness with Samuel Bolt

KENNETH OPPEL

behind you. You'll be free to pursue your true passion. I know you, my dear, better than you think. Right now you are in the throes of a passion yes yes, I know, even I know. But it will wane, and your circumstances will become a terrible burden. Poverty. A feckless, restless husband. Perhaps he's made you promises of education and opportunity. But I can deliver these things much more reliably."

I couldn't speak and knew I was on the verge of tears.

"There, there, my dear. Don't cry. Things can be made right."

"I am crying," I said, "because you would never have offered me these things normally. Even now I don't know whether to trust you. And you're unkind to try and tempt me when I've already made a hard choice."

"Look, there's something I brought to show you."

He'd taken my elbow and was leading me back to the camp. Withrow looked at me questioningly. I smiled weakly. Father bent down to his saddlebag.

"We've made some very promising finds near our new camp."

"You've moved?" I asked.

He undid the buckles. "Downriver. We needed better forage for the horses. And so I decided to take the Sioux boy at his word. His directions, you remember. We found the hoodoos he described and started digging. And look."

With both hands he lifted out a single bone, a massive vertebra. But what I noticed most was its color—the same silvery black as the Black Beauty's tooth.

• • •

"Who found that?" I demanded.

I'd just walked into camp, and there were Withrow and Browne huddled together with Rachel and Professor Cartland. The mere sight of him made me angry—and angrier still when I saw what he cradled in his hands.

Withrow answered, "The professor's showing us a bit of bone they dug up."

"Manganese oxide in the rock, no doubt," said Cartland, talking to Rachel like I wasn't there. "Reminds me yes yes of that tooth of yours? Seems that Sioux boy might have been telling us the truth."

I stepped closer, drawn by the black bone. I felt hollowed out, like some gutted bit of taxidermy. My mouth went dry. By the looks of it, it was a caudal vertebra from some creature's mighty tail. I wanted to touch it so badly. Our *rex*?

"How much have you dug up?" I heard Rachel ask, like she was in a trance.

"We found this only yesterday," Cartland replied. "We're just turning our full attention to the site now. We could use your help, my dear."

I looked at him sharply, then Rachel, waited a heartbeat, then another, for her reply. When it didn't come, I said, "Rachel's not going anywhere."

It sounded bullying, and when she turned to me, I wasn't sure if there was relief or dislike in her expression. I realized I'd never been very good at reading her.

"Or were you planning on kidnapping her?" I asked Cartland.

"If there was any kidnapping," the professor replied, "it was not done by me."

"We eloped," Rachel said. "I wasn't abducted." She glanced at me. "And I don't think Papa means to try now."

"I'm very encouraged by this find," Cartland said placidly, replacing the vertebra in his saddlebag. "A shame we lost the tooth, though. I suspect the Sioux boy took it when he escaped. Incredible that he knew to look in my tent!"

Cartland was watching me as he said this. I pretended my face was a fossil, and I was only looking out through the eye holes.

"He must have been very stealthy," Rachel said.

"The Sioux heads went missing too. The lieutenant thinks he likely had an accomplice. Setting free an army prisoner is a very serious offense."

"Why would anyone do that?" I asked.

"Maybe they were hoping to get something in return," Cartland replied.

I was good at staring. I learned it playing cards with my father. If Cartland knew, he had not a scrap of proof, or the lieutenant would have been here to arrest me. Cartland looked away first.

"Well, my dear, I must be off. Shall I wait while you gather your things?"

He smiled at his daughter, and I realized I'd never seen a smile on his face before. It contracted soon enough when Rachel slowly shook her head.

"I see. I want yes yes the best for you, but you must know it's impossible as long as you remain with young Bolt here. Quite impossible."

Her eyes were wet. "I am staying here."

Stiffly he said, "Well, if you change your mind, I'm not far."

As her father walked away to his horse, I went and put my hand on her shoulder, but she felt stiff and far away from me. She watched Cartland ride off with the Pawnee scout.

Withrow said, "What was that bone he showed us?"

"A vertebra. Maybe a piece of the lower spine, the tail. It could've come from all sorts of dinosaurs."

"The Black Beauty?"

I shrugged. "Maybe. I didn't measure it."

"Looked pretty big to me."

"Yes, it was big!"

"The color," he said.

"The color was right," Rachel said.

I said, "Doesn't mean he has the Black Beauty."

"We sure don't have it," Withrow said.

"Not yet," I said.

"You didn't tell us the Sioux boy spouted out two maps." He said it casually enough, but there was accusation in his voice.

"Because he was lying the first time," I replied. "Why would he tell the truth to someone who'd beaten him and tied him up?"

"To get untied maybe," said Hobart, who looked like he'd probably been tied up a few times himself.

"But *I* untied him," I insisted. "And got his things back. Why would he lie to me?"

Withrow stared into his tin cup. "I'll be honest; I'm starting to worry that your Sioux boy just made some squiggles in the sand."

Starting to worry. I'd been worried for days. Every time I took a break and stared out over the blistered landscape, I worried. The noise of the cicadas had become a song of worry in my head. I worried in time to the beat of my heart. I was a little boy again in my father's house, everyone watching and the clock running out and me not being able to piece the bones together.

I said, "There's still plenty of ground we haven't covered."

Of the three buttes, we'd prospected two of them pretty thoroughly, and the third we'd only started working.

"Maybe another two or three days," said Withrow.

I nodded.

"And if we don't find anything?" he asked.

"I could retrace the routes of your men—they might have missed something."

Hobart smiled at me unkindly.

Withrow said, "And after that we're in the shit, aren't we?"

When he touched me beneath the covers, I said, "It's my time of the month."

"Oh." He withdrew his hand. "Does it matter? Neither of us is squeamish."

"I'd rather not."

He pulled away and turned over, and I thought what a clod he was for not even holding me. He could still have kissed me, wrapped me up. I thought he was already asleep when he said, "Were you tempted to go with him?"

"No," I lied.

"I think you were."

I said, "Of course I was tempted."

"I could tell."

"He isn't much of a father, but he's the only one I have. My whole life he was the only person who took care of me!"

He turned over to face me. "*I* take care of you!"

"I *stayed*, didn't I?"

"Am I supposed to thank you? I'm your husband."

"And I stayed for *you*."

"I can't believe you were even tempted."

"Maybe it's easy for you to part with your father, but for me it's a wrench. Is that hard to understand?"

"He would've put our baby in an orphanage!"

All of a sudden my eyes welled up. My face crumpled. He kissed my eyes, put a hand to my cheek.

"It's all right," he said, his voice gentle at last. "He's not coming back. I'm going to take care of you. Our baby will not end up in an orphanage."

Before I could stop myself I said, "I don't want a baby."

The touch of his hand on my cheek changed. A sudden stillness, a stiffness, like something dying.

"What do you mean?" he said. "Why not?"

"I'm . . . not ready. Once I'm pregnant I'd have to stop

working, and I don't want to stop working."

"Only for a bit . . ."

"We were supposed to be partners. But when the baby comes, I'd have to look after it. I'll become just another person in a room. I didn't want to go from my father's rooms to yours. That's *not* what I wanted."

"All right," he said. "You don't want a baby yet."

"Every time we lie together I could have a baby."

"I can withdraw myself and . . . when we get to town I can buy a rubber."

"I think that would be a good idea," I said, and was quiet then.

But my mind roiled with all that I hadn't said. I thought of being poor; I thought of us fighting all the time; I thought of me being trapped in a room, while my husband went out and did the things I wanted to do. I thought of Professor Bolt, drinking and cavorting with a slattern on a train; I thought of Samuel's white knuckles on the geological hammer.

I thought about how I wasn't sure I wanted a baby with Samuel now—or ever.

That night I dreamed of the Black Beauty again. I dreamed of her silver-black bones laid out like jewels in a velvet case. Each bone was free of stone, all its surfaces polished smooth, gleaming, their identities so obvious that no labels were necessary. I could easily build her back together. There would be no trick pieces.

There would be not a single piece missing.

26.
THE SIOUX

DRAGGED BACKWARD, MY HEAD JOLTING against the ground, I cried out as I woke. Canvas smacked my face as I tried to twist round to see who was hauling me out of my tent, still inside my bedroll. Against the colorless dawn sky, an Indian loomed. He gripped my ankles, black and white feathers jutting from his braided hair.

A second Sioux man pulled out Samuel, kicking and swearing, his eyes wide with confusion and rage—and then fear. He saw me and tried to scramble closer, but the Indian grabbed him and threw him down so his head hit the ground hard. He went still.

I cried out his name, and after a few seconds he shifted and blinked. His eyes focused on me briefly and then darted back to the two Indians towering over us. The one with the most feathers held a four-foot club. At one end was a horsehair tassel; at the other was an oblong stone the size of an ostrich egg.

There were more Indians in the camp. Hollering, Withrow and Browne and Thomas were yanked from their tents. Hobart was already crumpled on the ground by the smoldering fire. Blood matted his hair. They must've snuck up on him and knocked him out. An Indian was coming out of an empty tent, collecting rifles. Another Indian hopped up into the wagon. Things flew out the back into the dirt. All of them had knives in beaded sheaths strapped to their breechclouts. They were bare chested, barefoot, and some wore buckskin on their legs.

"Thomas!" shouted Withrow from the ground. "Talk to them! Tell them we're not army!"

Standing slowly, hands out, Thomas spoke. The Sioux seemed startled at first. They turned and listened, but then it seemed to make them angry. They shouted at him, and he tried to keep talking, but they yelled over him. I didn't understand. Didn't they believe him? That we were just prospectors, that we had nothing to do with the army? Or maybe all they cared about was that we were *Wasicu*—and one of their own was a traitor for helping us. My eyes kept getting pulled back to the Indian's club, imaging the long arc of its swing, the impact of stone against skull.

Two Indians strode closer to Thomas, chests thrown out, faces belligerent. They plucked contemptuously at his cotton shirt. They yanked his short hair and slapped his face, then pushed him to the ground. One pulled a knife from his sheath and stepped on Thomas's chest, bending lower.

Thomas lashed out with his fists. The other Indian struck him hard, pinned his arms with his knees, and took hold of his hair.

"Stop!" I shouted. Everyone was shouting now, two languages battering against each another.

"Please! Don't! Wait!"

Samuel started to rise, and the Indian with the club glared at him. His fist tightened on his stone-headed club, lifted it high.

I heard another shout, rising above the others. The Indian with his knife at Thomas's scalp hesitated and pulled back. Everyone looked over as the Sioux boy walked into camp. It was the same boy who we'd beaten and tied up, the one Samuel had set free.

The Sioux boy's eyes flicked over me and rested on Samuel, then went to the Indian with the stone club. The boy pointed at Samuel while he spoke. Harshly the bigger man replied. Their words sounded like an argument to me, and I was amazed the boy could talk to his elder with such force.

Then, from the corner of my eye I saw Hobart shift near the campfire. I couldn't see his face, but I saw his hand twitch and reach for something under his clothing. I caught a glimpse of gunmetal. If Hobart started shooting now, we were all doomed. I couldn't catch his eye.

The Sioux boy and the older man were still talking, and the longer they talked, the more worried I got. Suddenly the boy looked at Sam and shouted in Sioux.

"What did he say?" Desperately he looked over at Thomas.

"He said, 'Go home.' He said there are many more coming,

and they won't know you. They won't know how you set him free."

I glanced at Hobart; he still had the gun in his hand, concealed in the folds of his clothing.

"We'll go!" I cried out. "Tell him, Thomas."

Why wouldn't Hobart look my way, the fool? I needed to shake my head at him, tell him not to shoot.

Fiercely the boy spoke again, and Thomas translated.

"He says you're on Indian land. There's a war coming. He says we'll be killed if we stay."

"Thank you," Samuel said. "Tell him thank you, Thomas."

With relief, I watched as Hobart hid his pistol in the folds of his clothing.

The Indians started to leave the camp. I knew I shouldn't, but I couldn't stop myself. The boy had just spared our lives, and I didn't want to anger him, but he was right here, right here at the spot he'd described to Samuel.

"Thomas, ask him where exactly his father found the tooth."

Samuel looked at me in surprise, and then at Withrow, who jerked his head at Thomas and said, "Go ahead. Do it; ask him!"

The boy was already walking away when Thomas spoke.

He stopped; the man with the club stopped too. They looked at each other, then turned back. It was impossible to know what they were thinking, but I worried I'd made a terrible mistake.

The boy ignored me and spoke to Samuel.

"He says he doesn't know why you look," Thomas translated. "There's no power in those bones without a vision."

Samuel nodded. "Yes. But do you know where?"

It was a wild hope I had that he would just point. *There,* he would say.

The Indian boy scoffed. He said he didn't know. Not even his father knew exactly where he'd fought his battle. It was in darkness, but he said the Sisters were the first thing he saw when he saw the sky again.

He turned and walked after the others. They'd taken all the rifles but left our horses.

Samuel rushed to me and held me tight. Everyone stayed on the ground for a bit, bewildered, like we'd just survived a tornado.

I touched Sam's temple, and he winced. There was a bit of blood. "Just another bruise for your collection," I said.

"Still got my pistol at least," said Hobart, looking at it happily. I wasn't too happy thinking our one gun was owned by the craziest-looking of Withrow's men.

I wrapped a blanket over my nightdress and stood, my legs shaky. I started up the slope of the closest butte.

"Where you going?" Samuel asked.

"I want to see them."

He came with me. From the first ledge I caught sight of the Indians down in a defile, now astride their horses. They must've left them down there so they could creep up and surprise us. Deeper in the distance, beyond a range of low hills I glimpsed a long convoy of Sioux. Some of the horses trailed pole sledges carrying bundled belongings. Dogs ran excitedly among the ponies. They were all heading north.

"They're going to die."

I turned to see Thomas beside me, watching them.

"There are too many of you," he said. By "you" I knew he meant *Wasicu*.

"They should know when they're beat," Hobart said, climbing up. It seemed everyone was coming up the slope now.

"We'd fight too," Samuel said, "if it were the other way round. Wouldn't we? You wake up one day and there's people you don't know, who look different and dress differently, coming through the streets and building on land that doesn't belong to them. And maybe they'd tell us they just wanted our houses, and they'd pay us something, but it wasn't really a fair trade. And they kept taking more. We'd probably try to kill them before more came. Maybe if we killed enough, they'd change their minds and leave us alone."

His eyes found mine, and I gave him a small, private smile. I didn't think there was one man in a thousand who would say something like this, especially after what had just happened to us.

"Sure we'd fight," Browne said. "And maybe one day it'll happen to us. But right now, seems to me there's plenty of land, and at least we're doing something with it. Railroads and farms and cities. The Indians can fit in if they want. Like Thomas here."

Thomas didn't say anything. I don't think he wanted to talk anymore. He started down the slope. We all headed back to the camp and dressed and started tidying up. The Sioux had taken some foodstuffs from the wagons, but not too much.

"So how long we gonna stick around?" Browne asked as he cooked up our breakfast.

Hobart's face twisted. "We're packing up now, ain't we?"

"I think we should finish up first," Samuel said.

"Finish up?" said Hobart. "You crazy? The only reason we're not dead is you knew that kid. He won't be around next time."

"We're in the right place," Samuel said to Withrow. "I thought Cartland might've found it, with those black bones. But it's here somewhere. The boy said it was *here*."

Withrow shook his head. "That's not what I heard. He said even his *father* didn't know. He was on a vision quest—hallucinating on some kind of smoke maybe. All he said was the buttes were the first thing his father *remembered*. He might've been staggering around a long time before then."

This was a very good point, and not one I liked very much. If we left now, empty-handed, how likely was it we'd get another chance? I knew how much Sam had counted on us making this find, claiming the fee, using that money to give us a start.

I waited for him to ask my opinion, and when he didn't, I said:

"I think we should go back. It's not safe. We can come out again next season."

"Thank you very much, little lady," said Hobart. "A voice of reason."

I hated being patronized, but what I hated even more was that Samuel wasn't even looking at me. Had he even heard me? He was turned to Withrow and said, "Three more days. Just to finish around the last butte."

"We've got *one* gun!" Browne exclaimed.

Withrow looked at his men, then back to Samuel. I didn't know if he was as desperate as Sam, or just feeling sorry for him, but he nodded. "Three days."

When Browne and Hobart started to protest, he held up his hand. "And that's it. I'm not planning on being the only white man out here when things get ugly. And I hope your fathers have the sense to get out too."

"Yours will be fine," Thomas told me. "He's got a lot of soldiers with him. The Sioux won't risk a battle."

"Mine, though," Samuel said, and I could tell it had just occurred to him. "It's just him with Ned and Hitch."

"Lieutenant Frye will warn him, won't he?" I said.

"If he knows what's going on, but he might not. Anyway, they've moved farther away. They can't protect them. I should go. Just to make sure they know what's going on. I can get there and back by late afternoon."

Withrow sighed. "Okay. Thomas can go with you."

"I know the way," Samuel said.

"Thomas'll go," Withrow insisted. "We need you back alive so you can find us this *rex*."

Samuel went to our tent to collect his things, and I followed him inside and closed the flap.

"You didn't even ask what I thought," I said.

"About giving up? I thought I knew. But I guess I was wrong. I thought you wanted the *rex* as much as me."

"You know I do, but—"

"If we don't get it now, we're sunk. Withrow probably wouldn't even hire us again. Maybe your father would find it first, or maybe there'll be a war and we won't be able to get near this place again. We need it now!"

"We could've been killed today. And now you're leaving me?"

"How else can I warn my father? You'll be fine. I trust Withrow. He'll keep you safe."

"We're in Indian territory! Even with you here I'm not *safe*!"

"Then go to your father!" he snapped. "Is that what you want?"

I stared at him, stunned by his sudden anger.

"Is that what *you* want?" I retorted. "Because it doesn't feel like you want me here at all. We're not *partners*. You criticize and ignore me. You don't even seem to want me much in bed."

"You're the one who doesn't want to get pregnant!"

"And I have very good reasons for that! I didn't marry you to become your servant. I married you so I could go to university and work with you in the field!"

"Is that the only reason?"

Before I could halt myself, I said, "It was a *very* big part of it!"

He nodded. His lips compressed, and I could see his tongue working behind them, like he was trying to form words, or bite them back.

"Then it seems to me," he said, each word cold and clipped, "that you've got a pretty easy decision. After all, now your father's promised to send you to university. *He's* got a big find. And sounds like he can take care of you much better than me."

I said, "Maybe we both made a mistake."

He said nothing.

"We were rash."

Still he said nothing. I felt like I was floating free of my body, like I was witnessing some terrible accident.

I said, "It wasn't a clearheaded decision."

I wanted him to say something, to prove me wrong. Instead he reached inside his pocket and took out the two halves of our marriage certificate. He handed them to me.

"Your father was right," he said. "There doesn't have to be any fossil record of our marriage. You can burn it. Just walk away, if that's what you want."

Then he left the tent to go find his father.

27.
YOUTHFUL PASSIONS

AS I RODE, I RAGED. I THOUGHT OF ALL the ways I'd shown her I loved her, all the loving things I'd said to her. She was cold, so coldhearted, like her bloodless father; there was a part of her missing. She didn't want a baby with me. She still hadn't told me she loved me. She didn't know how to love anyone.

"Looks like they're packing up," said Thomas, as we neared my father's camp. It was strange: It used to be my camp too, and now it was just Father's. Hitch, up on the wagon, saw us first and waved. I saw Ned turn from striking a tent, and then call out to Father, who was nailing a lid onto a crate.

I was nervous as they all walked to meet us. I was worried about Father's anger, worried he'd try to stop me. Thomas and I dismounted.

"Sam!" cried Hitch, giving me a surprisingly powerful hug. "You're married! Congratulations!"

I laughed. "Thanks, Hitch."

I didn't know what my father had told them; I supposed it would've been hard to keep it a secret, once Cartland and he rode off together to try to stop us. Ned smiled at me but said nothing. I guessed he didn't want to rile up Father by wishing me well. But I could tell by his kindly eyes he did.

"So," Father said. We did not shake hands or embrace. "I hear you've struck out with the Barnum boys."

"Cartland told you?" I asked.

He nodded. "And where is Rachel?"

"Back at camp. We just had a nasty run-in with some Sioux." I told him about it. "Wanted to let you know."

"Lieutenant Frye's giving us an escort back to Crowe," Ned said. "They're calling it quits for the season too. It's nearly September anyway. It'll be getting cold soon. What about you?"

"We'll be out a bit longer," I said. "We've got a lead on something good."

"The *rex*?" Father asked.

I wasn't going to tell him anything. "I'm sure Ethan Withrow would be very pleased if we found that."

"Any bone yet?" he asked.

I said nothing. My father waited a moment, then lifted his hands as if it didn't matter. Hitch and Ned headed back to their packing, and we were alone. Quiet, standing there. I don't know that I'd ever seen him so stingy with his words.

I tipped my head at the crate he'd been closing. "What did you find?"

"Aren't we competitors now?"

"Maybe. But the world is large."

"Spoken like a wise man. It might be a variety of hadrosaur. Its head is quite large and has a curious hollow crest on top. . . ." He trailed off, distracted. Then:

"I appreciate you coming, Samuel, but—"

"But." I'd been waiting for this. "She's not a Quaker, and she's the daughter of the man you hate, and you want me to leave this whole thing behind."

And for just a moment I felt a flicker of what Rachel must have felt—the temptation. To go back to what we'd had, to what we knew and was easiest.

Father looked at me curiously. "No. I was going to say you should get back to your wife now."

"Oh." I took off my hat, scratched at my hair. "I'm not sure she wants me back."

He said nothing. My talkative father, for once in his life, was waiting for me. And like some natural law of physics, my words rushed out to fill his silence.

"She thinks it was a mistake. I'm not even sure she loves me. She's never said so."

"She ran away to marry you. She risked a great deal."

"But I'd told her she could go to university and work with me. And just a few days ago, her father came to our camp and offered her the same things. *If* she left me."

"She stayed, though."

"Yes, but . . ."

There was so much in my head I didn't know what to say.

"When I was younger," Father said, "not quite as young as you, I met a young woman while studying in Washington. I thought her very beautiful and very bright, and we saw a great deal of each other. In my letters home, I wrote about her, and my parents knew I was getting very attached. She wasn't a Quaker. My parents wrote back and discouraged my affections. But I didn't care much for their way of thinking and carried on."

"Did you run away with her?" I asked in amazement.

"No, no. I was not always obedient, but when my parents summoned me home, I went."

It was hard for me to believe Father had ever done anything he didn't want to.

"They told me it was a youthful passion and it would spend itself and then I could marry a suitable Quaker woman. I was sent to Europe to study and forget about her."

I wasn't sure if this story was a reprimand, or where exactly it was going, but something suddenly came to me.

"This is where you met Cartland."

"Correct. But this was not the purpose of my story—"

"You never told me you knew him in Europe."

He sighed. "Because I now consider our friendship, if you can call it that, grotesque. We met at the university in Berlin and became friendly in the way Americans abroad do. He was a solid scholar, a bit plodding for my tastes, but we exchanged notes and even went on a few ambles looking for samples. Toward the end of the summer we named small specimens after each other. He got a mollusk, and I got a millipede."

I shook my head, astonished. Unthinkable.

"And now you will hear my side of the story Cartland told you."

He made it sound like he was telling it just because I forced him; but I knew he wanted to tell it.

"I was headed home to America a full month before him, so he asked me to deliver a package to Melissa, his fiancée, in New Haven. It was an easy enough stop to make. His fiancée, I was surprised, wasn't hideous. Surprisingly presentable, but not at all my type of woman. Her family invited me to stay before returning to Philadelphia—they wanted to hear all of the news of Frederick Cartland and goings-on in Europe. So I stayed, and Melissa grew attached to me."

"How attached?"

He puffed air from his cheeks. "She seemed to think she was in love with me—at least, that's what she told me in the letters she wrote when I was back in Philadelphia."

I looked at him hard. "You didn't do anything to lead her on?"

"I am flirtatious; this is no secret. But I'm flirtatious with *all* women. It's a despicable weakness on my part, I know, but I don't seem able to help myself. In any event, I made no special effort to woo her. And I certainly never seduced her, as Cartland said! She kept writing, though, even *after* she married Cartland!"

"But you never wrote back?"

"Only to return her letters. Which foolishly she kept—which is why Cartland seems to think we carried on an affair. You have my promise, Samuel. I'm sorry for Cartland—a terrible humiliation for him, of course. She was a fool to keep those letters."

My whole life I'd been watching Father, listening to him, learning from him, trying to please him, charting the weather of his many moods. I knew his expressions pretty well, his poker face, his foxy charm. I probably shouldn't have, but I did believe him right now.

All these years trying to make sense of his hatred for Cartland, and now I got to see its murky beginnings. This wasn't the only reason they hated each other. Given who they were—their natures, their circumstances, what they'd done to each other—it was inevitable they'd become enemies.

"I'm glad to hear your side of things," I said.

"This has become a rather long story," he admitted, sounding uncharacteristically apologetic, "and I've strayed from its main point. I went home. I met your mother, and we married. But there wasn't a single day I didn't think about that lady from Washington."

"You wish you'd married her instead?"

"I do. I wish I'd had your courage, or recklessness, or both. Whether we'd have been happy, who can say? Your mother was a fine woman, Samuel, but I was a poor husband. She was very intelligent, and took a great interest in my work, but I didn't share it with her. And when her health became poor, I neglected her all the more. My heart may have been beyond my control, but I denied her my companionship and a shared life of the mind. And once you've made your choice, and said your vows, that's a great betrayal."

He'd never talked this much about my mother. And I had so

few memories of her, it hardly ever occurred to me to ask. But it was the naked way he spoke that struck me. I'd never seen him so revealed. Being a husband seemed a lot more complicated than I'd imagined. Maybe the problem was I'd never even properly imagined it at all.

Father gestured to the cookstove. "There's some lunch."

"No thanks. I should get back."

He reached out and shook my hand. "You take care of your wife. You love her."

"I will. I do."

His grip was tight. "Come back with us," he said. For a moment I saw genuine fatherly concern etched into his face. But then it gave way to his familiar charming grin. "I mean the both of you. Next spring we can return, you and me and Rachel, and find this thing properly."

I smiled, even as I felt a sting behind my eyes. He was sly as a fox still, and it was far too tempting an idea. But I shook my head. "We're going it alone, the two of us."

"All right, then. You know, I'm starting to enjoy the idea of having Rachel as a daughter-in-law." He grinned. "I'm sure Cartland's mad as a hornet."

This was as much of a blessing as my marriage was going to get. It wasn't a lot, but it was more than expected, and it made me think I wasn't losing my father.

When Thomas and I got back, the camp was empty, and we set out to join the others at the buttes. My head was full of things

I wanted to say to Rachel. We spotted Hobart working along a ledge, and Thomas went off to join him. I said I'd catch up later. On the far side of the butte, prospecting one of its many wrinkled folds, were Withrow and Browne. I couldn't see Rachel.

"I think she went farther round," Withrow said when I asked where she was.

It was a towering monument of stone. I started around the base, shading my eyes, and I didn't see her, and then didn't see her some more.

"Rachel?" I called out.

Why the hell had Withrow let her go off on her own? She might've been spotted by more Sioux. Might've fallen. Might've decided to run off and join her father. I shouted her name again. Panic ballooned inside me, squeezing the air from my lungs. My voice echoed off the steep slopes.

"I'm here," she said.

She stood tall. She'd been crouched in a shallow crevasse. For a moment I just stared with mute relief. *There you are.* She watched as I came closer. With every step I just wanted her body against me. I climbed down beside her and held her tight. She put down her hammer and her arms encircled me and her palms pressed into my back hard. I felt her solid heat and breathed her hair and skin, and we didn't say anything for a while.

I spoke into her ear. "I did not make a mistake."

I felt her breathing against my chest.

"All the way back," I said, "I was thinking of those specimen boxes I'd fill up when I was young. Always trying to fill them all up. And there was always something else, some new empty space to fill. You're the thing I could never find."

Her fingers lightly touched the hollow of my throat, like she didn't want me to talk anymore.

"No," she said. "There'll be something else. With you there will *always* be something else to find."

"Maybe." I tried really hard to think, to be honest. "But maybe as long as I'm looking *with* you, it'll be all right. If we can at least be together, that's what I'll be happy with. I'll be a better partner, I promise."

Her words against my neck: "I wasn't just running from my father. I was running to you. I wanted to be loved by you, to be with you."

"So we're agreed?" I said. "We'll stay married?"

"Yes!"

From her pocket she took out the two halves of our marriage certificate and gave one half to me. "We'll each keep one. For safekeeping."

I heard the rattle and looked down to see the snake flicking its tongue against her boot. We both stood very still.

"It's a rattler," I said.

"It doesn't want to bite me." Her voice was amazingly calm. "It came for the shade."

The snake bellied onto the toe of her boot, lifted its head toward her ankle.

"How do we get it off?" I asked.

"Sam. Stay calm. I know about snakes. It'll go away."

"When?"

A faint rattle emanated from its tail.

"Stay still," she said. "You're scaring it."

It moved farther up her ankle toward her calf.

I darted out my hand, grabbed it right behind its head so it couldn't bite me, and flung it hissing into the sagebrush.

"There!" I said.

"Sam."

Gently she took my hand in both of hers. In the soft part of my wrist, twin puncture marks welled red.

28.
RATTLER

YOU IDIOT," I SAID TO HIM. "WHY DID you grab it?"

"Damn," he said. "Damn it."

I grabbed his arm, locked my mouth over the bite marks, and sucked. I tasted blood and spat, then did it again two more times.

"Just in case," I said. "It might be a dry bite. Sometimes they don't inject any venom at all, or very little—just as a warning. Sit down. Right here, against the rocks. Put your hand on the ground. You want to keep it lower than your heart."

He looked at me with a boy's panic-stricken eyes. I put my hand on his arm. His body felt hard, tensed for flight, like he could outrun the venom that might be spreading through his veins.

"Everything all right?" said a voice behind me, and I turned to see Mr. Withrow. "I heard him calling out for you."

"I found her," Sam said. "But I just got bitten."

"Rattlesnake?" said Withrow, coming closer. He saw the bloody marks on Sam's wrist. "I'll get Thomas. He knows about snakebites."

"He's on the east side of the other butte," Sam told him.

"Hold tight," Withrow said, and ran off.

"What happens now?" Sam asked me.

"Nothing," I said, searching my satchel for a clean rag for a bandage. "Just sit still."

If there was venom, every beat of his heart would speed it. I didn't tell him this, because that would make anyone's heart pound.

"Thank you," he said, forcing a smile across his pale face. "Good thing you know so much about snakes."

"Well, I never kept poisonous ones, but I've read lots about them. Does it hurt?"

"Like a hot vise," he said tightly.

"The swelling isn't too bad at all," I said. "That's good."

There was still a fair amount of blood as I tied the bandage around the wound.

I sat beside him, feeling helpless. I'd read stories about snakebites; they made irresistible reading. There were many treatments, many cures, but all of them disputed, and some of them downright dangerous. The only thing most people agreed on was trying to suck out the poison.

A few minutes later the others came running. Thomas knelt beside Samuel. He undid my bandage and stared at the puncture marks.

"You sucked out the poison?"

"Three tries," I said.

He pulled his knife free and, before I could say anything, cut two slashes across the wounds. Sam yelped and tried to jerked his arm back, but Thomas held it tight. He bent his mouth to the bite, and his cheeks caved in as he sucked hard, then spat out. Blood welled up alarmingly.

I'd read that cutting the bite marks did more harm than good, and told Thomas so.

"Helps it bleed out," he said. "It drains the poison with it."

I wasn't at all sure about this.

"Tourniquet now," he said, and took my bandage and knotted it a few inches up Sam's forearm. Sam winced.

This I had heard of. "But not so tight," I said. "You don't want to cut off the circulation to his hand."

"If the poison spreads, he could lose more than that."

"I'm going to lose my arm?"

"No," I told Sam, glaring at Thomas.

"There's an army surgeon at your father's camp," Withrow said. "We should get him there."

"No," Sam said, shaking his head. Even in the shade sweat beaded his forehead.

"The doctor will know better than us what to do."

"I'm not going!" Sam shouted.

"There's nothing more anyone can do," said Thomas. "He shouldn't move anyway."

"I read something about pouring milk into the wounds," Browne said.

"No," said Thomas.

"Whiskey's the trick," said Hobart. "Half a quart, swallowed neat."

"No," I said.

"I'm from New York City, for God's sake," said Withrow. "We don't have this problem. What else can we do?"

"Carry him back to camp," said Thomas. "We can use a blanket."

On the way back Sam was shivering; I wasn't sure if it was fever, or just fear. Walking alongside his blanket stretcher, I touched his head. It felt cool enough. But his skin looked greasy.

"It's more swollen," he said.

I checked. "It's not so bad." It really wasn't.

"I've seen it much worse," Thomas said, glancing over.

"Did they live?" Sam asked.

"Sometimes."

"How's the pain?" I asked him.

"Bearable."

"That's good too," I said. "Some people are doubled over with it."

Back at camp we got him into our tent and propped him up so his hand stayed lower than his heart. We got him some water, and he sipped a little. I stayed with him.

"So stupid," he said, and swore at himself.

"That's not meetinghouse language, is it?" I said, trying to make him smile. It didn't work.

"Feel sick," he said, and turned over and retched against the side of the tent.

"You're all right," I said. "That's normal."

"Sorry," he panted.

"That's fine." I threw one of my dresses over the mess and bundled it up. "It's been almost an hour, and the swelling's not getting any worse. I think this is the worst of it. Sip of water?"

He shook his head.

"There's a very interesting thing about snakes I read. They get more venomous the farther south and west you get. So that's a good thing."

"We're pretty far west," he mumbled.

"But only a third of the way down," I pointed out. "Anyway, you obviously didn't get much in you. You were very fast when you grabbed it. Its bite must've been quite shallow."

I'd never tended anyone before. There was always a maid for my father or me when we were ill. I'd never had a mother take care of me or teach me anything, so I just kept repeating things and telling Sam he was doing fine.

But he wasn't. As it got dark, he got sicker. The swelling worsened. He didn't want food or water. He vomited some more, but there wasn't much left to come up. For a while he wanted to talk about the Black Beauty and the places we hadn't looked yet, but it seemed to make him more agitated, and I said we would talk about it in the morning.

"I'm tired," he said. His eyes closed, and his breathing came faster. He was terribly pale. A cold sweat dewed his neck.

I wished it were morning now; I hated the dark coming on. I talked to him and told him everything was going to be all right.

He muttered, half-asleep, "Do you have it?"

"What?" I asked.

"It's supposed to . . . every hidden thing?"

I didn't know what he was talking about. The marriage license? So I just said, "Yes."

His head lifted a bit, eyes only half-open. "You've got it?"

"I've got it, Sam. I do."

His head dropped back. "Don't lose it," he said.

"I won't."

"You hardly ever get one. With nothing missing."

"I know," I said, understanding. "We've got every piece."

He went quiet.

You idiot. Grabbing the snake when it would have been best to do nothing. So like you to do something rash like that.

Your pulse raced, and your face was gray and filmed with sweat, and I knew you were going to die.

I went close to you, so I could hear your breathing, and I told you you must not die. I told you to live because I'd never felt loved the way you loved me. No one else would be as good at it. I am sorry if I've been stingy. Come back to me. I love you, Samuel Bolt. Please do not leave me.

I tugged at the tourniquet on my forearm. My fingers teased the knot loose so it fell away. That was much better. I didn't remember leaving the tent, but I was suddenly outside. Entering the night air like slipping into a cool lake. Breathing again. A quarter moon and so many stars.

My hand felt fat, a tight leather glove. Hot, too, but its heat kept me warm. There was no more pain. I was light enough to drift up into the sky. Had to concentrate to keep my feet on the ground, really plant them on the soil. My heart was jumpy.

It was good to be in the open, away from the stifling fake night of the tent. But I was sad to be getting farther away from Rachel. Dawn was still a little ways off. With every step, thread spooled out, connecting me to her, but the thread would run out eventually, it couldn't last forever, and then I might not be able to keep my feet on the ground anymore.

Oh, Rachel, I wish you could see the sky now. I want to burst up into it. Would you come with me? Even though we're like two different species and we only have a torn marriage certificate and you don't know how much I love you.

If I caught the Pennsylvanian from Philadelphia to New York, arriving at Penn Station, I could make a quick change to the New England line, which would bring me to New Haven in another two hours. Didn't you say your house was on a big hill? You'll be there, won't you?

I wanted to run, so I ran. It was a sloppy kind of run. Arm jangling loose and painful at my side. I tripped up on something, hit the ground, tasted blood between my teeth. Up again, stride, jangle, flop, stride, jangle. How good it felt to be going somewhere! Nothing in my way, the far hills hammered together into the same seamless sheet of blackness.

I was torn from a dream. I heard a coyote howl, an echo from all directions. Around me, things moved underfoot. All the earth's nocturnal smells were out to greet me. Still didn't know all their names yet. I staggered and clumped, afraid every sound I made was a thunderclap. Coyotes! Scorpions! Indians! Shhhh. Go to sleep.

How many stars was I seeing? I'd never seen so many blemishes on the moon's pockmarked face.

I had nowhere to go, so anywhere was good.

I know you think I'm terribly impulsive and you're right, or why else would I be staggering in the dark, at risk of breaking my ankle or falling into a gulch, or being scalped by some braves eager to prove their manhood again?

The boy, the Sioux boy. His father battled in the darkness before he saw the sky. Isn't that the way he put it?

I fell again. I liked it. The pain. I wished for a battle, something to fight.

I ran, head tilted to the sky. The stars wheeled, then disappeared altogether, and I was being dragged down, rock striking my spine and the back of my head. My arms and legs nearly wrenched from their sockets—but with each jarring blow I was aware I was still alive. I didn't know how long I fell, but there were snakes. Couldn't see them, but felt their coiled presence all around me. "Shhhh, shhhh," they said.

I kept falling, went deeper into time, flaying the earth to expose all its secrets. So much easier than prospecting! A single stutter of my heart and I was back a million years, and then a million more. When I finally stopped moving, I knew I was entombed, like all the fossils I'd searched after all my life. The stone was so tight, the darkness even tighter. Within the rock I felt a stirring and a tensing. Something was coming for me.

I should have been afraid. Instead I was elated. Finally! From above came a pale wash of light, and I saw the moon slanting down. I looked at my own bloodied hands, one swollen.

When I looked up, I was feverish with happiness. Lunging from the stone was the most beautiful and terrible face I'd ever beheld. It was the creature the Sioux boy's father had battled in darkness. My heart went *boom boom boom.*

The skull was built from black bones and its jaws were parted and its teeth were curving scythes the length of my forearm, and it was coming through seventy million years of stone to greet me.

29.
WHAT'S LEFT BEHIND

WHEN I WOKE AND HE WASN'T THERE, I knew something terrible had happened. He'd died in the night, and they'd taken his body out of the tent to spare me. Or he'd skulked off to die like a wounded animal. That wasn't like him—more like something I'd do. But the tent flaps were unbuttoned, showing the colorless sky of dawn. I had no idea how long he'd been gone, how long I'd slept. I burst out of the tent to see Withrow setting the fire going, calm and unhurried.

"Where's Samuel?" I demanded.

Alarmed, he said, "What do you mean?"

I started shouting his name then, looking all about.

"He wandered off?" Withrow said, standing. "Jesus."

He went to wake the other men, shouting at Hobart. "You didn't see him? You were on duty. He didn't disappear into thin air!"

In the pitch-darkness anything could have happened to him. The land was pockmarked with sinkholes that would break your ankle at best. There were drop-offs of thirty feet.

"Sam! Sam!"

I picked a direction and ran, his name echoing between the buttes and ricocheting through the defiles. And then I saw him, limping toward me from the west. I called out to him, and he shaded his eyes, for the sun had just cleared the horizon. He raised his hand high.

In it was the blackest, biggest tooth I'd ever seen.

I wasn't much use digging; my wrist was swollen, and pain still jolted my arm. But it didn't seem like my hand was at risk of falling off; it hadn't turned blue or black, and I could feel my fingers and move them all right. I felt weak from the fever. There'd be no shoveling for me for a little bit anyway.

Restlessly I watched as Rachel and the others opened up the sinkhole so we'd be able to get at least two bodies down there to dig. Tricky because there were several rattlesnakes coiled up on shady ledges inside, and it took some very careful spadework to scoop them up and fling them far away. It was a miracle I hadn't been bitten as I slid down in the dark.

At the end of the afternoon Withrow helped lower me down into the pit beside Rachel. For the first time in millions of years, the sun hit the jaws of the Black Beauty.

"What a brute," she said.

Protruding from the sandstone was a good portion of the upper jaw, bristling with teeth. Some of them were still deeply buried, others weathered out almost completely. There were two noticeable gaps where the teeth had been wrenched from the rock—one by the Sioux man decades earlier, and one by me in the early hours of daybreak. I put my good hand on the charcoal-colored bone, ran my fingertips over its smooth surface. I peered hard at the rock, imagining the shape of the entire skull, the orbit, the naris and nasal bones, imagined the window of the antorbital fenestra, and the orbit where its huge eye would have socketed. I could almost imagine its nostrils flinching to take in my scent.

"As big as we thought," I said to Rachel. "The skull must be almost five feet long."

"We're going to need a bigger wagon," Withrow called down to me with a happy grin.

"Mr. Barnum's going to have his American dragon," I said.

"How big?" Withrow wanted to know.

"A monster. Twenty feet high at least."

"But how long to dig it all out?" Thomas asked.

"If it's big as I think," said Rachel, "we could spend most of an entire season."

"You really think so, Sam?" Withrow asked.

"My partner's right," I said, and saw her smile.

"That's time we don't have," Hobart said sourly.

I thought for a moment. "We just take the skull now," I said. "We can come back in the spring for the rest. I think Mr. Barnum will be pretty pleased to see it, don't you?"

The second day digging, Thomas went scouting and said

he saw some campfire smoke rising to the south. Every day we stayed, it was a risk. We needed to beat it back to Crowe.

But the skull took several more days. It was beautifully preserved, and Rachel did a fantastic job, cutting around it on all sides, so we had a chance at taking it out as a single big chunk. I didn't like just watching, and several times Rachel asked me to shush because I was giving instructions too much from the edge of the quarry. It was the most magnificent piece of bone I'd ever set eyes on.

Rachel came up with the idea of making a kind of plaster cast from flour and water and scraps of cloth and jacketing the entire block for extra strength before we hoisted it up and out. While it dried, Withrow and his men built a wooden tripod over the sinkhole.

On the last day, my hand was healed enough so that I could finally help. We got rope around the huge block, ran it through a pulley, and let the team lift it. Getting it onto the back of the wagon took some doing.

Last thing, we filled in the sinkhole. Rachel even planted some brush on top, and we rolled some rocks over for good measure. Right afterward it looked about as secret as a fresh grave, but I knew within a couple days the sun would have baked all the moisture out of the soil. And in a couple more it would settle and crack like any other stretch of parched badlands.

I hoped the camouflage wasn't even necessary. I didn't think there'd be any prospecting parties working through the winter. Especially now that the Indians were on the move and everyone festering for a big battle.

Rachel made several drawings so we'd have no trouble

KENNETH OPPEL

finding the spot in spring when we came back.

And we would come back. Withrow promised. As a sign of good faith, he handed over a portion of the fee we'd agreed on in cash. Rachel and I would get the rest when we reached New York City. He said it was likely Mr. Barnum would put the two of us on retainer, to quarry out the Black Beauty in the spring, and after that who knew?

The next morning we rode for Crowe to catch the next train east.

That first night on the train, after the porters had closed all the curtains, and the lamps burned low, I slipped down from my berth into Sam's. His arms were waiting to guide me to him in the dark. His body was luxuriantly warm, and we spooned together.

"I'm looking forward to seeing New York," I whispered.

"We have enough money to rent a cozy apartment through the winter."

"And enough time to prepare the skull for Mr. Barnum."

"We're fossil hunters, you and me," he whispered back. "We can work for whoever we want. We can sell to museums, paleontologists, our own fathers."

We both giggled at this.

"I think we'll have a very eventful life together," I said.

He flexed his fingers. "I'm a bit worried about my hand. That I won't get all my feeling back."

I took his hand and placed it against me.

"I feel that," he said.

"You'll be fine, then."

We kissed each other for a long time, and as the train shuddered and pulled and rocked through the darkness, our hands moved over each other, exploratory, gentle at first. We were patient with each other, and then neither of us could be patient anymore. Your right hand still hurt, but we figured it out—we were very clever, both of us, with our hands—and the only difficult part for me was not crying out.

You were the first to fall asleep.

I nestled with my back against your chest and stomach, your legs folded with mine, your arm across my breast, enclosed on all sides by you, and your unique marinade of desert and sweat and rarely laundered clothes, and yet you still managed to smell good.

As the train moved us east across the prairie, across that ancient inland sea, I thought how little of us got left behind after death. How none of the most important parts survived. It all decomposed: kisses, caresses, tongues, mouths. Passion spent itself in our animal heat, dissipated as vapor, left no permanent record. No echoes of spoken words, moans, gasps, endearments would be stored in the earth's layers.

You said I wasn't one bit romantic, and you were right mostly. But I knew that bones remained, like the terrible lizards who left their teeth and vast femurs for the jigsaw-puzzle pleasure of us paleontologists.

I hoped that when they found us, me and you, we'd be entwined together just like this, among the dinosaurs, in the ruins of the world.

ACKNOWLEDGMENTS

EVERY HIDDEN THING WAS INSPIRED, IN PART, by two pioneering American paleontologists, Edward Drinkwater Cope and Othniel Charles Marsh. Their rivalry in the late nineteenth century was famous, and has been referred to as the "Bone Wars," during which each scientist tried to outdo, undermine, and even destroy the reputation of the other. Nonetheless, between them they found and named over a hundred new species of dinosaurs—though today, a much smaller number of them are considered valid.

Researching this book was fascinating, and I'm very grateful to Donald Henderson, Curator of Dinosaurs at the Royal Tyrrell Museum; Donald Brinkman, Director of Preservation and Research; and Dennis Braman, a Research Scientist in Palynology, for allowing me to tag along with them during a dig at Dinosaur Provincial Park in Alberta, Canada. They were generous with their time, and patient in answering my many questions.

Two books in particular were invaluable to me in researching Cope and Marsh, and the history of American paleontology. The first was *The Gilded Dinosaur* by Mark Jaffe, an enthralling history of the fossil war between Cope and Marsh, and a great primer in the evolution of American science. The second book was *The Life of a Fossil Hunter* by Charles H. Sternberg. Sternberg was largely self-taught, and became an indispensable fossil hunter for Cope, before striking out as an independent collector. In 1912 Sternberg moved to Canada with his three sons and they prospected for dinosaurs in Alberta for decades.

The period in which my book is set was incredibly eventful not just scientifically, but politically and socially as well. The Civil War had ended just years before; the Union Pacific Railway had just bound the nation coast to coast, and American expansion was pushing farther west, displacing the Plains Indians, breaking territorial treaties and promises, and pursuing a policy whose aim was to confine the Indians to ever smaller and poorly maintained Reserves, while deliberately exterminating their traditional food source, the bison. *Black Elk Speaks, as told through John G. Neihardt*, helped give me an insight into this period of American Indian history, and the culture of the Lakota Sioux. Thomas King's *The Inconvenient Indian* was an excellent overview of the collision between First Nations people and white European settlers. Since my story contains several Lakota and Pawnee characters, it was very important to me that my depictions of them be as accurate as possible—so I am very grateful to Brandy Tuttle, a member of the Lakota people, for agreeing to read and comment on the manuscript before its publication.

Finally I'd like to thank my editors, Justin Chanda, Hadley Dyer, and Bella Pearson, who, as always, helped me to write a much better book.